Dear Reader,

Your response last ye~~~~
Birds, Bees and Babi~~~~
enthusiastic. This mo~~~~
another winner, *to Mo*~~~~
Linda Howard, Cheryl~~~~ ~~~~ Carr—
three fabulous authors, ~~~~ ~~~~ a wonderful
story to share.

The theme of this collection is motherhood, but
each author tells a totally different, uniquely
appealing tale. In "So This is Love,"
Cheryl Reavis's lonely Vietnamese adoptee will
touch your heart as she tries to fit into her new
world—and some of her outrageous ideas of how
to bring her father and would-be mother together
will make you laugh out loud. You'll enjoy it
when one of Robyn Carr's bridge-playing crew of
scheming grandmothers gets a well-deserved
comeuppance for meddling in her daughter's life
in "Backward Glance." And master storyteller
Linda Howard pulls out all the stops in
"The Way Home," sending you on a roller-
coaster ride of emotions when you see how even a
heart of ice can be melted.

If you haven't bought this book, buy it. I think
you'll enjoy it. If you have, let me say I think
you've made an excellent purchase.

All the best,

Isabel Swift
Editorial Manager
Silhouette Books

to Mother with Love

LINDA HOWARD
ROBYN CARR
CHERYL REAVIS

Published by Silhouette Books New York

America's Publisher of Contemporary Romance

SILHOUETTE BOOKS
300 East 42nd Street, New York, NY 10017

ISBN: 0-373-48235-3

First Silhouette Books printing May 1991

Contents

The Way Home

LINDA
HOWARD

A Note from Linda Howard

The subject of motherhood, of course, reminds me of my mother, with her common sense and good humor, both of which, with six children, she desperately needed. She was a little goofy in some things and downright eerie in others, such as the way she unerringly knew, without a shred of evidence, whenever one of us was hurt or in trouble or, unfortunately, doing our darnedest to *get* in trouble. We didn't even have to be there for her to sense when something was going wrong with us. On the other hand, sometimes she cheerfully joined in our mischief as if she were no older than we were.

Our friends from school loved to stay over at our house because of our mother. She was fun to be with and answered all of our questions, on any subject, with honesty and without embarrassment. She wasn't a good housekeeper or a particularly good cook, though she had "specialties" that were mouthwatering, but those things weren't important to either us or our friends. She was our rock.

But what makes me smile the most when I remember her isn't the things she did, but rather, the things she didn't do. Like the time she *didn't* kill me when I set the living room floor on fire. See, I was four years old and I wanted to paint a picture, but I didn't have any paint, so I decided to melt my crayons. To make a long story short, the floor caught fire before the crayons even got soft. I stomped the floor and extinguished the flames, then fetched her to show her the scorch marks and to confess what I'd been trying to do not because I was noble, but because I was highly indignant that those stupid crayons were so hard to melt and I obviously needed her help to paint my picture. Like I said, to her credit, she didn't kill me. She warned me that I was never to try that again (I didn't; after all, it obviously didn't work), and took me outside to show me how to pick poke berries and mash them up to use the purple dye for painting.

She *didn't* kill my brother Butch and me for taking the screens off the windows to use to sift dirt so we could make a really high-quality road system for our toy cars. Or for trying to dig a hole to China beneath the big oak tree, which also sheltered our road system. Actually, the hole totally escaped her notice until we missed our youngest brother, Tim, and finally traced these small cries for help to the hole to China. I remember being irritated that it was Tim instead of a little Chinese boy coming through from the other side.

She *didn't* kill Paul when he decorated the dining room with every tube of lipstick that he could find.

She *didn't* kill us when she returned from buying groceries to see, as she topped the hill, this enormous fire in the front yard. It hadn't rained in a while, so we'd decided to do a rain dance. To do a rain dance, you have to have a fire, right? Anyway, she was totally calm as she pulled into the driveway, picked up the bag of groceries and started into the house. As she passed us she casually asked, "What's the fire for?"

"We're doing a rain dance!"

"Put it out."

We put it out, and eventually, the grass grew back. It also rained the next day, to our pride.

So this is to our mother, who managed to keep her sanity despite six stubborn, brawling, inquisitive and highly unorthodox children. All of the good times are what I remember best about her.

Linda Howard

Prologue

The Beginning

Saxon Malone didn't look at her as he said, "This won't work. You can be either my secretary or my mistress, but you can't be both. Choose."

Anna Sharp paused, her nimble fingers poised in suspended animation over the stack of papers she had been sorting in search of the contract he had requested. His request had come out of the blue, and she felt as if the breath had been knocked out of her. *Choose,* he'd said. It was one or the other. Saxon always said exactly what he meant and backed up what he'd said.

In a flash of clarity she saw precisely how it would be, depending on which answer she gave. If she chose to be his secretary, he would never again make any move toward her that could be construed as personal. She knew Saxon well, knew his iron will and how completely he could compartmentalize his life. His personal life never bled over into business, or vice versa. If she chose to be his lover—no, his *mistress*—he would expect to completely support her, just as sugar daddies had traditionally done over the centuries, and in exchange she would be sexually available to him whenever he had the time or inclination to visit. She would be expected to give him total fidelity while he promised nothing in return, neither faithfulness nor a future.

Common sense and self-respect demanded that she choose the upright position of secretary as opposed to the horizontal position of mistress, yet still she hesitated. She had been Saxon's secretary for a year, and had loved him for most of that time. If she chose her job, he would never allow her to get any closer to him than she was right now. As his mistress, at least she would have the freedom to express her love in her own way and the hours spent in his arms as a talisman against a future without him, which she would eventually have to face. Saxon wasn't a staying man, one with whom a woman could plan a life. He didn't tolerate any ties.

She said, her voice low, "If I choose to be your mistress, then what?"

He finally looked up, and his dark green eyes were piercing. "Then I get a new secretary," he said flatly. "And don't expect me to ever offer marriage, because I won't. Under any circumstances."

She took a deep breath. He couldn't have stated it any plainer than that. The wildfire physical attraction that had overtaken them the night before would never become anything stronger, at least not for him. He wouldn't permit it.

She wondered how he could remain so impassive after the hours of fierce lovemaking they had shared on the very carpet beneath her feet. If it had been one hasty mating, perhaps they would have been able to ignore it as an aberration, but the fact was that they had made love over and over again in a prolonged frenzy, and there was no pretending otherwise. His office was permeated with sexual memories; he had taken her on the floor, on the couch, on the desk that was now covered with contracts and proposals; they had even made love in his washroom. He hadn't been a gentle lover; he'd been demanding, fierce, almost out of control, but generous in the way he had made certain she'd been as satisfied as he by each encounter. The thought of never again knowing that degree of passion made her heart squeeze painfully.

She was twenty-seven and had never loved before—never even, as a teenager, had the usual assortment of crushes or gone steady. If she passed up this chance she might never have another, and certainly never another with Saxon.

So, in full possession of her faculties, she took the step that would make her Saxon Malone's kept woman. "I choose to be your mistress," she said softly. "On one condition."

There was a hot flare in his deep-set eyes that just as quickly cooled at her last words. "No conditions."

"There has to be this one," she insisted. "I'm not naive enough to think this relationship—"

"It isn't a relationship. It's an arrangement."

"—this *arrangement* will last forever. I want to have the security of supporting myself, earning my own way, so I won't suddenly find myself without a place to live or the means of making a living."

"*I'll* support you, and believe me, you'll earn every penny of it," he said, his eyes moving down her body in a way that made her feel suddenly naked, her flesh too hot and too tight. "I'll set up a stock portfolio for you, but I don't want you working, and that's final."

She hated it that he would put their relationship—for it *was* a relationship, despite his insistence to the contrary—on such a mercenary basis, but she knew it was the only basis he could agree to. She, on the other hand, would take him on any basis he desired.

"All right," she said, automatically searching for the words he could accept and understand, words that lacked any hint of emotion. "It's a deal."

He stared at her in silence for a long minute, his face as unreadable as usual. Only the heat in his eyes gave him away. Then he rose deliberately to his feet and walked to the door, which he closed and locked, even though it was after quitting time and they were alone. When he turned back to her, Anna could plainly see his arousal, and her entire body tightened in response. Her breath was already coming fast and shallow as he reached for her.

"Then you might as well begin now," he said, and drew her to him.

Chapter One

Two years later

Anna heard his key in the door and sat up straight on the sofa, her heart suddenly beating faster. He was back a day earlier than he'd told her, and of course he hadn't called; he never called her when he was gone on a trip, because that would be too much like acknowledging a relationship, just as he insisted, even after two years, on maintaining separate residences. He still had to go home every morning to change clothes before he went to work.

She didn't jump up to run into his arms; that, too, was something that would make him uncomfortable. By now, she knew the man she loved very well. He couldn't accept anything that resembled caring, though she didn't know why. He was very careful never to appear to be rushing to see her; he never called her by a pet name, never gave her any fleeting, casual caresses, never whispered love words to her even during the most intense lovemaking. What he said to her in bed were always words of sexual need and excitement, his voice guttural with tension, but he was a sensual, giving lover. She loved making love with him, not only because of the satisfaction he always gave her, but because under the guise of physical desire she was able to give him all the affection he couldn't accept outside of bed.

When they were making love she had a reason for touching him, kissing him, holding him close, and during those moments he was free with his own caresses. During the long, dark nights he was insatiable, not just for sex but for the closeness of her; she slept every night in his arms, and if for some reason she moved away from him during the night he would wake and reach for her, settling her against him once more. Come morning, he would withdraw back into his solitary shell, but during the nights he was completely hers. Sometimes she felt that he needed the nights as intensely as she did, and for the same reasons. They were the only times when he allowed himself to give and accept love in any form.

So she forced herself to sit still, and kept the book she'd been reading open on her lap. It wasn't until the door had opened and she heard the thump of his suitcase hitting the floor that she allowed herself to look up and smile. Her heart leaped at the first sight of him, just as it had been doing for three years, and pain squeezed her insides at the thought of never seeing him again. She had one more night with him, one more chance, and then she would have to end it.

He looked tired; there were dark shadows under his eyes, and the grooves bracketing his beautiful mouth were deeper. Even so, not for the first time, she was struck by how incredibly good-looking he was, with his olive-toned skin, dark hair and the pure, dark green of his eyes. He had never mentioned his parents, and now she wondered about them, about the combination of genes that had produced such striking coloring, but that was another thing she couldn't ask.

He took off his suit jacket and hung it neatly in the closet, and while he was doing that, Anna went over to the small bar and poured him two fingers of Scotch, neat. He took the drink from her with a sigh of appreciation, and sipped it while he began loosening the knot of his tie. Anna stepped back, not wanting to crowd him, but her eyes lingered on his wide, muscled chest, and her body began to quicken in that familiar way.

"Did the trip go all right?" she asked. Business was always a safe topic.

"Yeah. Carlucci was overextended, just like you said." He finished the drink with a quick toss of his wrist, then set the glass aside and put his hands on her waist. Anna tilted her head back, surprise in her eyes. What was he doing? He always followed a pattern when he returned from a trip: he would shower while she prepared a light meal; they would eat; he would read the newspaper, or they would talk about his trip; and finally they would go to bed. Only then would he unleash his sensuality, and they would make love for hours. He had done that for two years, so why was he breaking his own pattern by reaching for her almost as soon as he was in the door?

She couldn't read the expression in his green eyes; they were too shuttered, but were glittering oddly. His fingers bit into her waist.

"Is something wrong?" she asked, anxiety creeping into her tone.

He gave a harsh, strained laugh. "No, nothing's wrong. It was a bitch of a trip, that's all." Even as he spoke, he was moving them toward the bedroom. Once there, he turned her around and began undressing her, pulling at her clothes in his impatience. She stood docilely, her gaze locked on his face. Was it her imagination, or did a flicker of relief cross his face when at last she was nude and he pulled her against him? He wrapped his arms tightly around her, almost crushing her. His shirt buttons dug into her breasts, and she squirmed a little, docility giving way to a growing arousal. Her response to him was always strong and immediate, rising to meet his.

She tugged at his shirt. "Don't you think you'd be better off without this?" she whispered. "And this?" She slipped her hands between them and began unbuckling his belt.

He was breathing harder, his body heat burning her even through his clothes. Instead of stepping back so he could undress, he tightened his arms around her and lifted her off her feet, then carried her to the bed. He let himself fall backward, with her still in his arms, then rolled so that she was beneath him. She made a tight little sound in her throat when he used his muscular thigh to spread her legs, and his hips settled into the notch he'd just made.

"Anna." Her name was a groan coming from deep in his chest. He caught her face between his hands and ground his mouth against hers, then reached down between their bodies to open his pants. He was in a frenzy, and she didn't know why, but she sensed his desperate need of her and held herself still for him. He entered her with a heavy surge that made her arch off the bed. She wasn't ready, and his entry was painful, but she pushed her fingers into his hair and clasped his head, trying to give him what comfort she could, though she didn't know what was wrong.

Once he was inside her, however, the desperation faded from his eyes and she felt the tension in his muscles subside. He sank against her with a muted groan of pleasure, his heavy weight crushing her into the bed. After a moment he propped himself on his elbows. "I'm sorry," he whispered. "I didn't mean to hurt you."

She gave him a gentle smile and smoothed his hair. "I know," she replied, applying pressure to his head to force him down within kissing range.

Her body had accustomed itself to him, and the pain of his rough entry was gone, leaving only the almost incandescent joy of making love with him. She had never said it aloud, but her body said it, and she always echoed it in her mind: *I love you.* She said the inner words again as he began moving, and she wondered if it would be for the last time.

Later, she woke from a light doze to hear the shower running. She knew she should get up and begin preparations for a meal, but she was caught in a strange inertia. She couldn't care about food when the rest of her life depended on what happened between them now. She couldn't put it off any longer.

Maybe tonight *wouldn't* be the last time. Maybe. Miracles had happened before.

She might hope for a miracle, but she was prepared for a less perfect reality. She would be moving out of this chic, comfortable apartment Saxon had provided for her. Her next living quarters wouldn't be color-coordinated, but so what? Matching carpets and curtains didn't matter. Saxon mattered, but she wouldn't be able to have him. She only hoped she would be able to keep from crying and begging; he would hate that kind of scene.

Being without him was going to be the most difficult thing she had ever faced. She loved him even more now than she had two years before, when she had agreed to be his mistress. It always squeezed her heart the way he would do something considerate, then go out of his way to make it appear as just a casual gesture that had happened to present itself, that he hadn't gone to any trouble to do something for her. And there was the concern he had shown over minor colds, the quiet way he had steadily built up an impressive stock portfolio in her name so she would be financially secure, and the way he always complimented whatever she cooked.

She had never seen anyone who needed to be loved more than Saxon, nor anyone who rejected any sign of love so fiercely.

He was almost fanatically controlled—and she adored it when his control shattered when they made love, though never before had he been as frenzied, as *needy,* as he had been tonight. Only when they were making love did she see the real Saxon, the raw passion he kept hidden the rest of the time. She cherished all of his expressions, but her most cherished image was the way he looked when they made love, his black hair damp with sweat, his eyes fierce and bright, all reserve burned away as his thrusts increased in both depth and speed.

She had no photographs of him. She would have to keep those mental images sharp and polished, so she could take them out and examine them whenever the loneliness became too intense.

Later, she would painstakingly compare his beloved face with another that was equally precious, and search for the similarities that would both comfort and torment her.

She smoothed her hands over her stomach, which was still flat and revealed nothing yet of the child growing within.

She had had few symptoms to signal her pregnancy, though she was almost four months along. This last period was the first one she had skipped entirely; the first one after conception had been light, and the second one little more than heavy spotting. It was the spotting that had sent her to the doctor for a precautionary exam, which had revealed that she was in good physical condition and undoubtedly pregnant. She had had no morning sickness, only a few isolated bouts of queasiness that had held no significance except in retrospect. Her breasts were now becoming a bit tender, and she had started taking naps, but other than that she felt much as she had before. The biggest difference was in the almost overwhelming emotions she felt for this baby, Saxon's baby: delirious joy at its presence within her; fierce protectiveness; a powerful sense of physical possession; impatience to actually hold it in her arms; and an almost intolerable sense of loss, because she was terrified that she would lose the father as she gained the child.

Saxon had made it plain from the start that he would accept no strings, and a child wasn't merely a string, it was an unbreakable chain. He would find that intolerable. Just the knowledge of her pregnancy would be enough to drive him away.

She had tried to resent him, but she couldn't. She had gone into this with her eyes open; Saxon had never tried to hide anything from her, never made any promises, had in fact gone out of his way to make certain she knew he would never offer anything more than a physical relationship. He had done nothing other than what he'd said he would do. It wasn't his fault that their birth control had failed, nor was it his fault that losing him would break her heart.

The shower had stopped running. After a minute he walked naked into the bedroom, rubbing a towel over his wet hair. A small frown pulled his brows downward when he saw she was still in bed; he draped the towel around his neck and came over to sit beside her on the bed, sliding his hand under the sheet in search of her warm, pliant body. His hand settled on her belly. "Are you all right?" he asked with concern. "Are you sure I didn't hurt you?"

She put a hand over his. "I'm fine." More than fine, lying there with his hand resting over the child he had given her.

He yawned, then shrugged to loosen the muscles of his shoulders. There was no sign now of his former tension; his expression was relaxed, his eyes lazy with satisfaction. "I'm hungry. Do you want to eat in or go out for dinner?"

"Let's eat in." She didn't want to spend their last night together in the middle of a crowded restaurant.

As he started to get up, she tightened her hand on his, keeping him in place. He gave her a look of mild surprise. She took a deep breath, knowing she had to get this over with now before she lost her nerve, yet when the words came out they weren't the ones she had planned. "I've been wondering…what would you do if I happened to get pregnant?"

Like a shutter closing, his face lost all expression and his eyes frosted over. His voice was very deep and deliberate when he said, "I told you in the beginning, I won't marry you, under any circumstances, so don't try getting pregnant to force my hand. If you're looking for marriage, I'm not the man, and maybe we should dissolve our arrangement."

The tension was back, every line of his big body taut as he sat naked on the side of the bed and waited for her answer, but she could see no sign of worry in his face. He had already made his decision, and now he was waiting to hear hers. There was such a heavy weight crushing her chest that she could hardly bear it, but his answer had been no more than what she had expected.

But she found that she couldn't say the words that would make him get up, dress and walk out. Not right now. In the morning. She wanted to have this last night with him, held close in his arms. She wanted to tell him that she loved him just one more time, in the only way he would allow.

Chapter Two

Saxon woke early the next morning and lay in the dim light of dawn, unable to go back to sleep because of the echo of tension left behind by the question Anna had asked the night before. For a few nightmarish moments he had seen his entire life caving in around him, until Anna had smiled her quiet smile and said gently, "No, I'd never try to force you to marry me. It was just a question."

She was still sleeping, her head pillowed on his left shoulder, his left arm wrapped around her, his right hand resting on her hip. From the very first he hadn't been able to sleep unless she was close to him. He had slept alone his entire adult life, but when Anna had become his mistress he had abruptly found, to his surprise, that sleeping alone was almost impossible.

It was getting worse. Business trips had never bothered him before; he had, in fact, thrived on them, but lately they had been irritating the hell out of him. This last trip had been the worst yet. The delays, glitches and aggravations hadn't been anything out of the ordinary, but what he had once taken for granted now grated almost unbearably. A late flight could send him into a rage; a mislaid blueprint was almost enough to get someone fired; a broken piece of equipment had him swearing savagely; and to top it off, he hadn't been able to sleep. The hotel noises and unfamiliar bed had been particularly annoying, though he probably wouldn't have noticed them at all if Anna had been there with him. That admission alone had been enough to make him break out in a sweat, but added to it was a gnawing need to get back home to Denver, to Anna. It wasn't until he had had her beneath him in bed, until he had felt the soft warmth of her body enfold him, that he had at last been able to relax.

He had walked through the door of the apartment and desire had hit him like a blow, low down and hard. Anna had looked up with her customary smile, her dark eyes as calm and serene as a shadowy pool, and his savage mood had faded, to be replaced by pure sexual need. Walking through that door had been like walking into a sanctuary to find a woman made specifically for him. She had poured him a drink and brushed close to him, and he had smelled the sweet scent of her skin that always clung to their sheets, the scent that had been maddeningly absent from the hotel linens. The ferocity of the desire that had taken hold of him still left him a little shaken this morning.

Anna. He had noticed that serenity, and the feminine scent of her, from the very first day when he had hired her as his secretary. He had wanted her from the beginning, but had controlled his sexual urges because he had neither wanted nor needed that sort of complication on the job. Gradually, though, the wanting had grown stronger, until it had become an unbearable need that gnawed at him day and night, and his control had begun crumbling.

Anna looked like honey, and he had been going mad wanting to taste her. She had silky, light brown hair, streaked with blond, and dark-honey eyes. Even her skin had a smooth, warm, honey tone to it. She would never be flashy, but she was so pleasant to look at that people continually turned her way. And those honey eyes had always been warm and calm and inviting, until finally he had been unable to resist the invitation. The frenzy of that first night still startled him, even in memory, because he had never lost control—until then. He had lost it with Anna, deep inside her hot, honeyed depths, and sometimes he felt that he had never gotten it back.

He had never let anyone get close to him, but after that first night he had known that he couldn't walk away from her as he had from the others. Acknowledging that simple fact had terrified him. The only way he had been able to handle it had been to completely separate her from the other parts of his life. She could be his mistress, but nothing else. He couldn't let her matter too much. He still had to constantly guard against letting her get too close; Anna could destroy him, and something deep inside him knew it. No one else had ever even threatened his defenses, and there were times when he wanted to walk out and never come back, never see her again, but he couldn't. He needed her too much, and he constantly fought to keep her from realizing it.

But their arrangement made it possible for him to sleep with her every night and lose himself over and over in her warm, pliant body. In bed he could kiss her and smooth his hands over her, wrap himself in her scent and touch. In bed he could feed his craving for honey, his savage need to touch her, to hold her close. In bed she clung to him with abandon, opening herself to him whenever he wanted, her hands sliding over him in bold, tender caresses that drove him wild. Once they were in bed together, it seemed as if she never stopped touching him, and despite himself, he reveled in it. Sometimes it was all he could do to keep from groaning in a strange, not completely physical ecstasy as she petted and stroked and cuddled.

Yet for all that they had virtually lived together for two years—the small distance that he insisted on retaining, so necessary for him, was in fact negligible in terms of time—he knew little more about her now than he had before. Anna didn't bombard anyone with the details of her past or present life, and he hadn't asked, because to do so would give her the same right to question him about his own past, which was something he seldom allowed himself to even think about. He knew how old she was, where she had been born, where she had gone to school, her social security number, her former jobs, because all that had been in her personnel record. He knew that she was conscientious, good with details and preferred a quiet life. She seldom drank alcohol, and lately seemed to have stopped drinking altogether. She read quite a bit, and her interests were wide and varied in both fiction and nonfiction. He knew that she preferred pastel colors and didn't like spicy foods.

But he didn't know if she had ever been in love, what had happened to her family—in her personnel file, "None" had been listed in the next-of-kin column—if she had been a cheerleader or ever gotten into trouble for childish pranks. He didn't know why she had moved to Denver, or what her dreams were. He knew only the surface facts that were there for anyone to see, not her memories or hopes.

Sometimes he was afraid that, because he knew so little about her, she might someday slip away from him. How could he predict what she would do when he knew nothing of her thoughts and had only himself to blame? He had never asked, never encouraged her to talk to him of those parts of her life. For the past two years he had lived in quiet terror, dreading the day when he would lose her, but unable to do anything to stop it. He didn't know how to reach out to her, how to hold her, when even the thought of letting her know how vulnerable he was to her had the power to make him physically sick.

The hunger grew in him as he thought of her, felt her lying so soft against his side, and his manhood swelled in response. If they had no other form of contact, they at least had this, the almost overwhelming sexual need for each other. He had never before wanted anything from a woman except sex; it was bitterly ironic that now he was using sex to give him at least the semblance of closeness with her. His heartbeat kicked into a faster rate as he began stroking her, easing her awake and into passion so he could ease himself into her and forget, for a while, everything but the incredible pleasure of making love to her

It was one of those sunny days when the brightness seemed almost overwhelming, the air was clear and warm for late April, a perfect day, a mockery of a day, because she felt as if her heart were dying inside of her. She cooked breakfast, and they ate it on the terrace, as they often did during good weather. She poured him another cup of coffee and sat down across from him, then folded her hands around her chilled glass of orange juice so they wouldn't shake.

"Saxon." She couldn't look at him, so she focused on the orange juice. She felt nauseated, but it was more a symptom of heavy dread than of her pregnancy.

He had been catching up on the local news, and now he looked up at her over the top of a newspaper. She felt his attention focus on her.

"I have to leave," she said in a low voice.

His face paled, and for a long minute he sat as if turned to stone, not even blinking. A slight breeze rattled the newspaper, and finally he moved, folding the pages slowly and painstakingly, as if every movement were painful. The time had come, and he didn't know if he could bear it, if he could even speak. He looked at Anna's lowered head, at the way the sun glinted on the pale, silky streaks, and knew that he had to speak. This time, at least, he wanted to know why.

So that was the question he asked, that one word, and it came out sounding rusty. "Why?"

Anna winced at the raw edge to his voice. "Something has happened. I didn't plan it. It—it just happened."

She had fallen in love with someone else, he thought, fighting to catch his breath over the knot of agony in his chest. He had always trusted her completely, had never even entertained the thought that she might be seeing other men during his absences, but obviously he'd been wrong.

"Are you leaving me for another man?" he asked harshly.

Her head jerked up, and she stared at him, stunned by the question. He looked back at her, his eyes fierce and greener than she had ever seen them before.

"No," she whispered. "Never that."

"Then what?" He shoved himself away from the table and stood, his big body taut with barely controlled rage.

She took a deep breath. "I'm pregnant."

Just for an instant his fierce expression didn't change; then all of a sudden his face turned to stone, blank and hard. "What did you say?"

"I'm pregnant. Almost four months. It's due around the end of September."

He turned his back on her and walked to the terrace wall to look out over the city. The line of his shoulders was rigid with anger. "By God, I never thought you'd do this," he said, his voice harshly controlled. "I've been suckered all the way, haven't I? I should have known what to expect after the question you asked last night. Marriage would be more profitable than a paternity suit, wouldn't it? But you stand to make a good profit either way."

Anna got up from the table and quietly walked back into the apartment. Saxon stood by the wall, his fists knotted as he tried to deal with both blind rage and the cold knot of betrayal, as well as the pain that waited, crouched and ready, to come to the fore at the least abatement of anger.

He was too tense to stand there long; when he couldn't bear it any longer, he followed her, determined to find out the depths of his own stupidity even though that would only deepen the pain. It was like the way a tongue would continually probe a sore tooth, in search of the pain. No matter how she tore him to shreds, he had to know, and then he would be invulnerable; no one would ever get to him again. He had once thought himself invulnerable, only to have Anna show him the chink in his emotional armor. But once he got over this, he would truly be untouchable.

Anna was calmly sitting at her desk, writing on a sheet of paper. He had expected her to be packing, at the very least, anything but sitting there scribbling away.

"What're you doing?"

She jerked a little at his harsh voice, but continued writing. Perhaps it was only that his eyes hadn't adjusted to the dimmer light, but she looked pale and drawn. He hoped savagely that she was feeling just a fraction of what he was going through right now.

"I said, what are you doing?"

She signed her name to the bottom of the page and dated it, then held it out to him. "Here," she said, using an enormous effort to keep her voice calm. "Now you won't have to worry about a paternity suit."

Saxon took the paper and turned it around to read it. He skimmed it once, then read it again with greater attention and growing disbelief.

It was short and to the point. *I swear, of my own free will, that Saxon Malone is not the father of the child I carry. He has no legal responsibility, either to me or my child.*

She stood up and moved past him. "I'll be packed and gone by tonight."

He stared down at the paper in his hand, almost dizzy with the conflicting emotions surging back and forth inside him. He couldn't believe what she had done, or how casually she had done it. With just a few words written on a sheet of paper she had prevented herself from receiving a large sum of money, because God knew he would have paid any amount, even bankrupted himself if necessary, to make certain that baby was taken care of, not like—

He started shaking, and sweat broke out on his face. Rage welled in him again. Clutching the paper in his hand, he strode into the bedroom just as she was tugging her suitcases out of the closet.

"That's a damn lie!" he shouted, and threw the crumpled paper at her.

Anna flinched but hung on to her calm demeanor. Privately she wondered how much more she could take before she broke down and began sobbing. "Of course it's a lie," she managed as she placed the suitcases on the bed.

"That baby is mine."

She gave him an odd look. "Did you have any doubt? I wasn't admitting to being unfaithful, I was trying to give you some peace of mind."

"Peace of mind!" It seemed as if all his control had been demolished. He was shouting at her again, when in the entire three years they had known each other he had never before even raised his voice to her. "How the hell am I supposed to have any peace of mind knowing that my kid...my kid—" He stopped, unable to finish the sentence.

She began emptying her dresser drawers into the open suitcases, neatly folding and placing each garment. "Knowing that your kid—what?" she prompted.

He shoved his hands into his pockets and knotted them into fists. "Are you even going to have it?" he asked raggedly.

She went stiff, then straightened to stare at him. "What do you mean by that?"

"I mean, have you already planned an abortion?"

There was no warmth or softness at all in her brown eyes now. "Why do you ask?" she questioned evenly.

"It's a reasonable question."

He really had no idea, she thought numbly. How could he even consider the idea that she might abort his child if he had any inkling at all about the way she felt? All of the love that she had expressed during those long, dark hours might as well have been kept hidden for all the notice he'd paid it. Maybe he had just accepted her passion as the skillful act of a kept woman, designed to keep a sugar daddy happy.

But she didn't say any of that. She just looked at him for a moment before stating abruptly, "No. I'm not having an abortion," then turning back to her packing.

He made an abrupt motion with his hand. "Then what? If you're going to have it, then what are you going to do with it?"

She listened to him with growing disbelief. Had she gone crazy, or had he? What did he think she was going to do? A variety of answers occurred to her, some obvious and some not so obvious. Did he expect her to list the numerous activities involved in caring for a baby, or was he asking what her plans were? Given Saxon's usual precision of speech, always saying exactly what he meant, she was even more bewildered.

"What do you mean, 'what am I going to do with it?' What mothers usually do, I suppose."

His face was grayish and covered with a sheen of sweat. "That's my baby," he said, striding forward to catch her shoulders in his hard hands. "I'll do whatever it takes to keep you from throwing it away like a piece of garbage!"

Chapter Three

Cold chills of horror trickled down her spine, rendering her momentarily incapable of speech. All she could do was endure his tight grip on her shoulders, wide eyes fastened on him and her mouth slightly parted in disbelief. She tried several times to speak, and when she finally managed it, her voice was a hoarse croak. "*Throw it away?* Dear God! That's *sick!* Why on earth would you ever say something like that?"

He was shaking. She could feel it now, in his hands; see it in the visible tremors of his big body. His distress had the effect of relieving her own as she suddenly realized that he was upset and in need of reassurance even more, perhaps, than she was, though she didn't know why. Instinct took over and ruled her actions as she placed her hands on his chest.

"I would never do anything to harm your baby," she said gently. "Never."

His trembling intensified. His green eyes were stark with some savage emotion that she couldn't read, but he took a deep breath and locked his jaw as he fought to regain control. She saw the battle, saw what it cost him to win it, but in just a moment his hands were steady and his face, if still colorless, was as blank as rock. With great care he released her shoulders and let his hands drop to his sides.

"You don't have to leave here," he said, as if that was what they had been discussing. "It's a good apartment. You could take over the lease...."

Anna whirled away from him to hide the sharp upthrust of pain, all the more hurtful because, just for a moment, she thought he had meant that things didn't have to change. But he wasn't offering to preserve the status quo; he still intended to sever the relationship. "Don't," she said, warding off the words with a hand held back toward him. "Just...don't."

"Don't what?" he challenged. "Don't try to make it comfortable for you?"

She inhaled raggedly and let her head drop as she, in turn, tried to marshal her own control, but all she could find was weariness and a need for the truth. If this was the end, why not tell him? Pride? That was a pitiful reason for hiding something that had changed her life. She took another deep breath. "Don't ask me to stay here without you," she said. "You're the reason I'm here. Without you, I have no reason to stay." She turned and faced him, lifting her head so she could see him as she said in a clear, deliberate voice, "I love you. If I hadn't, I never would have come here at all."

Shock rippled across his face, turning it even whiter. His lips moved but made no sound.

"I planned to leave because I thought that was what you would want," she continued steadily. "You made it more than plain from the beginning that you didn't want any ties, so I didn't expect anything else. Even if you wanted to continue our—our arrangement, I don't think it's possible. I can't be a mother and continue to be your undemanding mistress, too. Babies tend to have their own priorities. So, under the present circumstances, I have to leave. That doesn't mean I'll stop loving you." *Ever,* she added in her thoughts.

He shook his head, either in disbelief or denial, and moved jerkily to sit down on the bed, where he stared unseeingly at the open suitcases.

Concern welled in her as she watched him. She had expected him to react with anger or cold retreat, but he truly seemed in shock, as if something terrible had happened. She walked over to sit beside him, her gaze fastened on his face in an effort to catch every fleeting nuance of expression. Saxon was hard enough to read when he was relaxed; his face looked like marble now.

Anna gripped her fingers tightly together. "I never expected you to act like this," she murmured. "I thought . . . I guess I thought you just wouldn't care."

His head jerked up, and he gave her a look like a sword edge, sharp and slicing. "You thought I'd just walk away and never give another thought to either you or the baby?" His tone was harsh with accusation.

She didn't back down. "Yes, that's exactly what I thought. What else could I think? You've never given me any indication that I was anything more to you than a convenient sexual outlet."

His heart twisted painfully, and he had to look away. She thought she was only a convenience, when he measured his life by the time he spent with her. Not that he had ever let her know; she was right about that. He had gone out of his way to keep her from knowing. Was that why he was losing her now? He felt as if he had been shredded, but he was in too much pain to be able to tell which was hurting worse, the knowledge that he was losing her or that he had fathered a baby who was also lost to him.

"Do you have a place to go?" he asked numbly.

She sighed inaudibly, releasing the last frail grasp of hope. "No, not really, but it's okay. I've looked around a little, but I haven't wanted to commit on anything until I talked to you. I'll go to a hotel. It won't take me long to find another apartment. And you've made certain I won't be strapped financially. Thank you for that. And thank you for my baby." She managed a faint smile, but he wasn't looking at her and didn't see it.

He leaned forward and braced his elbows on his knees, massaging his forehead with one hand. Lines of weariness were cut into his face. "You don't have to go to a hotel," he muttered. "You can look for another place from here. There's no point in moving twice. And we have a lot of legal stuff to get sorted out."

"No we don't," she said. He slanted his head to the side to give her another of those incisive looks. "We don't," she insisted. "You've made certain of my financial security. I'm more than able to provide for my baby. If you think I'm going to be bleeding you dry, you can just think again!"

He straightened. "What if I want to support it? It's my kid, too. Or didn't you plan on ever letting me see it?"

She was frankly bewildered. "Do you mean you *want* to?" She had never expected that. What she had expected was a cold and final end to their relationship.

That look of shock crossed his features once again, as if he had just realized what he'd said. He gulped and got to his feet, striding restlessly around the room. He had so much the look of a trapped animal that she took pity on him and said softly, "Never mind."

Instead of reassuring him, her words seemed to disturb him even more. He ran his hands through his hair, then turned abruptly toward the door. "I can't—I have to think things through. Stay here as long as you need."

He was gone before she could call him back, before she truly realized he was leaving. The front door slammed even before she could get up from the bed. She stared at the empty space where he had stood, and recalled the haunted look in his eyes. She recognized that he was more deeply disturbed than she had ever considered possible, but had no clue as to why. Saxon had kept his past so completely private that she knew absolutely nothing about his childhood, not even who his parents were. If he had any family at all, she didn't know about them. But then, it didn't necessary follow that she would; after all, he still had his own apartment, and his mail still went there. Nor did she think it likely that he would have given out his mistress's telephone number so his family could contact him if he didn't answer his own phone.

She looked around at the apartment she had called home for two years. She didn't know if she would be able to stay here while she looked for someplace else, despite his generous offer. She had been telling him nothing less than the truth when she had said that she didn't want to stay here without him. The apartment was permeated with his presence, not physical reminders so much as the sharp memories that would be a long time fading. Her child had been conceived in the very bed she sat on. She thought about that for a moment; then her lips curved in a wryly gentle smile. Perhaps not; Saxon had never felt the need to limit their lovemaking to the bed, though they had usually sought it for comfort's sake. It was, she supposed, just as likely to have happened in the shower, or on the sofa, or even on the kitchen counter, one cold afternoon when he had arrived while she was cooking dinner and hadn't been inclined to wait until bedtime.

Those days of wondrous passion were over now, as she had known they would be. Even if Saxon hadn't reacted as she had anticipated, the end result was the same.

Saxon walked. He walked automatically, without aim or care. He was still reeling from the twin blows Anna had dealt him, incapable of ordering his thoughts or controlling his emotions. He had controlled every aspect of his life for so long, closing a door in his mind on the things that had happened years before, and he had thought the monster tamed, the nightmare robbed of horror. Yet all it had taken to destroy his deceptively fragile peace was the knowledge that Anna was pregnant. And she was leaving him. God, she was leaving him.

He felt like raising his fists to the sky and cursing whatever fate had done this to him, but the pain was too deep for that. He would have crouched on the sidewalk and howled like a demented animal if it would have relieved even a portion of the swelling agony in his chest and mind, but he knew it would not. The only surcease he would find would be where he had always found it: with Anna.

He couldn't even begin to think of the future. He had no future, no anchor. The image of endless days stretching before him refused to form; he simply couldn't face even one more day, let alone an eternal procession of them. A day without Anna? Why bother?

He'd never been able to tell her how much she meant to him. He could barely tolerate even admitting it to himself. Love, in his experience, was only an invitation to betrayal and rejection. If he allowed himself to love, then he was making himself vulnerable to a destruction of the mind and soul. And no one had loved him, not ever. It was a lesson he had learned from the earliest reaches of memory, and he had learned it well. His very survival had depended on the hard shell of indifference he had cultivated, so he had formed layer after layer of armor.

When had it changed from protection to prison? Did the turtle ever long for freedom from its boxy shell, so it could run unhindered? Probably not, but he wasn't so lucky. Anna had said that she loved him, and even if it wasn't true, in saying it she had given him the opportunity to stay just a little while longer, if only he had dared to take it. He hadn't, because it would have meant shedding at least a few layers of his armor, and the prospect filled him with a terror founded in earliest childhood and strengthened through long years of abuse.

When he arrived in front of his apartment door he stood staring at it in bewilderment, not quite certain of his location. When he finally realized that he was, in fact, at his own apartment, that he had walked several miles to reach it, he fumbled in his pocket for the keys.

The apartment was silent and musty when he entered, without any sweet welcoming presence. Anna had never been here, and it showed. He could barely stand to spend any time here. It was dark and empty, like a grave, and he was incapable of bringing any light into it. The only light he'd ever known had been Anna's, and he had shared it for too short a time, then driven her away with his own unbridled lust. He'd never been able to keep his hands off her. He had made love to her far more often than he ever would have thought possible, his male flesh rising again and again for the incredible sweetness of sinking into her and joining his body to hers. He had made her pregnant, and because of it he had lost her.

What would he do without her? He couldn't function, couldn't find it in himself to give a damn about contracts, or whether the job got done or not. Even when he had spent days on a job, he had always done it knowing that she was waiting for him. By working so hard, even if it took him away from her, he was able to take care of her and make certain she never had to do without anything. Every time he had expanded the stock portfolio he had set up for her, he had felt an intense satisfaction. Maybe he had thought that his diligent efforts in that would keep her with him, that they would show her that she was better off with him than with anyone else, or out on her own.

He couldn't let himself think, even for a moment, that she might have stayed with him only because he *was* establishing her financial security. If he thought that about Anna, then he truly had nothing left to live for. No, he had always known that she had disliked that part of their arrangement.

There had been no reason at all for her to stay... unless she *did* love him.

For the first time, he let himself think about what she had said. At the time, it had been too much for him to take in, but now the words circled tentatively in his consciousness, like frail birds afraid to light.

She loved him.

He sat in the silent apartment for the rest of the day and into the night, too far withdrawn into himself to feel the need for light or noise, and sometime during the dark hours he crossed an internal barrier. He felt as if he were pinning his desperate hopes on the slimmest of chances, as if he were shooting for the longest odds, but he faced the cold gray fact that he could do nothing else.

If Anna loved him, he couldn't let her go like this.

Chapter Four

Anna had a bad night. She couldn't sleep; though she hadn't expected to sleep well, neither had she expected to lie awake for hours, staring at the dark ceiling and physically aching at the empty space beside her. Saxon had spent many nights away from her before, on his numerous business trips, and she had always managed to sleep. This, however, was different, an emptiness of the soul as well as of space. She had known it would be difficult, but she hadn't known it would leave this wrenching, gnawing pain inside. Despite her best efforts, she had cried until her head had started throbbing, and even then she hadn't been able to stop.

It was sheer exhaustion that finally ended the tears, but not the pain. It was with her, unabating, through the long dark hours.

If this was what the future would be like, she didn't know if she could bear it, even with the baby. She had thought that his child, immeasurably precious, would be some consolation for his absence, and though that might be so in the future, it was a hollow comfort now. She couldn't hold her baby in her arms right now, and it would be five long months before she could.

She got up toward dawn without having slept at all, and made a pot of decaffeinated coffee. Today of all days she needed the kick of caffeine, but her pregnancy forbade it. She made the coffee anyway, hoping that the ritual would fool her brain into alertness, then sat at the kitchen table with a thick robe pulled around her for comfort while she sipped the hot liquid.

Rain trickled soundlessly down the glass terrace doors and jumped in minute splashes on the drenched stone. As fine as the day before had been, the fickle April weather had turned chilly and wet as a late cold front swept in. If Saxon had been there, they would have spent the morning in bed, snuggled in the warmth of the bed covers, lazily exploring the limits of pleasure.

She swallowed painfully, then bent her head to the table as grief welled up overwhelmingly again. Though her eyes felt grainy and raw from weeping, it seemed there were still tears, still an untapped capacity for pain.

She didn't hear the door open, but the sound of footsteps on the flagstone flooring made her jerk upright, hastily wiping her face with the heels of her hands. Saxon stood before her, his dark face bleak and drawn with weariness. He still had on the same clothes he'd worn the day before, she saw, though he had thrown on a leather bomber jacket as protection against the rain. He had evidently been walking in it, because his black hair was plastered down, and rivulets of moisture ran down his face.

"Don't cry," he said in a raw, unnatural tone.

She felt embarrassed that he had caught her weeping. She had always taken pains to hide any bouts of emotion from him, knowing that they would make him uncomfortable. Nor did she look her best, with her eyes swollen and wet, her hair still tousled from a restless night, and swaddled from neck to foot in a thick robe. A mistress should always be well-groomed, she thought wryly, and almost burst into tears again.

Without shifting his gaze from her, he took off his jacket and hung it over the back of a chair. "I didn't know if you had stayed," he said, the strain still evident in his voice. "I hoped you had, but—" Then, abruptly, he moved with that shocking speed of his, scooping her up in his arms and carrying her quickly into the bedroom.

After a small startled cry, Anna clung to his shoulders. He had moved like that the first time, as if all his passion had been swelling behind the dam of his control and the dam had finally given way. He had swept her off her feet and down to the floor in the office almost in the same motion, then had come down on top of her before her surprise could give way to gladness. She had reached for him with desire that rose quickly to match his, and it had been hours before he had released her.

She could feel the same sort of fierceness in his grip now as he placed her on the bed and bent over her, loosening the robe and spreading it wide. Beneath it she wore a thin silk nightgown, but evidently even that was too much. Silently she stared up at his intent face as he lifted her free of the robe, then tugged the nightgown over her head. Her breath quickened as she lay naked before him, and she felt her breasts tighten under his gaze, as hot as any touch. A warm, heavy pooling of sensation began low in her body.

He opened her thighs and knelt between them, visually feasting on her body as he fumbled with his belt and zipper, lowering his pants enough to free himself. Then his green gaze flashed upward to meet the drowning velvet brown of hers. "If you don't want this, say so now."

She could no more have denied him, and herself, than she could willingly have stopped breathing. She lifted her slender arms in invitation, and he leaned forward in acceptance, sheathing himself in both her body and her embrace with one movement. He groaned aloud, not just at the incredible pleasure, but at the cessation of pain. For now, with her slender body held securely beneath him, and himself held just as securely within her, there was no distance between them.

Anna twisted under the buffeting of a savagely intense sensual pleasure. The shock of his cold, damp clothing on her warm bare body made her feel more naked than she ever had before. The single point of contact of bare flesh, between her legs, made her feel more sexual, made her painfully aware of his masculinity as he moved over and inside her. It was too overwhelming to sustain, and she arched into climax too soon, far too soon, because she wanted it to last forever.

He stilled, holding himself deep inside her for her pleasure, holding her face and planting lingering kisses over it. "Don't cry," he murmured, and until then she hadn't known that there were tears seeping out of her eyes. "Don't cry. It doesn't have to end now."

She had cried it aloud, she realized, had voiced her despair at the swift peaking.

He brought all the skill and knowledge of two years of intimacy into their lovemaking, finding the rhythm that was fast enough to bring her to desire again, but slow enough to keep them from reaching satisfaction. There was a different satisfaction in the lingering strokes, in the continued linking of their bodies. Neither of them wanted it to end, because as long as they were together like this they wouldn't have to face the specter of separation. Withdrawal, right now, would mean more than the end of their lovemaking; it would be a parting that neither could bear.

His clothing became not a sensual pleasure, but an intolerable barrier. She tore at the buttons on his shirt, wanting the wet cloth out of the way, needing the pressure of his skin on hers. He rose enough to shrug his wide shoulders out of the garment and toss it aside; then he lowered his chest, and she whimpered in delight at the rasp of his hair on her sensitive nipples.

He cupped her breasts in both hands and pushed them together, bending his head to brush light kisses over the tightly drawn nipples. They were a bit darker, he noticed, and the pale globes were a little swollen, signs of his baby growing within her flat belly. He shuddered with unexpected excitement at the thought, at the knowledge that the same act he was performing now had resulted in that small life.

He had to grit his teeth in an effort to keep from climaxing right then. His baby! It seemed that knowledge wasn't quite the same thing as realization, and he had just been hit by the full realization that the baby was his, part of him, sharing his genes. Blood of his blood, bone of his bone, mingled inseparably with Anna, a living part of both of them. He felt a wave of physical possession like he'd never known before, never even dreamed existed. His baby!

And his woman. Honey-sweet Anna, smooth warm skin and calm, gentle dark eyes.

The crest had been put off too long to be denied any longer. It swept over them, first engulfing her, then him, her inner trembling too much for him to bear. They heaved together in a paroxysm of pleasure, crying out, dying the death of self and surfacing into the quiet aftermath.

They lay entwined, neither of them willing to be the first to move and break the bond of flesh. Anna slid her fingers into his damp hair, loving the feel of his skull beneath her fingers. "Why did you come back?" she whispered. "It was hard enough watching you leave the first time. Did you have to put me through it again?"

She felt him tense against her. Before, she would never have let him know her feelings; she would have smiled and retreated into her role of the perfect mistress, never making demands. But she had left that shield behind, baring herself with her declaration of love, and there was no going back. She wasn't going to deny that love again.

He rolled to his side, taking her with him, wrapping his arm around her hip to keep her in place. She shifted automatically, lifting her leg higher around his waist for greater comfort. He moved closer to deepen his tenuous penetration, and they both breathed infinitesimal sighs of relief.

"Do you have to go?" he finally asked. "Why can't you just stay?"

She rubbed her face against his shoulder, her dark eyes sad. "Not without you. I couldn't bear it."

She felt the effort it took him to say, "What if... what if I stay, too? What if we just go on as before?"

She lifted her head to look at him, studying his beloved features in the rain-dimmed light. She wasn't unaware of what it had taken for him to make such an offer; he had always been so diligent in shunning even the appearance of caring, yet now he was actually reaching out to her, asking for the ties of emotion. He needed to be loved more than any man she had ever seen, but she didn't know if he could tolerate it. Love brought responsibilities, obligations. It was never free, but required a high payment in the form of compromise.

"Can you?" she asked, the sadness as evident in her tone as in her eyes. "I don't doubt that you would try, but could you stay? There's no going back. Things have changed, and they'll never be the same again."

"I know," he said, and the stark look in his eyes hurt her, because she could see that he didn't really believe he could succeed.

She had never before pried into his past, just as she had never before told him that she loved him, but their insular little world had unraveled with frightening speed and turned things upside down. Sometimes, to make a gain, you had to take a risk.

"Why did you ask me if I would throw our baby away?"

The question hung in the air between them like a sword. She felt him flinch, saw his pupils contract with shock. He would have pulled away from her then, but she tightened her leg around him and gripped his shoulder with her hand; he stopped, though he could easily have moved had he wanted to pit his strength against hers. He stayed only because he couldn't bring himself to give up her touch. She bound him with her tenderness when strength couldn't have held him.

He closed his eyes in an instinctive effort to shut out the memory, but it didn't go away, couldn't go away with Anna's question unanswered. He had never talked about it before, never wanted to talk about it. It was a wound too deep and too raw to be eased by "talking it out." He had lived with the knowledge his entire life, and he had done what he'd had to do to survive. He had closed that part of his life away. It was like tearing his guts out now to answer, but Anna deserved at least the truth.

"My mother threw me away," he finally said in a guttural tone; then his throat shut down and he couldn't say anything else. He shook his head helplessly, but his eyes were still closed, and he didn't see the look of utter horror, swiftly followed by soul-shattering compassion, on Anna's face. She watched him through a blur of tears, but she didn't dare break down and begin crying, or do anything else that would interrupt him. Instead she gently stroked his chest, offering tactile comfort rather than verbal; she sensed that words weren't adequate to the task, and in any case, if she tried to speak, she would lose her battle with her tears.

But as the silence stretched into minutes, she realized that he wasn't going to continue, perhaps couldn't continue without prompting. She swallowed and tried to regain her composure; it was an effort, but finally she was able to speak in a voice that, if not quite normal, was still soft and full of the love she felt.

"How did she throw you away? Were you abandoned, adopted ... what?"

"Neither." He did twist away from her then, to lie on his back with his arm thrown up to cover his eyes. She mourned his loss, but gave him the distance he needed. Some things had to be faced alone, and perhaps this was one of them. "She threw me into the garbage when I was born. She didn't put me on the church steps or leave me at an orphanage so I could make up little stories about how much my mother had really loved me, but she had been really sick or something and had had to give me away so I'd be taken care of. All the other kids could make up stories like that, and believe them, but my mother made damn sure I was never that stupid. She dumped me into a trash can when I was a few hours old. There's not much way you can mistake an action like that for motherly love."

Anna curled into a little ball on her side, her fist shoved into her mouth to stifle the sobs that kept welling up, her streaming eyes fastened on his face. He was talking now, and though she had wanted to know, now she had to fight the urge to clap her hand over his mouth. No one should ever have to grow up knowing about such ugliness.

"She wasn't just trying to get rid of me," he continued in an emotionless voice. "She tried to kill me. It was winter when she threw me away, and she didn't bother to wrap me in anything. I don't know exactly when my birthday is, either January third or fourth, because I was found at three-thirty in the morning, and I could have been born either late on the third or early on the fourth. I almost died of exposure anyway, and I spent over a year in the charity hospital with one problem after another. By the time I was placed in an orphanage, I was a toddler who had seen so many strangers come and go that I wouldn't have anything to do with people. I guess that's why I wasn't adopted. People want babies, infants still wrapped up in blankets, not a thin, sickly toddler who screams if they reach for him."

He swallowed and took his arm down from his eyes, which stared unseeingly upward. "I have no idea who or what my parents are. No trace of my mother was ever found. I was named after the city and county where I was found. Saxon City, Malone county. Hell of a tradition to carry on.

"After a few years I was placed in a series of foster homes, most of them not very good. I was kicked around like a stray puppy. Social services got so desperate to place me that they left me with this one family even though I was always covered with a variety of bruises whenever the caseworker came around. It wasn't until the guy kicked in a couple of my ribs that they jerked me out of there. I was ten, I guess. They finally found a fairly good foster home for me, a couple whose own son had died. I don't know, maybe they thought I'd be able to take their son's place, but it didn't work, for them or me. They were nice, but it was in their eyes every time they looked at me that I wasn't Kenny. It was a place to live, and that was all I wanted. I made it through school, walked out and never looked back."

Chapter Five

What he had told her explained so much about the man Saxon had become and why it was so hard for him to accept any semblance of love. If the first eighteen years of his life had taught him anything, it was that he couldn't depend on what others called love but which he'd never known himself. As he had said, there was no fooling himself with pretty stories that his mother had loved him when her actions had made it plain that she not only hadn't cared, but she had deliberately left him to die. Nor had he received any real affection from the overworked staff of the charity hospital. Children learn early; by the time he had been placed in an orphanage, he had already known that he couldn't trust anyone to take care of him, so he had retreated into himself as the only surety in his life. He had depended on no one except himself for anything.

It was a lesson that had been reinforced by his childhood, shunted from one foster home to another, meeting with abuse in some of them and fitting in at none of them. Where did an outcast learn of love? The simple, heartbreaking answer was that he didn't. He had had to rise above more than simple poverty. He had needed to surmount a total lack of the most simple human caring. When she thought of what he had accomplished with his life, she was awed by his immense willpower. How hard had he had to work to put himself through college, to earn not only an engineering degree but to finish so high in his class that he'd had his choice of jobs, and from there go on to form his own company?

After the gut-wrenching tale of his childhood, they had both been emotionally incapable of probing any deeper. By mutual consent they had gotten up and gone through the motions of a normal day, though it was anything but. The past twenty-four hours had taken a toll on both of them, and they had retreated into long period of silence, punctuated only by commonplace matters such as what they would have for lunch.

He was there. He showed no indication of leaving. She took that as a sign of hope and did no packing herself. Right now, all she asked for was his presence.

It was late afternoon on that rain-drenched day when he said flatly, "You never really answered my question this morning. Can we go on as we did before?"

She glanced at him and saw that though stress was still visible on his face, he seemed to have come to terms with it. She wasn't too certain of her own reaction, but she would rather bear the strain herself than take the risk of putting him off now at a time when that might be enough to drive him away again.

She sat down across from him, trying to marshal her thoughts. Finally she said, "For myself, I would like nothing better. It nearly killed me to lose you, and I'm not too certain I can go through that again. But I can't just think of myself. We can't just think of our own arrangement. What about the baby? At first, nothing will matter to it but Mommy and Daddy, but assuming that we stay together for years, what happens when it starts school and finds out that other mommies and daddies are married? This is Denver, not Hollywood. And though no one frowns on a couple living together, the circumstances change when a baby is involved."

He looked down at his hands and said very carefully, "How is it different if you move out? Its parents still won't be married, but you'll be trying to raise it alone. Is that supposed to be better for it? I don't know what kind of a father I'd make, but I think I'd be better than nothing."

Her lips trembled, and she fiercely bit down on them. Dear God, was she making him *beg* to be included in his child's life? She had never intended that, especially in light of what he'd told her that morning. "I think you'd be a wonderful father," she said. "I've never intended to prevent you from seeing your child. It's our living arrangement I'm not sure of."

"I am. I want you, and you . . . you want me."
He still couldn't say that she loved him. "We don't
have to do anything right now. Like you said, it'll
be years before it's old enough to compare us with
other parents. You still have a pregnancy to get
through, and God knows I won't sleep at night if
I don't know you're okay. At least stay until the
baby's born. I can take care of you, go with you
to those childbirth classes, be with you during delivery." Though his tone was confident, his eyes
were pleading, and that was what broke down her
resolve. If she pushed him away now, he might
never recover.

"There's nothing I'd like better," she said hus-
kily, and saw the lightning flash of relief in his eyes
before he masked it.

"I'll move my clothes in tomorrow."

She could only blink at him in surprise. She had
expected him to return to the status quo, sleeping
almost every night with her but returning to his
own apartment every morning to change clothes
before going to work. The thought of his clothes
hanging next to hers in the spacious closet made
her feel both excited and a little alarmed, which
was ridiculous, because she had never wanted
anything as much as she had wanted a full, complete life with him. But things were changing so
swiftly, and her life was already in upheaval with
her pregnancy. Control of her body was slipping
further from her grasp with every passing day, as

the baby grew and demanded more of her. Though her early symptoms had been scant, she could now see definite changes.

She had been fighting one of those changes all day, and it was all suddenly too much. Tears welled in her eyes as she looked at him, and began to roll down her face. Instantly he was beside her, putting his arms around her and tucking her head against his shoulder. "What's wrong?" he demanded, sounding almost frantic. "Don't you want me to move in? I thought I could take care of you better."

"It isn't that," she sobbed. "Yes, it is. I'm happy, damn it! I've always wanted you to move in with me, or ask me to move in with you. But you didn't do it for my sake, you did it because of the baby!"

Saxon tilted her face up and used his thumbs to wipe away her tears. His black brows were drawn together in a scowl. "Of course I'm doing it for you," he said impatiently. "I don't know the baby. Hell, I can't even see much evidence of it yet! I don't want you to be alone any more than necessary." The scowl intensified. "Have you been to a doctor?"

She sniffed and wiped her eyes. "Yes, I didn't realize I was pregnant until I saw the doctor. I went because my last period was just spotting, and the one before that was really light. I've hardly had any symptoms at all."

"Is that normal?"

"As normal as anything else is. The doctor told me everything looked fine, that some women spotted for the first few months and some didn't, that some women had morning sickness and some didn't. All I've really noticed is that I get tired and sleepy and that I want to cry a lot."

He looked relieved. "You mean you're crying because of the baby?"

"No, I'm crying because of you!"

"Well, don't." He pulled her close and pressed a kiss to her forehead. "I don't like it when you cry."

There was no way he could know how it felt to be coddled and cuddled like that, how she had yearned for it. Love had been in short supply in her life, too, though she had never known the direct brutality Saxon had suffered. Her most cherished dreams had always been about having a home with him, just an ordinary home, with the sweet security of routine and the sure knowledge that he was coming home to her every day. In her dreams he had always held her and shown her how much he cared, while in reality he had offered her physical intimacy and an emotional desert. This sudden turnaround was so much like a dream come true that she was afraid to believe in it. Even so, she wasn't going to do anything to end it prematurely. For as long as he stayed, she intended to savor every moment.

True to his word, he moved in the next day. He didn't say anything to her about it, but a couple of phone calls, one from someone interested in leasing his other apartment and another from a utility company double-checking the address for the forwarding of his bill, made it obvious that he was completely giving up his official residence. That, more than anything, told her how serious he was about preserving their relationship.

She watched him closely for signs of edginess, because their relationship had changed in far more fundamental ways than simply that he no longer had dual residences. She had told him that she loved him, words that couldn't be erased or forgotten; by his reaction to their short estrangement, he had revealed a lot more about how much he cared than he ever had before. Though they had been physically intimate for two years, this sort of closeness was totally new to him, and she could tell that sometimes he didn't know how to act. It was almost as if he were in a foreign country where he didn't speak the language, cautiously groping his way about, unable to read the road signs.

He was increasingly curious about the baby and insisted on going with her to her next doctor's appointment, which was scheduled for only a few days after he'd moved in. When he discovered that an ultrasound photo later in her pregnancy might tell them the baby's sex, he immediately wanted to know when they would be able to do it, and how often the doctors were mistaken. Since it was the first interest he had shown in the baby's sex, she wondered if he was imagining having a son. He hadn't indicated a preference either way, and she had no decided preference, either, so they had somehow always referred to the baby as "it" rather than "he" or "she."

How would a son affect him? He would see more of himself in a boy, and it would be, in a way, a chance for him to correct the horror of his own childhood by making certain his own son never knew anything but love. In her mind's eye she saw him patiently showing a grubby, determined little boy how to swing a bat or field a pop fly. There would probably be years of attending a variety of ball games and watching with fierce pride every move the boy made. Every hit would be the best hit ever made, every catch the most stupendous, because the boy making it would be *theirs*.

Despite the dampening whispers of her common sense, she couldn't stop dreaming of a future with Saxon. One miracle had already happened: he hadn't disappeared when he'd learned of her pregnancy. She would continue hoping for another miracle.

Lying in bed that night, she nestled her head on his chest and listened to the strong, steady boom-*boom* of his heart. Her hand strayed down to her abdomen; the baby was hearing her own heart steadily pumping in the same rhythm, soothing and reassuring it just as Saxon's heartbeat soothed her. It was a wonderfully satisfying sound.

"You seemed really interested in the ultrasound," she said sleepily.

"Mmm," he grunted by way of a reply. Her head moved as she glanced up at him, though all she could see was his chin, and that not very well in the darkened room.

"Are you anxious to know what the baby is?"

He shifted restlessly. "I'd like to know, yeah. What about you? Do you have your heart set on a little girl?"

"Not really," she said, and yawned. "I just want a healthy baby, boy or girl, though it would be convenient to know ahead of time so we can have a name picked out and a nursery decorated without having to use greens or yellows."

"A nursery," he said in a faintly surprised tone. "I hadn't thought that far ahead. All I can picture is this little person about the size of a skinned rabbit, all wrapped up in a blanket. It'll stay where we put it and won't take up much space. Why does something that small need an entire room for itself?"

She grinned in the darkness. "Because otherwise the entire apartment would be cluttered with all the paraphernalia necessary for taking care of a baby. And where did you think it would sleep?"

The question startled him; then he laughed, the rare sound booming under her ear. "With us, I guess. On whichever arm you weren't using. I would say it could sleep on my chest, but I understand they aren't housebroken."

She snickered, and he laughed again. More content than she could ever remember being in her life, she snuggled even closer. "I imagine you want a boy. All day today I kept having daydreams about you teaching him how to play baseball."

Saxon stiffened, his body going rigid all along her side. "Not especially," he finally said in a strained voice. "I'd really rather have a girl."

Surprise kept her silent, particularly because she didn't know what about the question had upset him. He didn't say anything for a while, and she began to drift off to sleep, but all drowsiness left her when he said quietly, "Maybe if it's a girl you'll love it more."

Chapter Six

"What about your family?" he asked carefully the next morning, as if wary of treading on unstable ground. In his experience, family was something other people had and, from what he'd seen at his foster homes, it wasn't desirable. But he wanted to know more about Anna, wanted to find out all he could about her in case some day he came home to find her gone. "Have you told them that you're having a baby, or anything about me?"

"I don't have any family," she replied as she poured skim milk over her cereal. Her manner was casual, but his interest sharpened immediately.

"No family? Were you an orphan?" He had seen a lot of orphans, sad and terrified children who had lost their entire world and didn't know what to do. Maybe his situation, dire as it had been, was preferable to theirs. At least he hadn't lost someone he loved. His mother hadn't died; she had simply dumped him in the trash. Probably both she and his father were still alive somewhere, though he sincerely doubted they were together. He was more than likely the result of a short affair, at best, and more probably a one-night stand.

"Yes, but I was never in an orphanage. My mother died when I was nine, and my dad said he couldn't take proper care of me, so he sent me to live with his half sister. To tell the truth, he simply didn't want the responsibility. From what my aunt said, he'd always been irresponsible, never holding down a job for long, spending his money in bars and chasing after other women. He died in a car accident when I was fourteen."

"What about your aunt?" he asked, remembering the "None" she had listed beside the next-of-kin information. "Do you still see her?"

"No. She died about a year before I went to work for you, but I doubt I'd ever have seen her again anyway. It wasn't a fond relationship. She and Uncle Sid had seven kids of their own. I was just an unwelcome extra mouth to feed, especially since she had never gotten along with Dad anyway. Aunt Cora looked as if she had posed for the painting 'American Gothic,' all prune-faced and disapproving, soured on life. There was never enough money to go around, and it was only natural that she provided for her own children first."

Anger swelled in him as he pictured her, a thin, lost little girl with big honey eyes, standing off to the side as he had often stood, never quite a part of a family unit. That had been the better part of his childhood, but it infuriated him that Anna had been subjected to such treatment. "What about your cousins? Don't you ever see them, or hear from them?''

"No, we were never close. We got along as well as most children who have been thrown together, but we never had much in common. They've all moved off the farm, anyway, and I don't know where they are. I suppose I could trace them if I wanted, but there doesn't seem any point in it.''

Somehow he had never pictured Anna as being alone in the world, or of having a background in common with him. It shook him to realize that, in a different way, she had been just as deprived of nurturing as he had. She had never suffered the physical abuse, and perhaps that was why she was still able to reach out, to express her love. Even before he could remember, he had learned not to expect, or hope, or offer anything of himself, because that would leave him open to hurt. He was glad Anna hadn't known a life like that.

Even so, it couldn't have been easy for her to tell him that she loved him. Had she been braced for rejection? That was what he'd done, panicked and thrown her love back in her face. He had been terrified the next morning that she wouldn't be able to stand the sight of him after the way he'd run out on her. But she had taken him back, and thank God, she not only loved him, but she seemed to love his baby. Sometimes it seemed impossible.

"What about the foster family you stayed with?" she asked. "Do you ever call them, or visit?"

"No. I haven't seen them since the day after my high-school graduation, when I packed and left, but they didn't expect me to keep in touch. I told them goodbye and thanked them, and I guess that was good enough."

"What were their names?"

"Emmeline and Harold Bradley. They were good people. They tried, especially Harold, but there was no way they could turn me into their son. It was always there, in their eyes. I wasn't Kenny. Emmeline always seemed to resent it that her son had died but I was still alive. Neither of them ever touched me if they could prevent it. They took care of me, provided me with a place to stay, clothes, food, but there wasn't any affection there. They were relieved when I left."

"Aren't you curious if they're still alive, or if they've moved?"

"There's no point in it. There's nothing for me there, and they wouldn't be overjoyed to see me."

"Where did they live?"

"About eighty miles from here, in Fort Morgan."

"But that's so close! My cousins lived in Maryland, so it's at least reasonable that we haven't kept in touch."

He shrugged. "I left the state when I went to college, so it wasn't exactly convenient for me to visit. I worked two jobs to pay my tuition, and that didn't leave a lot of free time."

"But you came back to Colorado and settled in Denver."

"There's more demand for engineers in a large city."

"There are a lot of cities in this country. The point is, you're so close, but you never called them to tell them how college turned out, or that you were back in the state."

Temper edged into his voice. "No, I didn't, and I don't intend to. For God's sake, Anna, it's been fifteen years since I got out of college. They sure as hell haven't kept a candle in the window for me all this time. They knew I wouldn't be back."

She dropped the subject, but she didn't forget it. Harold and Emmeline Bradley. She committed their names to memory. Despite what Saxon thought, they had spent years raising him and were likely to be more than a little interested in what had become of him.

He left for work in silence, and returned that afternoon in the same brooding mood. She left him alone, but his silence made her quietly panic. Had her questions bothered him so much that he was considering terminating their arrangement? But he had started it by asking about her family, so he had only himself to blame. In the few days since she had told him of the baby she had become accustomed to thinking of him as more approachable, more *hers,* but suddenly she was very much aware of the wall that still surrounded him. She had knocked a few chinks out of it, but it was far from demolished.

Saxon hadn't liked all that talk about his foster family, but it had started him thinking. Unless he and Anna took steps to prevent it, this baby wouldn't have much of a family, either. He couldn't picture them having other children under their present circumstances, and to his surprise, he liked the idea of more children. He wanted them to be a family, not just live-in lovers who happened to have a baby.

He hadn't had pretty fantasies about his mother, but he had often wondered, with a child's bewildered pain, what it would be like to have a real family, to belong somewhere and have someone who loved him. It was a fantasy that hadn't lasted long under the merciless weight of reality, but he still remembered how he had imagined it, the feeling of security that was at the center of it and held everything together. He hadn't been able to picture parents, beyond tall shadowy figures that stood between him and danger. He never wanted his baby to have those kinds of fantasies; he wanted it to have the reality of a stable home.

Less than a week ago, just the idea of what he was now considering would have been enough to make him break out in a panicky sweat, but he had since learned that there were worse things. Losing Anna was worse. He hoped he never in his life had to live through another day and night like he'd endured then, because he didn't think his sanity could take it. In comparison, what he was thinking now was a snap.

Thinking it was one thing, actually putting it into words was another. He watched Anna with troubled eyes, though he knew it was useless trying to predict her answer. Behind her customary serenity she was deep and complicated, seeing more than he wanted her to see, understanding more than was comfortable. With so much of her thought processes hidden from him, he wasn't at all certain how she would react, or why. If she loved him there should be no hesitation, but that wasn't necessarily the case. She was capable of sacrificing her own happiness—assuming he could make her happy—for what she thought best for the baby.

It was strange what an impact the baby had had on their lives months prior to its birth, but he didn't regret the changes. It was frightening; he had the sense of living on the edge, where any false move could send him over, but at the same time the increased openness and intimacy he shared with Anna were, without a doubt, worth every minute of worry. He didn't think he could go back to the previous loneliness he had taken for granted, even embraced.

Still, it was a decision that racked him with nerves. In the end, he couldn't say the words that would be an offer of himself, a statement of his feelings and vulnerability; instead he threw them out couched as a suggestion. "I think we should get married."

There was nothing he could have said that would have astounded her more. Her legs went weak, and she sat down heavily. "Marriage!" she said with a mixture of disbelief and total surprise.

He wasn't pleased that the solution hadn't occurred to her. "Yes, marriage. It makes sense. We're already living together, and we're having a baby. Marriage seems the logical next step."

Anna shook her head, not in refusal but in a futile effort to clear her head. Somehow she had never expected to receive a marriage proposal couched as "the logical next step." She hadn't expected a marriage proposal, period, though she had wanted one very badly. But she had wanted him to propose for different reasons, because he loved her and couldn't live without her. She suspected that was the case, but she would never know for sure if he never told her.

It wasn't an easy decision, and she didn't rush into speech. His face was impassive as he waited for her answer, his green eyes darkened and watchful. Her answer meant a lot to him, she realized. He wanted her to say yes. She wanted to say yes. The question was whether she was willing to take the chance that he did love her and marry him on blind faith. A cautious woman wouldn't want to make a hasty decision that would affect not only the two of them, but their child as well. A broken marriage inevitably left its scars on all concerned.

She had taken a leap of blind faith in quitting her job to become his mistress, and she didn't regret it. The two years of loving him had been the best of her life, and she could never wish them undone. Pregnancy altered everything, she thought with a faint curving of her lips. She couldn't just think of herself now; she had to think of the baby. What was logical wasn't necessarily the best choice, even though her heart clamored for a quick acceptance.

She looked at him, her dark eyes grave. "I love you, you know," she said.

Once such a statement would have made his face go blank in a refusal to hear. Now he steadily returned her gaze. "I know." The knowledge didn't make him panic; instead he treasured it, savored it, as the most precious gift of his life.

"I want to say yes, more than anything I've ever wanted, but I'm afraid to. I know it was your idea for us to stay together, and you've been wonderful, but I'm not certain that you'll still feel the same after the baby's born. As the old saying goes, then it becomes a whole new ball game. I don't want you to feel trapped or unhappy."

He shook his head as if to forestall the answer he sensed was coming. "There's no way to predict the future. I know why you worry about the way I'll react, and to tell you the truth, I'm a little scared myself, but I'm excited, too. I want this baby. I want you. Let's get married and make it official." He smiled wryly. "The baby could have Malone for a last name. The second generation of a brand-new family."

Anna took a deep breath and denied herself what she had wanted more than anything else. "I can't give you an answer now," she whispered, and saw his face tighten. "It just doesn't feel right. I want to say yes, Saxon, I want that more than anything, but I'm not certain it would be the right thing to do."

"It is," he said roughly.

"Then if it is, it will still be the right thing a month from now, or two months from now. Too much has happened too fast—the baby...you. I don't want to make the wrong decision, and I think I'm operating more on my emotions now than on brainpower."

The force of his willpower shone out of his eyes, intensely green and focused. "I can't make you say yes," he said in a slow, deep voice. "But I can keep asking. I can make love to you and take care of you until you won't be able to imagine life without me.''

Her lips trembled. ''I can't imagine that now.''

''I don't give up, Anna. When I go after something, I don't stop until I've gotten it. I want you, and I'm going to have you.''

She knew exactly what he meant. When he decided something, he focused on it with a fierce tunnel vision that didn't let him rest until he had achieved his objective. It was a little daunting to think of herself as the object of that kind of determination.

He smiled then, a smile that was more than a little predatory. ''You can take that to the bank, baby.''

Chapter Seven

Marriage. The thought of it hovered in her consciousness during the day and crept into her dreams at night. Several times every day she started to throw caution to the winds and tell him yes, but there was a part of her that simply wasn't ready to take such an immense step. She had been willing before to settle for being his mistress, but now she was unable to settle for being his wife; she wanted him to love her, too, and admit it to both her and himself. She might be certain that he did love her, but until he could come to terms with his feelings, she couldn't rely on that. He could say "I want you," but not "I love you."

She couldn't blame him for having difficulty with the emotion. Sometimes when she was alone she cried for him, at first a discarded infant, then a lonely, frightened toddler, and finally an abused youngster with no one he could turn to for help. No one could have endured such a childhood without emotional scarring, without losing the ability both to give and accept love. When she looked at it clearly, she saw that he had reached out to her far more than could reasonably be expected.

She didn't really expect more, but she wanted it.

She couldn't get the Bradleys out of her mind. From what he had said, he had spent six years with them, from the time he was twelve until he was eighteen. Six years was a long time for them to keep him and not feel something for him. Was it possible that they had offered him more than duty, but at the time he hadn't been able to see it for what it was? And how had they felt at not hearing from him ever again?

Surely they had worried, if they had any hint of human warmth about them. They had raised him from a boy to a young man, given him the only stable home life he had ever known until Anna had become his mistress and made a sanctuary for him in the apartment. It was always possible that it had been exactly as he remembered it, that losing their son had prevented them from feeling anything for him beyond duty and a sense of pity. Pity! He would have hated that. If he had sensed that they pitied him, no wonder he hadn't gone back.

But though she fretted about it for several days, she knew that she wasn't accomplishing anything with her worrying. If she wanted to know for certain, she would have to drive to Fort Morgan and try to find the Bradleys. It might be a useless trip, since nineteen years had passed; they could have moved, or even died.

Once she made the decision to go, she felt better, even though she knew Saxon would be adamantly against the idea. However, she didn't intend to let his opposition stop her.

That didn't mean she intended to be sneaky about it. After dinner that night she said, "I'm going to Fort Morgan tomorrow."

He tensed, and his eyes narrowed. "Why?"

"To try to find the Bradleys."

He folded the newspaper away with an angry snap. "There's no point in it. I told you how it was. Why are you worried about it, anyway? That was nineteen years ago. It's nothing to do with us now. You didn't even know me then."

"Curiosity, partly," she answered with blunt honesty. "And what if you're wrong about the way they felt? You were young. You could have misread them. And if you were wrong, then they've spent nineteen years feeling as if they lost two sons instead of just one."

"No," he said, and from the command in his voice she knew he wasn't refuting her suggestion but issuing an order.

She lifted her brows at him, mild surprise in her eyes. "I wasn't asking permission. I was letting you know where I'd be so you wouldn't worry if you called and I wasn't here."

"I said no."

"You certainly did," she agreed. "But I'm not your mistress anymore—"

"It sure as hell felt like you were last night," he interrupted, his eyes turning greener as anger intensified the color.

She didn't intend to argue with him. Instead she smiled, and her soft face glowed as she sent him a warm look. "That was making love." And it had been wonderful. Sex between them had always been hot and urgent, but since he had moved in with her it had taken on an added dimension, a shattering tenderness that hadn't been there before. Their lovemaking was more prolonged; it was as if, before, he had always been aware that he was going to have to get up and leave, and the knowledge had driven him. Now he was relaxed and leisurely in a way he hadn't been before, with increased pleasure as a result.

There was a flicker of tension across his face at the word "love," but it was quickly gone, with no lingering echoes.

"I'm not your mistress," she repeated. "That arrangement is over with. I'm the woman who loves you, who lives with you, who's having your baby."

He looked around at the apartment. "You may not think you're my mistress anymore," he said with soft anger, "but things look pretty much the same to me."

"Because you support me? That's your choice, not mine. I'll find a job, if it will make you feel better. I've never enjoyed being a kept woman, anyway.''

"No!" He didn't like that idea at all. It had always been in the back of his mind that, if he kept her totally dependent on him, she would be less likely to leave. At the same time he had invested in stocks in her name to make certain she would be financially secure. The paradox had always made him uneasy, but he wanted her to be taken care of in case something happened to him. After all, he traveled a lot and spent a lot of time on construction sites, not the safest of places. He had also made a will a year ago, leaving everything to her. He'd never told her.

"I don't want you driving that far by yourself," he finally said, but he was grasping at straws, and he knew it.

"It's less than a two-hour drive, the weather forecast is for clear and sunny conditions tomorrow. But if you want to go with me, I can wait until the weekend," she offered.

His expression closed up at the idea. He had never been back, never wanted to go back. The Bradleys hadn't mistreated him; they had been the best of all the foster homes he'd been in. But that part of his life was over. He had shut the door on it when he'd left, and he'd spent the following years working like a slave to make himself into someone who would never again be helpless.

"They may have moved," she said, offering comfort. "I just want to know."

He made a weary gesture. "Then pick up the telephone and call information. Talk to them, if they're still there. But don't involve me in it. I don't want to talk to them. I don't want to see them. I don't want anything to do with this."

She wasn't surprised at his total rejection of the past; it was hardly the type of memory he would embrace. And she hadn't expected him to go with her.

"I don't want to talk to them over the telephone," she said. "I want to drive up there, see the house. I may not approach them at all. It depends on what I find when I get there."

She held her breath, because there was one appeal he could make that she wouldn't be able to deny. If he said, "Please don't go, for my sake," then she wouldn't go. If he actually asked for anything for himself, there was no way she could turn him down. He had been rejected so much in his life that she wouldn't add to it. But because of those prior rejections, she knew he wouldn't ask in those terms. He would never put things in the context of being a personal consideration for him. He would order, he would make objections, but he wouldn't simply ask and say, "Please don't."

He refused to talk about it anymore and got up restlessly to stand at the terrace doors and look out. Anna calmly returned to her own section of the paper, but her heart was beating fast as she realized this was the first normal domestic quarrel they had ever had. To her delight, they had disagreed, and nothing major had happened. He hadn't left, nor did he seem to expect her to leave. It was wonderful. He was already able to trust her enough that he wasn't afraid a disagreement could end their relationship.

She had worried that he would overreact to arguments, since they were part and parcel of every relationship. Normal couples had disagreements; probably even saints had disagreements. Two years ago, Saxon wouldn't have been able to tolerate such a personal discussion.

He was really trying, even though it was extraordinarily difficult for him to open up. Circumstances had forced him into revealing his past, but he hadn't tried to reestablish those protective mental walls of his. He seemed to accept that once the emotional boundaries had been crossed, he couldn't make them inviolate again.

She didn't know what she could accomplish by finding the Bradleys again. Perhaps nothing. She just wanted to see them, to get a feel for herself of what that portion of Saxon's formative years had been like. If they seemed interested, she wanted to reassure them that their foster son was alive and well, that he was successful and would soon be a father himself.

With his back still to her, Saxon asked, "Are you afraid to marry me because of my past? Is that why you want to find the Bradleys, so you can ask them questions about me?"

"No!" she said, horrified. "I'm not *afraid* to marry you."

"My parents could be anything—murderers, drug users. My mother may be a prostitute. The odds are pretty good she was. There may be a history of mental illness in my background. *I'd* be afraid to marry me. But the Bradleys won't be able to tell you anything, because no one knows who my parents were."

"I'm not concerned with your parents," she said levelly. "I know you. You're rock solid. You're honest, kind, hardworking and sexy."

"So why won't you marry me, if I'm such a good catch?"

Good question, she thought. Maybe she was being foolish in waiting. "I don't want to rush into something that might not be right for either of us."

"I don't want my baby to be born illegitimate."

"Oh, Saxon." She gave a sad laugh. "I promise you I'll make a decision long before the baby is born."

"But you can't promise me you'll say yes."

"No more than you can promise me our marriage would work."

He gave her a brief, angry look over his shoulder. "You said you love me."

"And I do. But can you say that *you* love *me?*" she asked.

He didn't answer. Anna watched him, her eyes sad and tender. Her question could be taken in two ways. He did love her, she thought, but was incapable of actually *saying* it. Maybe he felt that as long as he didn't say the words aloud, he hadn't made the emotional commitment.

Finally he said, "Is that what it'll take for you to marry me?"

"No. It isn't a test that you have to pass."

"Isn't it?"

"No," she insisted.

"You say you won't marry me because you don't know if I can handle it, but I'm willing to try. You're the one who's resisting making a commitment."

She stared at him in frustration. He was too good at arguing, agilely taking her previous arguments and using them against her. She was glad that he felt sure enough of her to do it, but she could see what she'd be up against in the future if they did get married. It would take a lot of determination to win an argument against him.

She pointed her finger at him, even though his back was still turned and he couldn't see her. "I'm not resisting making a commitment, I'm resisting making it *now*. I think I have a right to be a little cautious."

"Not if you trust me."

That turned back was making her suspicious. She gave him a considering look, then suddenly realized he had turned his back so she wouldn't be able to read his expression. Her eyes narrowed as she realized what he was doing. He wasn't as upset or even as indignant as he sounded; he was simply using the tactic as a means of maneuvering her into agreeing to marry him. It was all part and parcel of his determination to have his way.

She got up and went over to him, wrapping her arms around his lean waist and leaning her head against his back. "It won't work," she said softly. "I'm on to you."

To her surprise, she felt his chest expand with a low laugh; then he turned within the circle of her arms and looped his own around her. "Maybe you know me too well," he muttered, but his tone was accepting.

"Or maybe you need acting lessons."

He chuckled again and rested his cheek against the top of her head. But all humor was absent from his tone a minute later when he said, "Go see the Bradleys, if you have to. There's nothing there to find out."

Chapter Eight

Fort Morgan was a small town of about ten thousand people. Anna drove around for a little while to get her bearings, then stopped at a phone booth to look up the Bradleys' address. What she would do if they weren't in the book, she didn't know. It could mean they had moved or died, or it might just mean that their number wasn't listed.

She could have asked Saxon, but she hadn't wanted to ask him for information to help her to do something of which he didn't approve. Besides, it had been nineteen years, and there was no guarantee the Bradleys would still live in the same house, even if they had remained in Fort Morgan.

The phone book wasn't very big. She flipped through it to the *B*s, then ran her finger down the column. "Bailey...Banks...Black...Boatwright...Bradley. Harold Bradley." She wrote down the address and phone number, then debated whether she should call them to get directions. She decided not to, because she wanted to catch them unawares, as it were. People could mask their true reactions if they were given warning.

So she drove to a gas station, filled up and asked directions of the attendant. Ten minutes later she drove slowly down a residential street, checking house numbers, and finally stopped at the curb in front of a neat but unpretentious house. It looked as if it had been built a good forty or fifty years before, with an old-fashioned roofed porch across the front. The white paint showed signs of wear but wasn't at the point where one could definitely say the house was in need of repainting. An assortment of potted plants was sunning on the porch, but there weren't any ornamentals in the small yard, which gave it a bare look. A one-car, unconnected garage sat back and to the side of the house.

She got out of the car, oddly reluctant now that she was here, but she walked up the cracked sidewalk and climbed the three steps to the porch. A porch glider, with rust spots showing where the thick white paint had chipped, was placed in front of the windows. Anna wondered if the Bradleys sat out there during the summer and watched the neighbors go about their business.

There wasn't a doorbell. She knocked on the frame of the screen door and waited. A gray-and-white cat leaped up onto the porch and meowed curiously at her.

After a minute, she knocked again. This time she heard hurried footsteps, and her pulse speeded up in anticipation. With it came a wave of nausea that had her swallowing in desperation. Of all the times to have one of her rare bouts of morning sickness! She only hoped she wouldn't disgrace herself.

The door opened, and she found herself face-to-face with a tall, thin, stern-faced woman, only the thin screen separating them. The woman didn't open the screen door. Instead she said, "Yes?" in a deep, rusty-sounding voice.

Anna was dismayed by the lack of friendliness and started to ask for directions as an excuse for being there, planning to leave without ever mentioning Saxon. But the tall woman just stood there with her hand on the latch, patiently waiting for Anna to state her business before she opened the door, and something about that strength of will struck a cord.

"Mrs. Bradley?"

"Yes, I'm Mrs. Bradley."

"My name is Anna Sharp. I'm looking for the Bradleys who used to be foster parents to Saxon Malone. Is this the right family?"

The woman's regard sharpened. "It is." She still didn't unlatch the door.

Anna's hopes sank. If Saxon hadn't been exposed to any sort of love even here, where he had grown up, he might never be able to give or accept it. What sort of marriage could she have under those conditions? What would it do to her own child to have a father who always kept at a distance?

But she had come this far, so she might as well
carry on. She was aware, too, of the compelling
quality of the woman's steely gaze. "I know
Saxon," she began, and with an abrupt movement the woman flipped the latch up and swung
the screen door outward.

"You know him?" she demanded fiercely.
"You know where he is?"

Anna moved back a step. "Yes, I do."

Mrs. Bradley indicated the interior of the house
with a jerk of her head. "Come inside."

Anna did, cautiously, obeying an invitation that
had sounded more like a command. The door
opened directly into the living room; a quick look
around told her that the furniture was old and
threadbare in spots, but the small room was spotless.

"Sit," said Mrs. Bradley.

She sat. Mrs. Bradley carefully relatched the
screen door, then wiped her hands on the apron
she wore. Anna watched the motion of those
strong, work-worn hands, then realized that it was
more of a nervous wringing than it was a deliberate movement.

She looked up at her reluctant hostess's face and
was startled to see the strong, spare features
twisted in a spasm of emotion. Mrs. Bradley tried
to school herself, but abruptly a lone tear rolled
down her gaunt cheek. She sat down heavily in a
rocker and bunched the apron in her hands. "How

is my boy?'' she asked in a broken voice. "Is he all right?''

They sat at the kitchen table, with Mrs. Bradley drinking coffee while Anna contented herself with a glass of water. Mrs. Bradley was composed now, though she occasionally dabbed at her eyes with the edge of the apron.

"Tell me about him,'' Emmeline Bradley said. Her faded blue eyes were alight with a mixture of joy and eagerness, and also a hint of pain.

"He's an engineer,'' Anna said, and saw pride join the other emotions. "He owns his own company, and he's very successful.''

"I always knew he would be. Smart! Lordy, that boy was smart. Me and Harold, we always told each other, he's got a good head on his shoulders. He always got A's in school. He was dead serious about his schooling.''

"He put himself through college and graduated near the top of his class. He could have gone to work with any of the big engineering firms, but he wanted to have his own business. I was his secretary for a while.''

"Fancy that, his own secretary. But when he made up his mind to do something, he done it, even when he was just a boy.''

"He's still like that,'' Anna said, and laughed. "He says exactly what he means and means exactly what he says. You always know where you stand with Saxon.''

"He didn't talk much when he was here, but we understood. The child had been through so much, it was a wonder he'd talk at all. We tried not to crowd him, or force ourselves on him. It about broke our hearts sometimes, the way he would jump to do every little thing we mentioned, then kinda hold himself off and watch to see if we thought he'd done it right. I guess he thought we were going to throw him out if he didn't do everything perfect, or maybe even kick him around the way they'd done in some of those other homes."

Tears welled in Anna's eyes, because she could see him all too plainly, young and thin and still helpless, his green eyes watchful, empty of hope.

"Don't cry," Emmeline said briskly, then had to dab at her own eyes. "He was twelve when we got him, bone-thin and gangly. He hadn't started getting his height yet, and he was still limping where the woman who had him before us knocked him off the porch with a broom handle. He twisted his ankle pretty bad. He had some long, thin bruises across his back, like the broom handle had caught him there, too. I guess it was a regular thing. And there was a burn mark on his arm. Mind you, he never said anything about it, but the caseworker told us a man ground out his cigarette on him.

"He never acted scared of us, but for a long time he'd get real stiff if we got too close to him, like he was getting ready to either fight or run. He seemed more comfortable if we stayed at a distance, so we did, even though I wanted to hug him close and tell him no one was ever going to hurt him again. But he was kinda like a dog that's been beat. He'd lost his trust of people."

Anna's throat was tight when she spoke. "He's still distant, to some extent. He isn't comfortable with emotion, though he's getting better."

"You know him real well? You said you used to be his secretary. Don't you still work for him?"

"No, I haven't worked for him for two years." A faint blush stained her cheeks. "We're having a baby, and he's asked me to marry him."

The color of Emmeline's eyes was faded, but her vision was still sharp. She gave Anna a piercing once-over. "In my day we did things in reverse order, but times change. There's no shame in loving someone. A baby, huh? When's it due? I reckon this is as close to a grandchild as I'll get."

"September. We live in Denver, so we aren't that far away. It'll be easy to visit."

A sad look crept over Emmeline's lined face. "We always figured Saxon didn't want to have nothing to do with us again. He said goodbye when he graduated from high school, and we could tell he meant it. Can't blame him, really. By the time we got him, his growing-up years had marked him so deep we knew he wouldn't want to think about any foster home. The caseworker told us all about him. The woman who gave birth to that boy has a lot to answer for, what she did to him and the living hell she caused his life to be. I swear, if anyone had ever found out who she was, I'd have hunted her down and done violence to her."

"I've had the same thought myself," Anna said grimly, and for a moment her velvet brown eyes didn't look so soft.

"My Harold died several years back," Emmeline said, and nodded in acknowledgment of Anna's murmur of sympathy. "I wish he could be here now, to hear how well Saxon's turned out, but I guess he knows anyway."

Her rough, simple faith was more touching than any elaborate protestation could have been. Anna found herself smiling, because there was something joyous in Emmeline's surety.

"Saxon said you lost your own son," she said, hoping she wasn't bringing up a source of grief that was still fresh. Losing a child was something a parent should never have to experience.

Emmeline nodded, a faraway expression coming over her face. "Kenny," she said. "Lordy, it's been thirty years now since he took sick that last time. He was sickly from birth. It was his heart, and back then they couldn't do the things they can now. The doctors told us from the time he was a baby that we wouldn't get to keep him all that long, but somehow knowing don't always help you prepare for it. He died when he was ten, poor little mite, and he looked about the size of a six-year-old.''

After a minute the dreamy expression left her face, and she smiled. ''Saxon, now, you could tell right off, even as thin and bruised up as he was, he was a strong one. He started growing the next year after we got him. Maybe it was having regular meals that did it. Lord knows I poked all the food down him I could. But he shot up like a bean pole, growing a foot in about six months. Seemed like every time we got him some jeans, he outgrew them the next week. He was taller than Harold in no time, all legs and arms. Then he started to fill out, and that was a sight to behold. All of a sudden we had more young gals walking up and down the street than I'd ever imagined lived within a square mile of this house, giggling to each other and watching the door and windows, trying to get a glimpse of him.''

Anna laughed out loud. ''How did he take being the center of attention like that?''

''He never let on like he noticed. Like I said, he was real serious about his schooling. And he was still leery about letting folks get close to him, so I guess dating would have been uncomfortable for him. But those girls just kept walking past, and can't say as I blame them. He made most boys his age look like pipsqueaks. He was shaving by the time he was fifteen, and he had a real beard, not a few scraggly hairs like most boys. His chest and shoulders had gotten broad, and he was muscled up real nice. Fine figure of a boy.''

Anna hesitated, then decided to touch on the subject of Kenny again. Emmeline tended to get carried away talking about Saxon, perhaps because she had been denied the privilege for so many years. Now that she had finally met somebody who knew him, all the memories were bubbling out.

''Saxon told me that he always felt you resented him because he wasn't Kenny.''

Emmeline gave her a surprised look. ''Resented him? It wasn't his fault Kenny died. Let me tell you, you don't ever get over it when your child dies, but Kenny had been dead for several years before we got Saxon. We'd always planned to either adopt or take in foster kids, anyway, after Kenny left us. Kenny's memory laid a little easier after Saxon came to live with us. It was like he was happy we had someone else to care about, and having Saxon kept us from brooding. How could we resent him, when he'd been through such hell? Kenny didn't have good health, but he always knew we loved him, and even though he died so young, in some ways he was luckier than Saxon.''

''He needs to be loved so much,'' Anna said, her throat tightening again. ''But it's so hard for him to reach out to anyone, or let anyone reach out to him.''

Emmeline nodded. "I guess we should have tried harder, after he'd had time to realize we weren't going to hurt him, but by then we were kinda used to keeping our distance from him. He seemed more comfortable that way, and we didn't push him. Looking back, I can see what we should've done, but at the time we did what it seemed like he wanted.'' She sat for a minute in silence, rocking back and forth a little in the wooden kitchen chair. Then she said, "Resent him? Never for a minute. Land sakes, we loved him from the beginning.''

Chapter Nine

Saxon's face tightened when she told him Harold was dead, and the brilliant color of his eyes dimmed. She had expected him to refuse to listen to anything about the Bradleys, but he hadn't. If he was curious, though, he was hiding it well, because he hadn't asked any questions, either. The news of Harold's death jolted him into showing interest, though reluctantly. "Emmeline is still living in the same old house by herself?"

She told him the address, and he nodded. "It's the same house."

"She seems to be in good health," Anna said. "She cried when I told her I knew you." She took a deep breath. "You should go see her."

"No," he said shortly, dismissing the idea with a frown.

"Why not?"

She could feel him withdrawing, see his face closing up. She reached out and took his hand, remembering what Emmeline had said about letting him pull away when they should have pulled him closer. "I won't let you shut me out," she said. "I love you, and we're in this together."

His eyes were unreadable, but she had his attention. "If I had a problem, would you want to help me, or would you leave me to deal with it on my own?'' she pressed.

There was a flicker of expression, gone too fast for her to decipher. ''I'd take care of it for you,'' he said, and his hand tightened on hers. ''But I don't have a problem.''

''Well, I think you do.''

''And you're determined to help me with it whether I think it exists or not, is that it?''

''That's it. That's the way relationships work. People butt in on other people's business because they care.''

Once he would have thought it was an intolerable encroachment on his privacy, but though her determination was irritating him, at the same time it made him feel oddly secure. She was right; this was the way relationships worked. He'd seen it, though this was the first time he'd experienced it. Somehow their ''arrangement'' had become a ''relationship,'' full of complications, demands and obligations, but he wouldn't have chosen to go back. For the first time in his life he felt accepted as he really was; Anna knew all there was to know about him, all the hideous details of his birth and childhood. She knew the worst, yet she hadn't left.

On a sudden impulse he lifted her astride his lap so he could look full into her face while they talked. It was an intensely personal position for talking, both physically and mentally, but it felt right. "It wasn't a good time of my life," he said in an effort to explain. "I don't want to remember it, or revisit it."

"The way you remember it is distorted by everything that had gone before. You think of them as cold and resentful of you because you weren't their son, but that isn't at all the way they felt."

"Anna," he said patiently, "I was there."

She framed his face with her hands. "You were a frightened boy. Don't you think it's possible you were so used to rejection that you expected it, so that's what you saw?"

"So you're an amateur psychiatrist now?"

"Reasoning doesn't require a degree." She leaned forward and stole a quick kiss. "She talked for hours, telling me all about you."

"And now you think you're an expert."

"I *am* an expert on you," she snapped. "I've studied you for years, from the minute I went to work for you."

"You're pretty when you're mad," he said, abruptly enjoying this conversation. He realized with surprise that he was teasing her, and that it was fun. He could make her angry, but she would still love him anyway. Commitment had its advantages.

"Then I'm about to get a lot prettier," she warned.

"I can handle it."

"You think so, big guy?"

"Yes, ma'am." He cupped his hands on her hips and moved her suggestively. "I'm pretty sure I can."

For a moment her eyelids drooped heavily in response; then she opened her eyes wide and glared at him. "Don't try to distract me."

"I wasn't trying."

No, he was accomplishing, without effort. She was far from finished with her efforts to convince him, though, so she started to get up. His hands tightened on her hips and kept her in place. "Stay right where you are," he ordered.

"We can't talk in this position. You'll get your mind on sex, and then where will we be?"

"Probably right here on this couch. Not for the first time, either."

"Saxon, would you please be serious about this?" she wailed, then stopped in astonishment at what she had just said. She couldn't believe she had just had to plead with him to be serious. He was the most sober of men, seldom laughing or even smiling. She had probably seen him smile more in the past week or so than in the rest of the three years she had known him.

"I *am* serious," he said. "About this position, and about Emmeline. I don't want to go back. I don't want to remember."

"She loves you. She called you 'her boy,' and she said that our baby would be her grandchild."

He frowned a little, his attention caught. "She said that?"

"You should talk to her. Your memory is one-sided. They understood that you were wary of adults getting close to you, after the abuse you'd received, and that's why they didn't try to touch you. They thought they were making it easier on you."

A stark look came into his eyes as memories surfaced.

"Did you want them to hug you?" she asked. "Would you have let them?"

"No," he said slowly. "I couldn't have stood it. Even when I started having sex, in college, I didn't want the girl to put her arms around me. It wasn't until—" He broke off, his eyes unfocused. It wasn't until Anna that he had wanted the feel of arms around him, that he had wanted her to hold him close. With all the other women, he had held their hands above their heads, or he had been up on his knees out of their reach. But that had been sex; with Anna, from the very beginning, it had been making love, only it had taken him two long years to realize it.

He would never have allowed Emmeline or Harold to hug him, and they had known it.

Had his perceptions, and therefore his memories, been so distorted by his previous experiences? If what he had seen had been reflections in the carnival mirror of his mind, then nothing was as it had seemed. The beatings and general abuse he had suffered at the other foster homes had trained him to expect rejection, and he had been too young to be analytical.

"Can you really get on with your life unless you know for sure?" she asked, leaning closer to him. Those honey-dark eyes were pools he could drown in, and suddenly he pulled her tight against his chest.

"I'm trying to get on with my life," he muttered against her hair. "I'm trying to build a life, with you. Let the past go. God knows I've spent enough years trying to do that, and now that it's working, why dig it up again?"

"Because you can't let go of it! You can't forget your past. It's part of what made you the man you are. And Emmeline loves you. This isn't all for your sake. Part of it is for hers. She's alone in the world now. She didn't whine about it, or complain because you'd been gone for nearly twenty years and had never been back to see her. She just wanted to know if you were all right, and she was so proud to hear how well you've done."

Saxon closed his eyes, fighting to keep the images from forming in his mind, but it was a useless battle. Emmeline had always been the stronger personality; Harold had been softer, gentler. He could still see her face, strong-boned, plain, as spare as a desert landscape. Never malevolent, but stern and upright. Her standards of cleanliness had been of the highest; for the first time in his life, he had always had good, clean clothes, clothes he hadn't been ashamed to go to school in.

He didn't want to think that she had spent twenty years wondering about him, worrying. No one had ever worried about him before, so the possibility simply hadn't occurred to him. All he had thought about was making a clean break with his past, making something of himself and never looking back.

Anna thought you had to look back, to see where you had been, as if the landscape changed once you had passed it. And maybe it did. Maybe it would look different now.

From habit he thrust emotion away from him, and the logic of the thing was suddenly clear to him. He didn't want to go back. He wanted Anna to marry him. Anna wanted him to go back. The three ideas fell into place, and all at once he knew what he would do.

"I'll go back," he said softly, and her head jerked up, her doe-eyes big and soft and questioning. "On one condition."

They faced each other in silence for a moment. He remembered the beginning of their relationship, when she had said she would be his mistress on one condition, and he had refused it, forcing her to take him on his terms. She was remembering, too, and he wondered if she would refuse on principle. No, not Anna. She was infinitely forgiving, and wise enough to know that the one instance had nothing to do with the other. He also accepted that he wouldn't always win, but that was okay, as long as Anna was the victor. As long as she won, he won, too.

"So let's hear it," she said, though she already knew. "What's the condition?"

"That you agree to marry me."

"You'd reduce our marriage to a condition that has to be met?"

"I'll do whatever it takes, use whatever argument I have to. I can't lose you, Anna. You know that."

"You aren't losing me."

"I want it signed and sealed, on record in the county courthouse. I want you to be my wife, and I want to be your husband. I want to be a father to our kids." He gave her a crooked smile. "This is kind of like a way for me to make up for my own lousy childhood, to give my kids something better and have a real childhood through them."

Of all the things he could have said, that one got to her fast and hard. She hid her face against his neck so he wouldn't see the tears welling up in her eyes and swallowed several times so she would be able to speak normally. "All right," she said. "You have yourself a wife."

They couldn't go to Fort Morgan immediately, because of his business commitments. Looking at

the calendar, Anna smiled and made plans for
them to go the following Sunday, and called
Emmeline to let her know. It wasn't in Emmeline's character for her to bubble over with enthusiasm, but Anna could hear the pure joy in her
voice.

The day finally came. As they made the drive,
Saxon could feel himself tensing. He had been in
foster homes all over the state, but he had lived in
Fort Morgan the longest, so he had more memories of it. He could picture every room in that old
house, every piece of furniture, every photograph
and book. He could see Emmeline in the kitchen,
dark hair pulled tightly back in a no-nonsense
bun, a spotless apron protecting her plain house-
dress, while mouth-watering smells from the stove
filled the entire house. He remembered that she
had made an apple pie that was almost sinful, rich
with butter and cinnamon. He would have gorged
himself on that pie if he hadn't always been wary
of anything he liked being taken away, so he had
always restricted himself to one slice and forced
himself not to show any enthusiasm. He remembered that Emmeline had baked a lot of apple pies.

He drove to the house without any difficulty, its
location permanently etched in his mind. When he
parked at the curb, his chest tightened until he felt
almost suffocated. It was like being caught in a
time warp, stepping back almost twenty years and
finding nothing had changed. There *were* changes,

of course; the porch roof was sagging a little, and the cars parked in the street were twenty years newer. But the house was still white, and the undecorated lawn was still as neat as a hatbox. And Emmeline, stepping out on the porch, was still tall and thin, and her gaunt face was still set in naturally stern lines.

He opened the car door and got out. Without waiting for him to come around, Anna had climbed out on her side, but she made no move to walk forward and join him.

Suddenly he couldn't move. Not another step. With only the small expanse of lawn separating them, he looked at the woman he hadn't seen in two decades. She was the only mother he'd ever known. His chest hurt, and he could barely breathe. He hadn't known it would be like this, that he would suddenly feel like that terrified twelve-year boy again, brought here for the first time, hoping it would be better than the others, expecting more of the same abuse. Emmeline had come out on the porch then, too, and he had looked up at that stern face and felt only the old rejection and fear. He had wanted acceptance, wanted it so much that his heart had been pounding in his chest and he had been afraid he would disgrace himself by wetting his pants, but he hadn't let himself show it, because not having it at all was easier than facing another rejection. So he had closed himself off, protecting himself in the only way he knew.

Emmeline moved toward the steps. She wasn't wearing an apron; she had dressed up in one of her Sunday dresses, but she was wiping her hands on the skirt out of habit. She stopped and stared at the tall, powerful man who was still standing at the curb. It was Saxon, without a doubt. He had turned into a breathtaking man, but she had always known he would, with that olive-toned skin, black hair and eyes like the clearest emeralds. She could see his eyes now, and the expression in them was the same as it had been twenty-five years ago when the caseworker had brought him to them, scared and desperate, and needing to be loved so much it had wrung her heart. He wouldn't come any closer, she knew. He wouldn't have back then, either, except for the caseworker's grip on his arm. Emmeline had remained on the porch rather than frighten him by rushing at him. And maybe it had been a mistake, waiting for him to be brought to her. Saxon needed for people to reach out to him, because he didn't know how to make the first move.

Slowly her face relaxed into a smile. Then Emmeline, that stern, reserved woman, walked down the steps to meet her son, her mouth trembling and tears running down her cheeks, her arms outstretched. And she never stopped smiling.

Something broke inside him with an audible snap, and he broke, too. He hadn't cried since he'd been an infant, but Emmeline was the only anchor he had ever had in his life, until he'd met Anna. With two long strides he met her in the middle of the sidewalk, caught her in his arms, and Saxon Malone cried. Emmeline put her arms around him and hugged him as tight as she could, as if she would never let go, and she kept saying, "My boy! My boy!" In the middle of his tears he reached out to Anna, and she flew around the car and into his arms. He held them both tight in his embrace and rocked them together, the two women he loved.

It was the twelfth of May. Mother's Day.

Epilogue

Anna woke slowly from what seemed like the deepest sleep she'd ever had and opened her eyes. The first sight she saw kept her from moving for a long, long time, as she reveled in the piercing sweetness of it. Saxon was sitting beside her hospital bed, just as he had been beside her all during labor and delivery. She had seen his face taut with worry and torment over her pain, filled with jubilation when she finally gave birth, his green eyes brilliant with tears as he stared wordlessly at his tiny, squalling offspring.

He held the sleeping baby in his arms now, all his attention focused on the little creature. With infinite care he examined the tiny, perfect hands and minuscule fingernails, almost holding his breath as the little fingers folded over his big one in a surprisingly tight reflexive grip, even in sleep. He traced a finger over the almost invisible eyebrows, down the downy soft cheek, to the pink bud of a mouth. Their son fit almost perfectly in his big hands, though he had weighed in at a respectable seven pounds.

She eased around onto her side, smiling at Saxon when he snapped his attention to her. "Isn't he gorgeous?" she whispered.

"He's the most perfect thing I've ever seen." Awe was in his tone. "Emmeline has gone down to the cafeteria to get something to eat. I practically had to fight her to get him away from her."

"Well, he is her only grandchild. For now."

He looked incredulous, remembering her labor, but then he looked at the baby in his arms and understood how she could consider the result as being well worth the effort. Then he smiled at his wife, a slow smile that melted her bones. "As long as the next one is a girl."

"We'll try our best."

"We still haven't decided on a name for him," he said.

"You can pick out his first name. I've already decided on his middle name."

"What is it?"

"Saxon, of course," she said. "The second Saxon Malone. We're starting a new family tradition, remember?"

He reached out and took her hand, then eased himself onto the side of her bed, and together they admired their son.

*   *   *   *   *

Linda Howard

There are few things in life I hate more than doing a biography, and it's only a measure of my deep affection for my editor, Leslie Wainger, that I'm doing one now. Leslie, sweetie, please put this one on file; I don't think I'll need updating for at least ten years.

I've lived in or near Gadsden, Alabama, all of my life, usually near rather than in; I prefer rural life over city life, silence over noise, solitude over crowds.

I'm the second eldest of six children, one of the two "quiet" ones, though my friends and family will swear I'm anything but quiet. Let's just say that I bide my time around strangers, watching instead of talking. Looking back, I would say that I had a wonderful childhood, as only a childhood in the country can be.

I attended a small rural school in Walnut Grove, then the local community college, where I was the only journalism major, but I saw right away that journalism wasn't for me. Those people wanted only the facts! I wanted to add characterization and action, so never the twain shall meet. I dropped out of college and began working at a trucking company, a job that I loved because no two days were the same.

Let's see, what else is there? I married young, divorced young and showed much more sense in choosing the next time. Gary and I have been married now for sixteen years. He gave me three stepchildren whom I love, and the two oldest have now each given us a grandchild. (Grandchildren are *wonderful!*) Gary is preparing to join the professional bass-fishing-tournament trail next year, or the year after at the latest, which will be a huge change in lifestyle for us, as he will be gone two weeks out of every month. Wow, talk about honeymoons! I'll have twelve a year!

On one hand, my life is completely normal. I do all the things any woman does, like cook and clean, buy groceries. No one looking at me is going to think I'm a writer because I'm running around in jeans and sneakers and oversize shirts. On the other hand, my neighbor says I'm the most eccentric normal person she's ever known, with this other life that most people can't even imagine.

Of course, parts of the above paragraph are fiction. I dislike cooking, clean only under duress and *I'm* the one who will move heaven and earth to get back home in time to watch a ballgame. I sulk when football season is over, pout all the way through basketball season, except for the NCAA tournament, and perk up during baseball season. I insist on having an odd-numbered license plate on my car (it will crash if it has an even-numbered plate), can't stand the look, smell, taste or touch of mayonnaise because I had a traumatic experience with mayo when I was six, and detest the colors yellow and orange to the point that I automatically don't buy products that have those colors on the label. I will never forgive ABC if they cancel *China Beach* because of their stupid move in putting it on Saturday nights, and refuse to watch the show they put on Wednesday nights in its place. If they cancel it, I will move my allegiance to another network.

My husband loves me anyway.

Backward Glance

ROBYN
CARR

A Note from Robyn Carr

When asked to write a novella that had some link to motherhood, I was forced to think back on the more treacherous encounters with parenting that I've survived. When my second child was about to begin kindergarten, I attended a meeting of the parents. Mostly mothers, of course. It happened we lived in a rather upscale neighborhood at the time; it was a complete accident, and we didn't belong there. We weren't upscale at all and never did get anything but sheets to cover those windows. Our neighbors, though, were definite yuppies.

The principal addressed our group of kindergarten moms. During his program, he delicately suggested that the parents allow the teachers to take their time in discovering those students who would most benefit from the gifted programs. He had been overwhelmed with requests—out of sixty-seven five-year-olds entering school, over fifty parents thought their children were "gifted" and should be in accelerated programs.

I turned to my neighbor and said, "Over fifty! Gimme a break!"

And she solemnly replied, "If they are, they are."

I have never lived my own life through my children to that degree. Oh, sure, I use them to keep my weight down. And among my novelist friends, our children are still discussed as much as those other babies, the books. (You thought husbands? Naw.)

My kids have gifts, sure. I mean, amazing gifts. They're bright, good-looking, quite expensive, and they both have killer wits. They have to, of course, because around this house, there are only two categories—the quick and the dead. Simple survival of the fittest ensures us all of long lives; the competition to see who's got the most chutzpah should take a long, long time.

Also, they have special talents. My fourteen-year-old daughter can find anything. Even things she isn't supposed to know we have. She is not allowed in her brother's room, yet she knows where to find his golf tees, school schedule and, if need be, bankbook. We use her for this all the time—whether it's the soup ladle or the Phillips screwdriver.

And my son has perfect pitch. It comes in handy to know what note the doorbell is or the pitch of the car horn. In trying to develop this skill, we hired a good piano teacher to teach him to read music rather than play it by ear. My son's progress was astonishing. Then we learned that he had very politely asked the teacher to play his practice pieces through so he could tape the whole thing. He's still playing by ear, but now I get to pay thirty dollars a week for it.

I don't mean to imply that I drag my children kicking and screaming from highpoint to highpoint. Nothing of the sort. My refusal to pay the additional car insurance for a sixteen-year-old who couldn't maintain a B average, however, did have a marvelous effect on my son's schoolwork. A confession: I did tell him that it was illegal to operate a motor vehicle without a B average. Then he enrolled in driver's-training class and found out that in addition to being manipulative, his mother is a liar. But he chose to let it go because we have a saying around here: "Momma ain't happy, ain't nobody happy."

Gritty business, this mothering. All children are unique; this we know. They all have their very special gifts; they certainly all have their special needs. Well, here's a flash—all mothers are likewise unique. There are certain duties, worries and expectations that bond us, but each one of us has a special style.

That aside, there is one profound common link. We do know what's best for our kids. And don't you forget it.

Robyn Carr

Chapter One

John drove past Jess Wainscott's house regularly, his eyes always sharpened for a glimpse of her daughter, Leigh. It had been almost five years. He hated that he looked for her; he wanted to be over her. He looked in spite of himself—and he wasn't over her in the least.

Today he wasn't just driving past. Jess had called him to do a job. John owned his own business in Durango—McElroy Property Services—which included home maintenance and repairs, landscaping and a very fine nursery, and Jess wanted to know if now—early March—was too early to plant a flowering plum tree. Though his business had incidentally or accidentally become successful, he still considered himself a handyman and lawn maintenance person. He could not only bring her a flowering plum, but also change the faucet on the sink, hang wallpaper, install a hot tub, pour a cement patio. Or have one of his employees do it.

"No, it's not too early," he had said. "Not as long as you're willing to protect it from a possible late freeze and pay the price of having some poor slob try to dig into the hard ground."

"Only if that poor slob is you," she cheerfully replied. "I really have my heart set on seeing those blossoms outside my bedroom window this spring." And then she had sighed. John had never before heard a wistful sound from Jess. Sentimentality was not in her repertoire.

Jess Wainscott was sixty and had been widowed for eight years. At fifty-two, a ripe age for a woman of sound health and strong looks, she had lost her mate, but not her vitality. Jess chaired both the Friends of the Library board of directors and the Women's Council of the First Presbyterian Church. Additionally, she served on many committees and worked for several charitable causes. She could be found at almost every art fair, fund raiser, ball game, black tie dinner or barbecue in town. And she skied, which was where John saw her most often, because he was on the volunteer ski patrol.

"Cal told me if he came back after death he'd be a hummingbird and suck the nectar out of the blossoms outside my bedroom window," she told John. John grunted as he hauled the can holding the plum tree from the back of his pickup. He let it drop with a bang. "I have to get something planted and see if he was putting me on."

"You've been widowed quite a few years, Jess," John pointed out. She was the fourth and newest member of a group of vivacious women who referred to themselves as the widows' brigade. They were best friends, seen together all over town, and John did handiwork for all of them. Peg, Abby, Kate and Jess. He had many clients, not all widows, but these four women were his favorites. They all overpaid him, pestered him, tried to feed him like a son.

"Eight years," she said. "I tend to procrastinate," she laughed. "Until now, I didn't want his interference."

The cars lining the driveway indicated that Jess had company. "Meeting of the brigade?" he asked.

"Tuesday. Garden club. Or is it mah-jongg day? I never remember. We hardly ever do what we planned to do, anyway. Usually we just try to have something to do while we gossip," she said. She followed John to the side of the house where the tree would be planted and asked him questions the whole time he dug. Had he led the ski patrol again last winter? Did the nursery do much business winters? What softball team would he be on this summer so she could watch for one of his games? Did he still have that condo for rent at Purgatory? Not just questions. Also statements. The yard needed to be resodded. She was thinking of moving the piano upstairs. Leigh, her daughter, would be arriving soon.

The shovel paused in midair.

"My daughter, Leigh. Surely you've met her on one of her visits. She was here for two or three months the summer Cal died. She spent another whole summer here a few years...ah, five years ago, I guess. Maybe you met her then.''

"I...ah, might've. Yeah. Maybe."

"Oh, you'd remember, John. She's very striking. Rather unforgettable, actually."

Yes. Unforgettable. Completely. His brow began to bead with sweat. The temperature was fifty-two degrees, and there was still snow here and there in crevices around yards, at the edges of driveways, sidewalks, but he was sweating. His heart rate had been about one-ten from digging; the mention of Leigh Wainscott Brackon had caused it to shoot to two-sixty.

"You never mention her," he said.

"Don't I? Oh, nonsense, you just haven't been paying attention. I hardly talk about anything else."

But not to him. They didn't move in the same social circles, have mutual friends, or seek common amusements. Their only common trait was that they were equally well-known in town, for entirely different reasons. Everyone knew John McElroy because he was in charge of the volunteer ski patrol and A-Number-One Mr. Fix-it, and everyone knew Jess Wainscott because she belonged to every club, charity and social group in Durango. One of the town matrons and the town's best handyman. And although they liked each other fine, they weren't exactly friends.

Every time Jess called him out on a chore, he hung on her every word. Leigh never came into the conversation; it wasn't as though he would have missed it. The few times he had done indoor jobs, he had scanned the place for pictures, and there was only an old one—Leigh in her twenties. The same picture that had been there when he cleaned Jess's chimney, put up her new chandelier, unplugged the kitchen drain. It seemed to move around a lot, but there was never a new one. "Does she ski?" he asked, as if he didn't know.

"Leigh does many remarkable things, although athletically she isn't accomplished. She's kind of . . . uncoordinated. She hasn't been out here for a long time. Well, two years ago last October, and then only for a couple of days. She prefers that I visit her, since she has so many obligations, and she has plenty of room. Los Angeles is a nice place to get a tan in winter. That's about all I care to do there, anyway."

Los Angeles? It had been Los Altos when she was at Stanford University. But she had said there was a job at UCLA if she wanted it. He shook these thoughts from his mind. God, so long ago. She'd never looked back; what had she decided their relationship was? Dalliance? Panic attack? Mistake? He'd written her at her office, only to have letters returned. He'd called; a secretary took messages. Her home phone number in Los Altos, which had been difficult to find, was changed.

Shovel ready, he mentally scanned those events while he dug, and dug hard.

He plunked the tree into the hole and started pushing dirt in around it. "If she's coming for a long visit, I'll probably meet her," he said. He thought about getting drunk later.

"I'm practically forcing her to come. I've been trying to get her back here for a long, long time. Now the darnedest thing has come up. You just won't believe it. It seems I've developed some kind of heart problem." His eyes shot to her face; Jess was a breathtakingly robust sixty-year-old woman with the appearance of absolutely rude good health. Her hair had been thick gray for as long as he'd known her; her face was healthily tanned and only slightly wrinkled at the corners of her clear, intelligent blue eyes. Her cheeks were pink, her lips cherry red, and she looked smashing on skis. If it weren't for her shock of silver hair, she could pass for forty, maybe forty-five. She shrugged off his look of concern. "Not unheard of at my age."

"That's awful. What's Doc doing about it?"

"Heavens! Tom Meadows doesn't even *know*," she said, which instantly made John suspicious. Tom Meadows was seen with the widows often . . . with one or all of them. He must be some kind of late-in-life beau.

"You're not seeing Doc about this?" he asked. He had just assumed Doc was everyone's Doc.

"Well, now, Tom is a fine doctor, I'm sure, but he isn't a cardiologist."

"I really hate to hear this, Jess. Please, be careful. Do as you're told."

"Well, I'd rather it were something like a testy heart than all the things it could be. I've always been just a bit ticked off at Cal for the abrupt way he left us, but all things considered, if I could just nod off in the garden, I would rather do that than be sick. I feel all right, you see. I've just been diet-restricted as all hell. Can't eat anything truly enjoyable. However, besides eliminating strenuous exercise like skiing, my life-style is unchanged. I do watch cholesterol much better now. I thought I had watched it before, but now I *watch*. And I take long walks."

"Is it bad?"

"Bad tickers are getting to be a regular thing, John," she said philosophically. "They can check your cholesterol at the grocery store. Now that they know so much about hearts, seems no one just drops dead anymore—everyone is getting a bypass or something. The fact is, if I'm very conscientious I could live long enough to become a nuisance. On the other hand, I shouldn't get hooked on any serial novels right now."

"Jess!"

She laughed at him. A resounding, loud, hilarious laugh—typical. It made him flinch; he worried she might keel over. "You know, John, you could drop dead tomorrow, too. The only difference is that if I do, it won't be completely unexpected. I want to get that girl home and straightened out. She needs a keeper, that one. Lord, raising her was a job for ten mothers. Come in and I'll write you a check. You can have a glass of wine with the girls and me—it's my medication." For a moment he thought she had read his mind. The news that Leigh was coming had caused him to think he could use a glass—or ten. "It's the only nice thing about a tricky heart—a glass in the afternoon, a glass in the evening."

"I have to pass on the wine," he said. "But I'll take the check."

He followed her up the stairs to the redwood deck surrounding her large home, then in the back door to the kitchen. There, as predicted, were the other women at the kitchen table. What they were doing today was unclear; nothing but writing paper and coffee cups covered the surface between them. They could be planning a cotillion or writing book reviews for the local paper. Once, when he'd seen them around a table with writing tablets and impetuously enquired about their current project, they had said they were writing their wills. He hadn't asked since. "Hi, John," he heard three more times.

"Will you promise to drop by when Leigh and the boys are here?"

"Boys?" His voice had gone an octave higher. He had to concentrate to keep the shock from showing all over his face. So, Leigh had achieved motherhood. That had been one of her chief desires, children. At the time he had been with her, having children had been low on his list of wants, but hearing she had sons caused a pang of envy. Was Jess going to insist she'd been talking about "the boys" all these years, too?

"Mitch and Ty, my grandsons," she replied, digging into her purse for her checkbook. "You'd hit it off, I think. They're absolute hellions. Unlike their mother, they're quite athletic." She wrote his name on the line. "I wouldn't say Leigh is a bad mother. She adores them. But her mind wanders, and she's frequently off in la-la land. She's really no fun for little boys to play with. She's too prissy. She's the kind of woman who's...brilliant, but without a lick of sense, you know?"

He knew.

"I think she has burnout," Jess was saying as she wrote the check. "Pressures, deadlines, complications, work work work. Her housekeeper quit, leaving Leigh in charge, and Leigh's a slob. My fault. With all she learned, she was too busy to straighten up. Gad. Leigh never takes time off unless she's completely frazzled."

Like last time, he thought. "How old are your grandsons?" he asked.

"Four," she supplied, fishing her wallet out of her purse. "Twin boys." She flipped open the picture section of her wallet. John didn't audibly gasp, but his heart did flip around in panic. "I can't believe I haven't bragged about them, but maybe I just bore other people."

"She is an awful show-off about those boys," Kate said.

"We don't exactly get sick of hearing about them," Peg said, "but a change of subject once in a while wouldn't hurt."

John looked at the pictures. One was blond and blue eyed, one dark. Interesting. Leigh was blond and blue eyed. He himself, it so happened, had very dark brown hair and brown eyes. He gulped. "They look older than four," he tried a bit breathlessly, baiting her, his heart not only hammering, but racing. He hoped his voice didn't sound terribly unnatural.

"Oh, no, they just turned four." He almost fainted. His eyes did a long blink. "End of January, I think.... Yes, the twenty-eighth."

His eyes actually closed while he calculated, but he didn't drum his fingers one at a time; he wasn't the snap at math that Leigh was. At anything, for that matter. Seven months from the time he met her. An old pain shot through him and hurt slightly more. Oh, no. Oh, no. She had *already* achieved motherhood. And hadn't known? She couldn't have. She wouldn't have gotten involved with him if she . . .

"I wonder if I could impose on you to take them fishing or something? We have a fundamental absence of men here."

"Yeah. Sure," he said, suddenly exhausted. His eyes began to blur, and he acknowledged the remarkable presence of threatening tears. God, how he had loved her. "Let me know if there's anything more you need," he said, pocketing the check, dying to get back to his truck. He usually loved hanging around with the women, but this time he couldn't chance it. He could barely breathe. "And for God's sake, take care of yourself, Jess."

"I do need a crew, beginning soon, to spruce up the place. I'm planning to have a very large party here in mid-June, and I want some extensive landscaping and building done. I'm going to wait for Leigh to get here—just a couple of days from now—and get her input before I start, since she's going to live here for several months . . . though I do hope she stays on permanently now. You can do it, can't you? Handle a big job?"

"Permanently?" He nearly choked. "She's coming to live here permanently?"

She laughed, and the women joined her, stifling their chuckles. "Well, I admit I'm only calling it a long visit, but I fully intend to hang on to her this time. She loves Durango. No reason she can't stay. It's the perfect place to raise kids, and Leigh knows that."

"Sure," he said weakly. Imagine having her around all the time, running into her at the grocery store, at the Jaycee's Spring Art Fair...at the Steak House.

"Will you be able to do the yard this spring, John?"

"Yeah. Sure. Gotta run. Busy day. Lotta calls. Take it easy, ladies."

"Bye, John," was said, times four.

He let the back door slam shut, took the steps down from the deck two at a time and loped to his truck. At last he was alone. He waited a minute to start the engine. Leigh was burned-out and frazzled, he thought. That was what had been itching in her before, when he'd hoped it was *him*. It hadn't been, obviously.

Jess saw him sitting in his truck in front of the house as she watched from the living-room window. Abby came up behind her and reached over her shoulder to pull back the curtain for a better look.

"Don't do that," Jess whispered. "What if he sees us watching him."

"You don't have to whisper," Kate said. "He can't hear us."

"So? What do you think?" Jess asked.

"He just about fainted when you told him she had kids, but that doesn't mean anything. How did he react when you said she was coming home?"

"Oh, like he wanted to get in the hole he was digging."

"I don't think you'll know anything for sure until you see them together. Wouldn't it be just as easy to come right out and ask her if she just happened to be in love with our favorite handyman about five years ago when she was here for the summer getting pregnant?"

Jess scowled. "It's just not that simple. She nearly had a nervous breakdown. I was worried about her survival. Now I'm worried about her future and the future of those little cuties. But don't you think John would be good for them even if it's not him?"

"He'd be good for anyone." Peg sighed. "Oh, to be forty years younger."

"Look at him. He's just sitting there. He's in shock. I'd say that's a good sign," Kate said. "Doesn't that seem like a good sign?"

"He's in shock? That could be a bad sign," said Abby.

"Oh, to put a man in shock." Peg sighed. "Just once more."

"I just don't know if this is going to work," Jess mused, watching the truck just sit there.

"Logically, I don't think anyone can be tricked into getting married," Kate said.

"Of course they can't," Jess said. "I wouldn't even attempt that. I thought I'd just trick them into being together again. If they still care for each other, they'll do the getting married part themselves."

"They didn't before."

"Well . . . things were different then."

"Not as different as things are now," Kate said.

Chapter Two

John couldn't move. He would drive away in a minute, but not until his breathing began to smooth out and his heart quit leaping around.

Five years ago—just about the first of June, when everything was gloriously green, when Durango, Colorado, was as fresh and alive as a new baby—he had met her. Leigh, twenty-seven, long limbed, intelligent, monied, home to see her mother for a long visit. She had filed for divorce after a year-long separation from her husband. It was uncontested, mutually desired and would be no-muss, no-fuss, simple and quick. A mere formality, said Leigh, since she and her estranged husband had always been more student and teacher than husband and wife.

John had seen her in the Steak House, sitting alone at the bar, having a glass of white wine. She looked like one of a million long-legged beauties who visited Durango, except it was June. Most of the female visitors possessed of such blatantly powerful and photogenic looks made their appearance during ski season. Purgatory was a veritable smorgasbord of feminine delight. He introduced himself with nothing in mind but killing time with a knockout woman. That was when he found out she was Jess's daughter. He had done some repair and landscaping work for Jess Wainscott. So he had a couple of beers while Leigh mostly just twirled the stem of her wineglass in her fingers. They shared chitchat, and John began to tumble into incredible love. Then and there.

Her soon-to-be-ex-husband was a molecular biologist at Stanford University, a genetic engineer. She had met him when she was very young and doing some research for an advanced degree. She married him and began to work on his research projects with him, for him. John had thought she meant she had been his secretary. Although some members of his family were impressively educated, he didn't hang out with scientists.

Every time Max Brackon got a new project and new budget, Leigh explained, he hired his wife. Now she was home for a rest; she intended to change her life-style. A great deal was missing from her life.

So he asked her out.

"On a date? Should I be dating?" she asked.

"It's okay during a legal separation," he told her, as if he knew. All he really knew was a need to be with her.

"I need to be socialized," she said. "With Max, you see, I was isolated and I haven't—yes," she finally said. He told her to meet him Friday night for a drink, same time, same place. "Do you think I should tell my mother?" she asked him.

"Well, sure ... I guess. Why not? Or you could always tell her you've joined the Sierra Club because you've begun to love the environment." He'd been kidding. Sort of. Even though he didn't know much about Leigh, he wasn't sure Jess would approve of her dating the handyman.

Affairs probably always started that way, he thought now. A little bit by accident. He had expected her to change her mind, but she hadn't. They started by exchanging details of their failed relationships—John had had a serious relationship when he was twenty-one. He had met a San Francisco girl while he was in the Navy and brought her to Durango to live with him. That put a few gray hairs on his mother's head. But it didn't last long. She didn't like small-town life and had really wanted to be a rock star, even though she couldn't sing or play an instrument. She left him a note; it didn't take him all that long to get over her. He expected he might catch her on MTV one of these days, wearing underwear for a costume and belting out some deranged sonnet...off tune. Since then, he admitted unselfconsciously, he dated women who were just in town on vacation.

Commitment, said John, was not his bag.

Leigh had married a very successful, well-known stimulating older man. A scientist. A genius. She had been too young, she knew, and he had been too old. But her circumstances had been somewhat unusual—she didn't immediately explain how—and she had married her teacher, a father figure. "Did you know," she had asked John, "that my father did medical research? Biochemistry. Mom and Dad moved here to attempt retirement, although my dad just couldn't seem to slow down. My dad was pretty famous."

That had no impact on John; he didn't peruse any scientific journals. He hadn't attended one day of college and had no desire to get any smarter.

Now, Leigh had said, she realized her mistake. She wanted children and friends, for example, and her husband didn't feel so inclined at his age. His work was as demanding as any unruly child, and he really couldn't keep up a social life. In fact, Leigh's husband was not terrifically interested in having a wife. Assistant, protégé, student—yes. Wife? The only kind of wife he could conceive of was one with goals like his, schedules like his, and who would not distract him from his research, which was his first wife. He was too busy for marriage, really. He was married to his job.

Even when they had separated, drifted apart, Max still called her to come to the lab to do this or that for him; he couldn't count on anyone else the way he could count on her. She had finally filed divorce papers and come to Durango because, "He seems as disinterested in our divorce as he was in our marriage. It's as if he hasn't noticed. At least if I'm here with my mother he can't call me to come in to the lab.''

How *anyone* could take Leigh for granted was beyond John. He was already so shaken with adoration by their first date he believed he was in love. Well, maybe not *love*. But boy, he was in something. He almost had to sit on his hands at the bar to keep from fondling her. He knew he was going to love the way her skin felt, smelled, tasted.

For starters, the very sound of her voice sent him drifting; he loved her voice. Her skin was clear and fair, her eyes sparkled and her laugh was like music. He was falling.

''If you knew my father and how like him *I* am,'' Leigh had gone on, ''you would know what utter chaos our marriage *really* was. My mother predicted long ago that Max wouldn't favor our marriage with even a cursory glance and it would simply disappear. Mother, you see, is *not* like my father. She is an absolute rock with great common sense. She was the anchor in the raging sea that was my father's enormous intelligence. She's very intelligent, but not in the showy, extreme way my father was. She always knew the best thing for me would be an anchor, not a sail. She advised me not to marry someone so like my father, but I didn't listen.''

John had given her a bewildering frown and ordered another beer, letting her talk, intrigued by her expensive vocabulary. Then they had necked in his truck after drinks, indulging in kisses that were long, wet and the most exhilarating he had ever known. And he had known a few.

John had often pondered the whole concept of the physical chemistry between a man and a woman. It was like the meshing of fine gears, like waxing skis or tuning up a Porsche . . . and he said so. "What a great match of taste, texture, smell," he had said.

"Pheromones," she had replied.

John had more fun exploring the phenomenon than discussing it and closed her mouth with his. Whether it was pheromones or dumb luck, it could grab you by the neck and drag you across the room. That was how it had been with Leigh from the start, as it had never been with any other woman, ever. Though she was beautiful, it hadn't been her picture-perfect looks that had drawn him closer. In fact, he liked beauty but hated vanity. Leigh, he learned right away, didn't put much stock in her appearance. He had wanted her instantly; he wanted her still.

Jess never did know that Leigh was seeing a man in Durango. With the Sierra Club as a cover, Leigh could disappear for "hikes," "trail rides" and "camping trips" that took days. It was the closest thing to paradise John had ever experienced. But, he wondered, didn't Jess suspect something?

"She works very hard at not interfering in my personal life," Leigh had said. "My dad was an intellectual, a Bohemian, more so than my mom...and I'm a spoiled and indulged only child. They treated me like an adult from the time I was three. I don't want her to start worrying about me now.''

Over the next several weeks John began to understand that he had landed himself in a peculiar and extraordinary situation. When Jess had been twenty-one she had married a forty-year-old eccentric genius and produced one gifted child. Leigh. Cal, a very successful, prize-winning scientist, was so well-known and well traveled that Leigh had lived a privileged, highly educated life. She had graduated at the age of nineteen from Princeton and received a master's degree by twenty-one. Math and philosophy, a unique combination, were her specialties. She also spoke four languages, painted, sculpted, wrote poetry and plays, played the piano, to say nothing of all she had read.

Also she had two left feet and often seemed sidetracked by some huge idea; she lost things, missed turns, bounced checks. It made him laugh; she could work on some complex math theory containing more letters than numbers—not to mention strange symbols—but forget to balance her checkbook or make deposits. She was brilliant. John began to slowly understand that Leigh had been far more than Max's secretary; she had several degrees of her own, including a Ph.D. in Physics.

John, by contrast, had a high-school diploma and, when he met Leigh, was a ski bum who played Mr. Fix-it and Mr. Yardman from April to October so he could make just enough money to ski all winter. He was emotionally and materially unencumbered and led a loose, fast life. After Leigh left Durango, he found he was so much in demand that he hired young men with similar agendas to work in a little business that had since become a hefty operation. He had been raised in Denver by an airline mechanic and a housewife, and was the youngest of four boys. He did not like the big city and had never understood, nor cared to understand things like stock leveraging, quantum physics or DNA, nor did he read anything more complicated than the sports weeklies. But, boy, could he plant a flowering plum. If he died in summer, he would go to heaven with dirt under his nails.

They were together for just over two months. Through the high, green heat of summer he was amazed by how intensely he loved her. He knew that while Leigh had traveled the world and read *El Cid* in Spanish, she had never before had great sex. He knew because her response shocked her as much as it pleased him. Though multilingual, she had not been multi-that-other-thing before John—

and she told him so. Breathlessly, she said, "I thought there was only one to a customer."

"How many do you want, doll? I'm in no hurry."

"Oh...John...is everyone this good at this?"

"No," he told her, kissing every place he could think of. "Just me with you—it's the only combination that works this good."

"Well," she corrected. He didn't hear.

The true meaning of arrogance, John discovered, was believing you were the cause of another person's passion or pleasure. He believed he had invented sex for Leigh. She could paint and sculpt, but he had been the first man to undress her outside, beside the lake, and rock with her on a floating dock.

Around the first of August, just as John was beginning to believe he could not live without her, a series of events conspired to tear them apart. In retrospect, he could see that it was nothing but lousy luck that arrived before he was ready to deal with it.

First, Max Brackon had a heart attack and Leigh went to him. Though it didn't change the facts of the divorce and she returned to Durango in less than a week, it exacerbated John's jealousy and fear that he wasn't smart enough to be loved by her. It made him irritable, unfair and critical. He began to find things seriously wrong with being in love with a genius.

One—she had very few practical skills, having been told by a quorum of professors throughout her life that she had more to offer the world than her skill at cleaning and cooking. She should exercise her cerebellum and let someone else do the drudge work. She could, therefore, theorize and build a microwave oven, but she couldn't cook vegetables in one.

"That's just plain lazy," said John. Perhaps he raised his voice.

"I am *not* lazy," she replied, just as hotly. "You can't call someone who has three degrees and gets a Ph.D. by twenty-three *lazy*."

"I thought it was just a master's," he replied.

"That was at twenty-one."

Two—she obviously thought that because of her higher than average IQ, she had higher than average needs and should be indulged. Whenever they began to talk about never being apart, she naturally assumed they would go wherever *she* went. "What can I do in Durango?" she had asked. "I'll have to go somewhere where I can be challenged. Boredom terrifies me more than anything. I have an offer from UCLA to work on a design for a newborn CAT scan device that can be used to detect a predisposition for Sudden Infant Death Syndrome. You could come to L.A."

"And do lawns?" he asked. "While you win the Nobel Prize in scientific discoveries? Maybe I should clean pools."

"You could do anything you like," she replied, not understanding him or his ego problem. "I would be happy to support you financially. It would be no problem."

"Yes, it would," he had said. How could a woman so smart be so completely insensitive to a man's feelings? A man's needs? It never occurred to him to be more considerate of what *she* might need.

Three—there appeared to be exactly one place in which they were totally compatible; in all other places they were different. She wanted children right away, the sooner the better. He didn't. He loved athletics; she didn't even run to answer the phone. He liked the mountains and fresh air; she had her nose in a book. He was physical; she was mental. He was night; she was day.

"It works here, like this," he whispered to her when they had just made love.

"Yes," she said, her eyes tearing, "but will this be enough? I didn't have this with Max, but here in Durango, with you, there's nothing to do *after* this! I need work, family, challenge, mental stimulation, intellectual activity."

Those were not things John could offer.

Things fell apart at the last breath of summer. Leigh gave him books he didn't read; she talked about scientific research he couldn't fathom. Ecology was the only subject on which they could converse without him feeling like an idiot. He had trouble prying her loose from some sheaf of papers to hike. Their differences became more obvious. Tense. Leigh often lost track of things. She could begin to make a pot of coffee, think of some odd mathematical equation she had read about or have an unfinished poem pop into her mind, and become consumed, forget to put the pot under the coffee maker and flood the kitchen. She left Jess's car in Drive once because she had been thinking of something complex, and it rolled down a steep incline and into a ditch. The scatterbrain antics that had amused him at first began to strike him as inexcusable. It was like baby-sitting sometimes. John wasn't quite ready for the job but was definitely unprepared to give her up. The pain and frustration began to match the ecstasy.

Leigh became morose and restless all at once. She wanted to stay, wanted to go. Wanted to make love, but cried, sometimes during their loving. John couldn't stand to be so messed up over someone so messed up! Where were all the uncomplicated, silly, girlie girls? The ones looking for a man with muscles and no serious conversation?

In the panic of coming to the end of an affair they were filled with equal parts hunger and agony. It was exactly the kind of mood that made lovers demand impossible things of each other and suffer temporary insanity. He demanded she admit she couldn't cope with being in love with a ski bum who had no ambition beyond enjoying life as much as possible. She demanded he make an effort, at least, to fit into a world in which she would have the challenge she craved and he could fish, hunt, ski, boat and do anything he wanted on the money she would earn. He said he would cut his throat before he'd live off a woman, and she said she'd only die a painful death without intellectual stimulation. She needed long hours. Relaxation of the type he loved was harder for her than anything else in life. However impossible it was for him to understand, she relaxed by reading philosophy and physics.

John said that was garbage. And he honestly thought it was.

The way it ended was even more ridiculous than the rest of it had been. She said she was going to go back to Stanford to think things through, to at least get her divorce taken care of. And he said— it was still hard for him to believe—he actually said, "Good. Go. It was fun, but we're just from two different worlds. I'm not up to this, anyway."

When that made her cry, he didn't hold her and say he was sorry. He didn't try to take it back. For a brief moment he really believed he wanted someone "regular." That's what you think when you're twenty-seven and stupid.

Then, when she was gone, he had called, written, even braved asking Jess, "How are you getting on? Need anything done around the house?"

"No, my daughter was here, but she's gone home now," Jess had said, as if that were an answer.

John felt thoroughly rejected. After a hard-hitting four-month depression and more failed attempts to reach Leigh, he quickly married a pretty young woman named Cindy who was "regular" and whom, though he didn't now it at the time, he did not love. Their happiness had lasted only a month or so, although their divorce took much longer.

He often wished there was some way to find out if Leigh had really left because she wanted to or if he had driven her away.

When he thought about it rationally, he believed Leigh had been the smart one. They couldn't have made it work; she hovered above the average mind by about twenty feet. No matter how great their bodies worked together, it would have been unbearable to watch her grow bored and weary with someone like him—a simple man who didn't earn much money and couldn't discuss science. Unfortunately, he wasn't able to think about it rationally very often.

But now he knew she had twin sons, and he realized what else had been going on. That first night he met her, she had said one of her marital frustrations had been about children. Seven months after that first shared drink, after the first time they were intimate, she had had twins. She must not have been all that separated from her husband. She must have realized she was pregnant and taken herself guiltily home to Max, disconnecting from her summer affair. It made him feel slightly better to know that her inability to bridge the IQ gap hadn't been her only reason for leaving. Very slightly.

He was afraid to see her again, yet he wanted desperately to see her again. He was no braver. Also no smarter.

Jess was repotting a plant on her redwood deck. She could see her grandsons, Mitch and Ty, constructing a fort in the thick batch of trees behind the yard and garden. They had taken turns swinging on a rope swing; they had nailed boards together in a sad attempt to make a ladder up the crooked spine of a perfect tree-house tree. She predicted they would ask to sleep in a tent in the backyard before the end of the week. She would say no. But it was grand to know they were *average*. Active, curious, healthy, athletic boys... What a treasure. They could keep themselves busy and challenged. They could get into the same jams that all kids did—a ball through a window, swiped candy, a fight.

Leigh been such a handful to raise; she had been reading at the age of two, skipped grades and taken special classes and advanced lessons all through school. Leigh had been so relentlessly curious that she mixed cleaning supplies with fertilizers after she had picked the lock on the garden shed. It was amazing she hadn't killed herself; she *had* burned a hole through the floor.

Having her home was much like having Cal back. Ninety-five percent of the time Leigh was a joy and best friend—clever, funny, helpful. That other five percent she was like a wandering two-year-old. Jess hadn't yet encountered the five percent this visit; Leigh seemed to be improving at keeping her mind clear.

The first thing they had to get out of the way was the business of Jess's heart abnormality.

"I want to talk to your doctor," Leigh had said.

"No. This is *my* condition. It's manageable, and I will not have you involved. I've had a series of examinations, and I'm watching my cholesterol and my activities. I've been told I won't drop dead today, and I'm still a competent baby-sitter. In fact, if I'm careful of my diet, I'll probably be around to drive you crazy for years to come. I'm having another checkup in the fall. You're lucky I told you at all. And the only reason I did is that I really wanted to spend some time with you and the boys. Just in case."

"Is it angina?"

"What?"

"Mom," Leigh had said, "I could investigate, help with some treatment decisions...."

"Absolutely not. I'm well aware of your intelligence, but this is a matter that requires good instincts. You'll only get technical, pragmatic and annoying. Butt out."

"But I'm home because—"

"I hope you're home because you want to be, not just because you're afraid I'm short term!"

"Mother," Leigh had begun.

"Daughter," Jess had mimicked.

Now Jess saw Mitch, the dark one, take a wide swing on the rope that hung from a high branch. A good, big swing. What a guy. And then she smelled a nasty smell and cursed under her breath. The five percent! She made quick work of the steps to the kitchen and found macaroni burning in the pan. Then she heard a sound and looked up; a damp spot was spreading on the ceiling. She cursed again. She missed Cal, but not enough to go through all this again.

"If I had a serious heart condition," she grumbled as she raced up the stairs, "this girl would kill me in no time. And if I ever get a really important heart condition, she will be the *last* to know!"

The tub was overflowing. *"Leigh!"* she shouted. But of course she wasn't heard. Busy mind, blocked ears. She turned off the water and pulled the plug. The carpet was soaked, and her sneakers got so wet she sloshed. She went to the loft that had been Cal's study and saw Leigh, wearing her bathrobe, sitting in front of her computer screen, her fingers clicking keys at lightning speed. She touched Leigh's shoulder. "You've burned up a pan and flooded the bathroom!"

"Oh, Mom," Leigh said, startled and shaken. "Oh, I'm sorry! I really don't do that so much anymore, really! Damn, I'll clean it up, I'm so sorry.... I'm..."

"Never mind," Jess sighed wearily.

"Where are the boys?" Leigh asked over her shoulder.

"The boys are just fine. You need more watching than they do!" Oh, Leigh, she thought, where *is* your brain?

Much later, while drinking her afternoon glass of wine on the deck, Jess said, "Do you realize how much better you are when you have a social life? That summer you joined the Sierra Club, you had fewer mishaps. I think the fresh air helps clear your head."

"I had mishaps that summer. Remember?" Leigh said.

"They weren't as obvious," Jess said.

"To you," Leigh argued. And then, on the subject of mishaps who were now four years old, "The loveliest thing happened, Mom. Max remembered Mitch and Ty. Wasn't that dear of him?"

"In his will?" Jess asked, amazed.

"Yes. I can't think why. He rarely saw them. He must have done it for me, knowing how much I wanted children. Do you suppose that means he finally forgave me? Perhaps he loved me more than I knew. Am I being sentimental?"

Jess couldn't resist the urge to touch her daughter's golden hair, braided and falling over her shoulder. Sometimes Jess tried to imagine Leigh's pain, her feelings of inadequacy or the way she suffered in rejection. Men were afraid to date her; women friends were equally rare. It could be such a lonely life, being a fast-tracker. "Oh, Leigh, the boys *need* a father."

Leigh actually looked away. She rarely let her emotions show, was actually still in the learning stages of even allowing herself to have emotions. Jess thought it had a lot to do with returning to Durango. "Let's not go over that again, Mom. I don't have a father to offer them, and I can't help it."

Well, *I can,* Jess thought. "I'll need your advice with something, darling. I want to have a huge party this summer, partly to welcome you and the boys home and introduce you to all my friends, and partly because I don't know if I'll ever feel this well again. I've wanted to landscape the whole blasted yard for years now—make it a wonderland. You'll help me, won't you?"

"When did you start reading this?" Leigh asked, picking up a copy of a bridal magazine. What on earth was her mother doing with a bridal magazine?

"That? Oh, I think Abby or Peg left a lot of them here. We planned both their girls' weddings together.... What fun. Abby's daughter even left her gown here.... You're about the same size. You ought to try it on sometime.

"Now, I want flagstone walks, a gazebo and a big barbecue pit. I'd like a couple of birdbaths or statues . . . maybe even a fountain. Can you design something like that on your little machine?"

"I think so . . . yes, I'll have a go at it in the next day or two."

"When you have some plans, I want you to see this man who sometimes works for me—John McElroy. He's a very good builder and a landscape specialist. In fact, he's also great on skis and heads up the ski patrol. This winter I'll talk to him about teaching the boys."

Leigh focused an unusual amount of attention on the magazine, not responding to her mother.

"Why don't you make my last days easier and just marry him? I think he's stable enough to take care of you and the boys when I'm gone. He even looks a bit like Mitch."

Leigh was silent for a long time. "What an imagination you have," she finally said, sipping her wine and flipping the pages.

Chapter Three

"Hello, John."

He dropped a fifty-pound bag of compost on a pile of identical bags and whirled around to face her. All the anticipation and anxiety that had surrounded the thought of seeing her again seemed to drain out of him when the moment actually arrived. There she was. Beautiful as ever. Hardly aged. He was instantly self-conscious about whether he smelled of sweat and cow dung. This was not what he had planned. He'd known he would run into her at some point, but he hadn't been able to prepare for the experience. "Leigh," he said quietly. "Dr. Brackon."

She half smiled when he said her name, then flinched just slightly when he used her title. "I . . . ah . . . didn't mean to startle you. I'm sorry. I'm—"

"No, it's okay. I'm just surprised. It's been a long time."

"I've been back a couple of weeks. I'm living with my mother for now, maybe for good. She needs me, and I need a new kind of life-style. Jess . . . my mom . . . she has some kind of—"

"She told me." He took a handkerchief from his pocket and wiped the perspiration from his forehead. "She said she has a heart problem and was forcing you home."

"She didn't actually have to force me. I was ready to come. I wanted to come. I've been planning to for years. I just kept putting it off."

"This can't make your husband very—"

"Didn't she tell you about Max? Oh, my... I divorced him a long time ago and Max...well, he passed away about six months ago. He was sixty, Mom's age... Far too young."

"I didn't know," he said slowly. "I'm sorry."

"I don't know why I thought you'd know," she said in that slightly baffled, absentminded way of hers.

"How would I know?" he asked a bit more peevishly than he intended. Leigh had always been able to imply that everyone should be able to keep up with her thoughts. *I guess I thought we talked about that,* and *I didn't mean to take it for granted that you already knew when you didn't.* But he didn't want to get into all that again now. "What I mean is, we do a little work for Jess now and then, but she hasn't mentioned you.... Not once. In fact, I'm sure she just mentioned your children for the first time when I took out a tree to her. Congratulations. I know children were one of the things you wanted."

"That's impossible, her not mentioning the boys. She never shuts up about them. You must not have noticed."

"I *would* have noticed!"

"Oh-oh," she nervously replied.

"So, you're back to help Jess and learn a new kind of life-style," he said, the edge to his words unmistakable. "Haven't you already done that one?"

"Look, John, my mom wants some work done in the yard. And she wants it to be *you* who does the work. She obviously doesn't know how testy you can get, or she'd hire someone more agreeable." Leigh reached into her purse and pulled out a piece of paper that had a long list of items on it. "The job would mean you and I would run into each other quite a bit, since I happen to live there now. If you'd rather not, say so and I'll just get someone else." She stared him down. Maybe she didn't seem older, but she had gotten tougher somehow. Tougher underneath. More sure of herself. "So?"

After some long and serious eye contact he churlishly snapped the list out of her hand. He concentrated on it for a second. Brick gazebo, barbecue, flagstone walks, a birdbath with a *fountain*. He whistled. "A few things," he muttered. These people, it seemed, never ran out of big ideas, brains or money. It could get downright irritating.

"Yes, well, I realize it's quite a lot. My mom is so spontaneous. When she gets an idea like this, she wants it, and she wants it fast."

"For what? She isn't selling, is she?"

"No, no. She plans for me to have that house one day. She says she wants to throw a big summer party and invite half the town. She has two reasons. Reason one—because I have returned to live in Durango with the boys. Reason two—which I do not much like—she isn't sure how good she'll feel next summer. What do you know about this heart condition of hers?"

"How would I know anything?" he asked, walking to the countertop that he used as a desk. "I'm the handyman, Leigh, not her priest."

"Pardon me," she returned, just as cranky. "I'm only trying to find out what I can. She wouldn't tell me anything, and I'm worried."

John felt a bit contrite. "Sorry." The last thing he wanted was to get all nasty with her. "I don't know anything, though I did ask. It seems Doc Meadows doesn't even know about it. Which means, I guess, that she's seeing someone else, but I wouldn't even hazard a guess as to who. I thought Doc was taking care of all the widows. But I guess not medically."

"She said she doesn't see Tom professionally because they're good friends. But when I called him and asked him if he had recommended a cardiologist, he was silent a long time before he said he hadn't. Then he suggested I quiz the widows' brigade on this alleged heart condition. Alleged? She's acting very strangely. I think there's more wrong than her heart, although I can't get a drop of information out of her. I've snooped through all her cupboards and can't find any prescription bottles, insurance receipts, anything. She's being absolutely impossible and won't let me get involved."

"What did the widows tell you?"

She shrugged. "To mind my own business and let Jess have her way for once. Abby West said that mother thing. 'Now, dear, your mother made many sacrifices for you as you were growing up. Why not just indulge her for a while?' To forestall an enormous fight, Mother promised me that if I would leave her alone and get settled in, she would tell me all about it later, before her next checkup. She's adamant that she will not discuss her condition this summer."

He smiled in spite of himself. "Mighty pig-headed, isn't she?"

Leigh tapped the list. "I think she's getting some of these repairs and improvements out of the way so as not to leave anything—you know, undone." She swallowed and looked away.

"What a thought," he mumbled.

"Jess is that way—efficient, compassionate. I just hope she's completely wrong about this heart thing. I don't think I can live without her. She's my anchor. The lead in my shoes. You know...I just don't have anyone to turn to the way I can turn to Jess."

"Let's not bury her yet. Let's think about her yard before we worry about her plot. This is a lot of new landscaping and building. Expensive."

"Can you do all this? A brick gazebo with a shake roof? Brick barbecue pit? Flagstone walks? If I give you a blueprint to follow?"

He made a face. "No, Leigh. I'm the builder and landscaper. *I* give *you* the plans, and you approve or alter them. See, this is *my* business."

"It's *my* yard."

"For gosh sakes," he blustered, "do we have to argue about the damn *air?*"

Deep breath. Times two.

"Okay," she relented. "Your plans, my alterations. Can you do it?"

"You're in luck. We're having a special."

"What kind of special?"

"The one where we do anything for money."

She smiled indulgently.

"It's going to cost a lot if you want it to look good."

"Mom doesn't care about money. She's very well fixed and still getting royalties from my father's books. John? Does my mother...could she...have you...?" She gave up, then started over more slowly. "Does she know about that summer?"

"I don't know how she could. Why?"

"She asked me to ask you if you could either supervise or do most of the work yourself. She also happened to ask me if I couldn't just marry you and make her life easy."

He didn't think that was funny. "Did you tell her we've been over all that?"

"Of course not," she said. "That wouldn't be true. We never actually talked about marriage. We talked about being together, and even that was too much."

"Well, one of us *was* married, if you recall," he flung back.

She rolled her eyes in irritation. She'd been afraid of this, that he would really make her mad. She tried a change of subject. "You've really made something of this operation. The last time I saw it, it was a garage surrounded by a big old cyclone fence."

"When was that?"

"Oh, I don't remember the date," she lied. She remembered *exactly*. "You weren't here. You were on your honeymoon." Nuts. It was no longer going to be all his fault if they moved from general sniping into a full-fledged battle. So much for good intentions.

"My honey—! You *came* here? No one ever told me you came here!"

"Well, I didn't leave a message. You weren't here. You were indisposed, so to speak. So I left. Back to the yard—this whole thing is typical of Jess's spontaneous—"

"Why did you come here?" he asked.

"I said I would. I said I was going to get things together, straightened out. Don't you even remember?"

"That isn't what you said. You said you couldn't live here with me—I wasn't *challenging* enough!"

"Not *you*. There wasn't any work for me here. I had to have some kind of—"

"You said you had to go back to Stanford because—"

"Because that's where I lived. That's where my job was. My stuff. All my stuff was in Los Altos. I'd been offered a grant—I had to accept a grant to have a job. One of us had to have a job. You were a ski bum who occasionally cut grass for people. Besides, you said you were glad I was going away."

"Ski *Patrol*, if you don't mind. Ski Patrol and landscaping. It wasn't a big, fancy job maybe, but a couple of little, decent, *ordinary* jobs that *regular* people do. And I only said I was glad because I was too proud to say I couldn't stand it that you would just leave like that." He snapped his fingers. "Without a backward glance!"

"Without a—" She ran a hand over her hair. "Sorry if I offended," she sarcastically replied. "I needed a paying job somewhere. I was pregnant! The grant was offered by UCLA. I *had* to move, John."

"Oh. Oh, I get it. So, you just came by to say hello. It wasn't like you came back to see me or anything."

Leigh stared for a second and opened her mouth to speak, but it turned into a huff. She began again. Another huff. She put a hand on her hip. "I came back to see my mom and you. My divorce was final. I thought I'd ask again if you wanted to try L.A. But...if you didn't, I thought maybe we could work something out."

"Work something out?"

"A commute. I don't know. What's the difference, John? You weren't available. You were on your honeymoon!"

"I was on my honeymoon because I got married, which I did four months *after* you couldn't be bothered to answer any of my calls or letters."

"Calls and letters? You dummy! I didn't *get* any calls or letters!"

"I left messages! I wrote!"

"Well, I went back to Los Altos, packed up and moved. I didn't know I was supposed to somehow keep you *unmarried*. Most people get married because they want to, not because someone else doesn't answer the damn phone!"

"No one told me you moved! And don't call me a dummy! You know I already feel like a dummy just being in the same town with you, since your IQ is around four thousand and something! So, is there any particular reason why *you* didn't try writing or calling or something?''

"No, no particular reason," she shouted back. "Except I was a little *busy*. I was working on a scientific project, pregnant with twins and visiting with a psychologist to find out how in the world I had managed to be so smart and still mess up my life so badly! Now, I'd love to hang around and fight with you, but I have things to do! Are you going to do the damn yard for my mother? Or what?''

"Yes!" he shouted. "I'll be out tomorrow!"

"Great!" she shouted back, turning so dramatically that her long blond braid swung out so far behind her that it hit him in the nose. She stomped out the door.

John felt the scorching heat of red anger on his cheeks. Oh, boy, how he remembered the steam in their arguments. He pounded the counter twice, hard enough to make all the pencils bounce.

He put his elbow on the counter, lowered his forehead into his hand and took a few deep breaths. Boy, did she look good. Twenty-seven was pretty and nubile, but there was something about a few years on a woman. A couple of kids, a little maturity, and something a bit more steady settled around the chest and hips. She had changed from lovely to lush. What kind of dummy would fight with her? He could have been a nice guy and maybe asked her out. They were, after all, both single now.

Was he crazy? Wasn't that what started all this? Dating? The two of them came from two completely different worlds.

"John?" He looked up. "I . . . ah . . . locked my keys in my car. . . . I must not have been . . . you know."

A small laugh woofed out of him. He should have known. "You weren't paying attention. You were thinking about the mating cycle of the whooping crane or iambic pentameters." *Or me. Could you have been thinking about me, Leigh?* "Don't worry, I can get anything open."

"And I'm sorry about what just happened. The fight. I really didn't think that would happen," she said. "Anymore," she added.

"You weren't the only one at fault," he said. "Leigh, maybe we'd better get together, meet for a drink or dinner or something. We have this really messed-up karma, me and you, and if we don't get some of this straightened out, we're going to meet again in the next life as deadly enemies. Which would be okay if we ended up on opposing football teams, but if we're twin sisters or something, it could be disastrous. Maybe we ought to get it all talked out so we can press on as . . . friends. Huh?"

"Yes," she said in a breath, relieved. "Yes, that's what I wanted to do from the start—to make up and be friendly somehow. But you're the married one now."

"Me? No, I'm divorced, too. I've been divorced practically since I got married."

Her shocked expression was unmistakable. "I didn't know. I'm sorry."

"It was over before it started. We only lived together for a few months. Ski season," he added quietly, with the good grace to be somewhat embarrassed.

"Children?"

"Nope."

"Oh. Well, you said you didn't want children, so you're probably all right about that."

"I didn't want them back then. I was twenty-seven and self-centered. I was a skier with no ambition, for gosh sakes. I never thought about anything or anyone but myself. Surely you remember that."

She nearly smiled. That was the closest to an admission of imperfection or an apology as John had ever come. "We don't seem to have the best luck in romance, do we?"

"Well, how about if two unlucky people meet later?"

"I don't know...."

"You have someone? Some guy?"

She laughed in spite of herself. There were never any guys. Colleagues, Project managers. Probably the only reason she'd accidentally married

Max was fatigue; they had worked so hard and long together, marriage had seemed a natural progression. John was practically the only "guy" she'd ever had. Briefly. "I have a couple of guys. Four-year-old guys," she said.

"How about if, for now, it's just you and me?"

Leigh sighed. "I'm still not very good at this sort of thing, John. I'm so clumsy in relationships. I don't mean to be, and I don't want to be... I'm very quick with mathematical problems. I just—ugh—I'm a mother now. I have to be more careful, because when I get in over my head, the boys can get hurt."

"We had an affair that messed us both up," he said. "Since we're still fighting like we used to, maybe we're still not through this. Shouldn't we talk about it? Rationally?"

She looked into his dark brown eyes. He had eyes like Bambi. Eyes you could fall into and drown. Arms by Adonis, face by Prince Charming, temperament by Attila the Hun. She smiled at him. "You have a ponytail."

He had to think for a minute. "Oh, yeah. It's not a bad ponytail, though. Is it?"

"No," she said. Ponytails were in again, but with John it was unclear whether he was being fashionable or lazy. In her memory of him, fashion was low on his list of priorities. Fashion, children and commitment. But he was such a cute renegade. "The Steak House?"

"Yeah. Let's get your keys." He lifted his hand toward her elbow and let it sort of hover there, undecided. Then, with a contrite, helpless look, touched her briefly. She felt a tremor. She knew she was in up to her neck right now. If he touched her again, she would crumble.

Chapter Four

Leigh arrived at seven, and John was already there. She wore a silk jumpsuit with a decorative scarf slung over one shoulder, earrings made of shells, and beige flats. She looked fashionably chic according to Jess, who had cheerfully—maybe too cheerfully—checked her over before she went out the door. This time Leigh was not pretending to join the Sierra Club. "You'll be delighted to know that your favorite maintenance man has asked me to meet him for a glass of wine," she had said.

John wore jeans, but decent jeans without holes, and something resembling a polo shirt with a sweater over it. To look at them, no one would know how scared they both were of this meeting. And they were both terrified of the identical things, that their love affair would officially end—and that it would carry on from where they had left it. She had a glass of wine and he a beer. They were on their second round before their words began to work.

"So," he started, "what happened?"

"When?"

"You came back, you said, and found out I was married. I'll tell you what happened to me if you tell me what happened to you. So what happened before that, in Los Altos?''

"Oh, it was dreadful. Max, who was recovering from one heart seizure, almost had another one. He was furious with me.''

"Why?" he asked.

She just looked up at him with that blank, bewildered, aren't-you-able-to-keep-up-with-this? look of hers.

"For being pregnant?" he asked.

She nodded. "He said he felt betrayed.... That's what he said. I couldn't understand that at all. I mean, it isn't as though I did it on purpose. And there I was...pregnant. Part of me was thrilled beyond my wildest dreams.... The other half was amazed at how foolish I'd been. If it hadn't been for my mother, I don't know what I would have done.''

"Wait a minute, wait a minute," he said, remembering the way Leigh could get so far ahead of herself, or begin her stories at the end and go backward. He had no doubt she could deliver a dissertation in clear language, but when it came to real life, she meandered. "Slow down, Leigh. He was angry about your pregnancy? Didn't he want to be a father?''

"No," she answered in apparent surprise. "Of course not. I know I told you that.''

"I know he didn't *think* he wanted to, but after you told him you were..." She was shaking her head, looking stunned. "That's a damn shame," John said sincerely. "Even men who think they aren't ready for children usually act civilized when they find out their wife is expecting. I think I would."

Her eyes grew amazingly round, and she looked at him strangely, as if she didn't understand what he was saying. Finally, as though she had shaken herself free of some complex notion, she said, "You said *you* didn't want to be a father."

"Well, hell, I was being honest at the time. But I think I would have faced the prospect a bit more reasonably than Max did. I don't think I would have accused you of betrayal."

"Wait a minute here," she began. "What do you think *you* would have done? If you'd discovered your wife, for example, was pregnant?"

"We would have had to work on our marriage." He shrugged. "Harder," he added, in case anyone thought he hadn't tried.

"Oh, dear," she said. "John . . . have you seen the boys?" she asked.

"No. Just a picture. Jess asked me if I'd take them fishing sometime. They're pretty cute, but they don't look like twins. I guess the dark one looks like his father."

Leigh swallowed and nodded.

"Jess knows I coach Little League, and I still work the Ski Patrol in winter, part-time, and instruct kids in downhill. She said they're real hellions," he added, smiling. He rested his hand on her forearm.

"John," she said, twirling her wineglass by the stem. "I'm not sure which one of us messed up worse . . . you or me."

"How about if we just leave it in the past and go from here?"

"I don't know if that will work. The past is following us around. And besides . . . go where?"

"Take a little drink of that wine, Leigh. Let's get out of here for the rest of this conversation . . . in case it gets personal."

"I think the rest of this conversation is going to be real easy and involve one little word," she said softly. "No."

" 'No' to what?" John asked.

"I'm not willing to pick this up where we left it, John. It hurt me too much. Even though it was at least as much my fault as yours, it was still very painful."

John caressed her forearm. Boy, did he understand that. He was all through being belligerent and touchy; besides, she was right. All he wanted was to put an arm around her shoulders, maybe hold her hand, and talk about it. He had to resolve things with this woman for whom he'd carried a big, heavy torch for five years. Okay, he did want to see if being close to her caused him to feel the old feeling that he would never get close enough. But he only wanted to know. He wasn't going to go crazy. Right away.

"Let's go for a walk, huh? Alone? Talk a little. And I promise, you won't have to say 'no' again." He held up three fingers. "Scout's honor."

"You were never a Boy Scout, were you?" she asked later.

"No."

"I should have known," she said.

"It was only one kiss," he said. "I just wanted to check and see if it was as good as I remembered."

"And was it?"

"Yep. But what that means, I guess, is that it can be just as bad as it was, too. So we'd better finish that conversation."

They had abandoned their walk because the April night was a bit too brisk and chilled them into the shivers. They were in his truck, parked up on a ridge from which they could see a million miles out into the sky and across the land. If they'd been looking out, that is. With his lips on hers, it was inward that Leigh was looking.

There were things she had learned about herself since the last time they had kissed. She was going to have a lot of startling information for John . . . but, like a coward, she decided to start slow and sneak up on it.

For example, she explained, her adolescence had been very lonely. She was a woman who had reached her intellectual peak at eighteen and had entered puberty—at least emotionally—at twenty-seven.

John hummed in appreciation, though what he really wanted was to be kissing her neck. He was smart enough to keep that to himself.

Next she went on to explain her marriage, which she knew she had never adequately explained to John before. She and Max had rarely made love. They were a team in the lab; he was her mentor. Since she had never had any friends her own age, since she'd never had a boyfriend in her entire life, she hadn't realized her relationship with Max was peculiar. If she hadn't fallen into a "thing" with John, she might not know even now.

"But you're so gorgeous..."

She shook her head. "I didn't think of myself as attractive. Honest. I thought I was a freak. I never dated anyone. I was twenty before I realized my colleagues were intimidated by me, and women seemed to really dislike me. Well, except older, more matronly intellectual women, and scientists. But maybe the hardest thing about living that kind of life is that if you have a terrifically busy mind, it's fairly easy to avoid looking closely at your personal life. I never bothered to examine my unhappiness closely, because it was easy for me to find something else to think about. It's a dysfunctional behavior.''

"Maybe a lot of people would like to have something better to think about than their problems," he suggested.

"No, John, I'm not talking about avoiding self-pity. I'm talking about denying what's going on in your life. The problem with denial is its finite.... At some point you run out of it. Usually, by then, whatever you're denying is bigger than you are." She paused briefly and smiled at him. "I almost had what some people call a nervous breakdown when I found myself trying to juggle two tiny little boys," she said quietly. "Two five-pounders...counting on me. I couldn't give them a good life because I had no idea what a good life was. I didn't even know what good was. So Jess came to L.A. to help me, and I went to a counselor—a wonderful counselor who helps kids with abnormally high IQs adapt socially. I was her first twenty-eight-year-old kid."

John was quiet, and she wondered if he was able to understand, fully understand, the significance their relationship had held for her. But apparently he wasn't. "I guess I never thought of your life as hard. I guess I never thought of you as not smart enough to know what to do."

She chewed her lip a little. She should do a scholarly paper on this. She had felt—had *been*— a misfit. She never learned the eighth-grade boy-girl dynamic, because when other thirteen-year-old girls were finding out how to flirt, she was taking Physics II at the university as part of the gifted program. When other girls were crying because they didn't get asked to the prom, Leigh was crying because she hadn't been admitted to a master's program to which she had applied. One of the neighbor girls flunked her driving test; Leigh lost out on a major grant. When she got her first period her classmate, a twenty-year-old coed who was wearing an IUD, told her to "Stay cool, doll face, and just pin this little puppy in your panties like so, and pretty soon you'll graduate to tampons. . . ."

"Ever have a friend face you with his envy?" she asked John. "With real *hot* jealousy? Like when you win a medal skiing, and you complain a little because your muscles hurt, your bank account is dried up, your best girl left you because she wasn't getting enough attention while you trained, and you're exhausted. I mean, you worked so *hard* for it! And the friend says something like, 'Yeah, yeah, cry me a river. . . didja win or not?'"

John thought about that for a long time before he replied. He had never been gifted in anything except getting along. He was good at a lot of things, but he wasn't the best at much. He had to remember way back to just before he went into the Navy, when he had competed in downhill skiing.

He'd gotten into a fistfight with some loudmouth jerk who was taunting him about having some secret "advantage." Hell, John had about killed himself in training and had taken enormous risks. After a while he'd guessed the guy was just jealous. "Yeah. Yeah, I have."

"I never," she said seriously, "had otherwise."

"I was never *jealous* of you...."

"Oh, John, I know that. But I'd like you to understand why I have never known what to do with a boyfriend.... With a lover. I never had one. Never. Max wasn't a boyfriend or a lover. We married in a state of confusion and inertia. He was leaving a project at Columbia to take on a new one at Stanford. He wanted me to go along.... It wasn't exactly true love, though I suppose Max loved me as much as he could.

"Then I met you and had no idea what hit me. It was my very first acquaintance with real lovemaking. I think that's why we weren't able to salvage anything. Too complicated. Not enough experience on my part."

"What do you really want, Leigh?"

"Not a lot, actually. I want to be a good mother and have some friends. I just want to be okay like I am. Acceptable. There are a lot of reasons why I was disappointed that we weren't able to work things out. Just one is that I haven't had much fun since we went our separate ways. I know you think I'm a pain, clumsy, forgetful ... but I had fun camping and hiking. We used to laugh a lot. I think I might like to learn to ski...."

John frowned as the mental picture of Leigh tripping around the slopes, getting lost and falling down came to mind. Well, there were bunny slopes.... How did she imagine she was going to raise two boys?

"I'd at least like my kids to learn to ski and play ball.... They already love anything physical and don't read anything that isn't previewed on the Saturday morning cartoons. They're completely normal."

John had discovered, in the years since Leigh had left him, that he actually liked kids. He wouldn't mind taking her boys to a ball game or a ski lesson. Getting them early like this, they might do pretty well.

"You're going to stay here, then?" he asked.

"There's a trust from my father's estate that I could use to live modestly but comfortably, but I plan to work. I've been studying ethics. I'm doing a paper on the ethics of scientific research called *The Fear of New Knowledge*. It could turn into a book."

"How about the fear of old knowledge?" he asked. And old lovers? "What got you interested in ethics?"

"It's profoundly interesting, both simple and highly complex," she said. "What's your definition of ethics?"

He shrugged. "It isn't too complicated to me. Honesty, fairness, decency, knowing the difference between right and wrong. Treating people nicely, the way you'd want to be treated."

She leaned against the seat, looking out over the vast Colorado terrain, dimly lit by the moon. She was beginning to feel safe. She sighed deeply. She wouldn't bother to tell him that he was right—exactly, absolutely right—and that still she could make a whole profession out of the study. Part of the study would show that the real role models for ethical behavior were people who naturally did the "right thing" without studying the subject. It wasn't as though ethical people were flawless or never made mistakes; they sought rightness and rectified mistakes when they could. Like John.

Which was why she hadn't argued for one second when Jess called and said, "I need you to come home." She was grateful; she had needed a nudge. There were lots of "rights" in there. Of course you came home when your mother, who had been your life raft every time you ever got into trouble, called. And also, Leigh had already been thinking of returning to see if she could tidy things up with John, bury the hatchet and see if there was a way to get along. She'd expected to find him married and had prepared herself to negotiate friendship with him *and* his wife. And she hadn't made this decision during her preliminary study of ethics, either. Rather, she had known all along it was the right thing to do. However tough it was for her and John to see eye to eye, she knew he was a good and honest man who would naturally do the right thing—and she needed such a man to be a role model for her sons.

For his sons.

"So," John said, "what's next?"

"Do you think it's possible for us to be friends?"

"Well, anything's possible. But what might make it hard is that I remember," said John, "when I held you before. I remembered holding you at the weirdest times. I missed you so much, Leigh. I never told you how much you meant to me. I missed all my good chances to say all the right things, all the smart things. I was absolutely crazy in love with you, and scared to death.... You fascinated me. You terrified me. All I can say is thanks . . . for coming back and making an effort to be friends again, to work things out.... I'm such a—hey! Why are you crying?"

"It's nothing."

"Oh, Leigh, it's okay. C'mere. It's okay to come here so I can put an arm around you while you—"

"Easy does it, John. Let's go slowly.... Please . . . ?" But she was moving into the protective circle of his arm just the same. She felt so good, so secure, when she curled up against him like this and let herself pretend, for just a second, that there was someone to lean on, someone to care for her.

"Yeah, that's livin' right.... Let's pretend everything is okay. Okay?"

"Okay."

Leigh put a hand on Jess's shoulder to rouse her. "I'm home. You didn't have to wait up."

"Hmm? Oh, I didn't mean to wait up. I must have dozed off. Did you have a nice time, dear?"

"Yes, Mom. You feeling okay?"

"Sure," she said, and yawned. "Sure I am. Just dozed off. Did you discuss the landscaping with John?"

"Yes. I think we've covered everything."

"Isn't he a nice young man?" Jess pushed.

"Yes, Mom. I'm going to bed."

"Do you think you'll be seeing him again?"

"I'm sure I'll see a lot of him, since he'll be working on the yard for weeks. G'night."

Jess frowned. "Leigh, have you been crying? Your eyes are all red around the edges."

"Me? I never cry."

Never used to, Jess thought. Only love can really bring on the tears.

"It must have been the cigarette smoke in the Steak House."

"Ah," said Jess. But Leigh didn't smell of smoke. She smelled slightly of woodsy after-shave. Jess hid her smile.

Chapter Five

By the first of May, John's crew had cleared away most of the shrubbery that had to be torn out to accommodate the changes and had begun working in the yard. He arrived on site early each day to supervise the work.

Before the work started, he had joined Jess, Leigh and the two rambunctious little boys for dinner one night. The object of the meal was to go over the plans for the way the yard was going to look, review the labor and materials price list and, even though they were friends, sign a contract. It wasn't exactly a simple process, what with Mitch and Ty jumping up and down, spilling and shouting and, before the night was over, just before bed, getting into a fight.

It looked to John as though it was a regular brother thing. He had a brother two years older, and they had done the same kind of wrestling and tumbling that began with a tickle and a poke and escalated into warfare. He was just thinking about how it took him back, watching them, when someone started crying. Twins, he discovered, did everything double. Soon they were *both* crying.

"Mommy, Mitch poked my eye!"

"Mitch, did you poke Ty's eye?"

"He was tickling me when I told him to stop it, and I didn't poke it, I—"

"Did he ask you to stop, Ty?"

"But, Mom, he *told* me to tickle, and then I—"

"Mitch, did you *ask* Ty to tickle?"

John glanced over at Jess and rolled his eyes as if to say, "Listen to the genius," which he had the mental control not to say. "I bet it's bath time," he said instead.

"Nooooo."

"Not yet! Mommmm."

"Yes, it is!" she said, triumphant.

Later, in the blessed quiet of the evening over a little coffee, John advised Leigh, "I don't know much about kids, but I know one thing for sure. You'll *never* figure out who started it, no matter how far back the questions go. It's a lot easier if you don't get involved. If they can't fight it out, change the activity. Bench 'em."

"Is that how your mother handled things?" Jess asked.

"Wellllll, sort of," John said, somewhat uncomfortable. "Her way was a little more devious. I fought with one brother all the time. He was third, I was fourth. There were two years between us, but we were close to the same size. We both had a hand in starting them. She sent us outside or down to the basement to finish, depending on the weather."

"Oh," Leigh said, "then one of you got to win?"

"No winners," he said, sipping his coffee. "If no one got hurt, it was a draw. If someone did get hurt, the one who didn't got punished. Most of our fights ended with us competing to fake the best injury. My brother once stood on his own hand for so long I had already gone upstairs and to bed by the time he thought he had something good enough to show Mom." He paused as if to think. "Now that I think about it, he's still a little weird."

"But can he type?" Jess asked, chuckling.

"I think his hand made it all right. He's a surgeon. Dr. McElroy... Specializes in good looks. He claims to have helped create half the bodies that come skiing here each winter. When he sees a gorgeous woman, his wife has to threaten him to keep him from asking who her surgeon is."

Leigh realized that she knew very little about John's family. Was it possible she hadn't even asked? And she had accused him of being self-centered...

"So, Jess, we're a go on the yard?" John asked, moving onto safer ground.

They were on one condition, she said. That he take the boys fishing once. They had no uncles or cousins, no one to do that sort of thing with them.

John said he would be glad to.

Sometime between that first dinner and the first couple of weeks of work on the yard, the weather got warm enough for John to choose a Saturday for their fishing trip. And Leigh found an excuse to go along.

"I didn't realize until the first night you came over for dinner that I never asked about your family."

"I'm the youngest of four, and the only one, my mom says, who isn't ambitious. It's a pretty well-known fact that I don't like to work all that much. Well, I like work that feels like play. I found out accidentally that I like to fix things and make things look good. Lucky break, huh?"

"So, what about your family?" she asked. They were sitting together on the ground right behind the boys, who sat at the edge of the water with long cane poles.

"Bob is the oldest. He's about forty. He has his own tool and die business in Denver. He makes a great living and has a terrific wife and three kids. Judy, his wife, wanted ten kids until she had two. Number three, she says, was not her idea.

"Mike, the second one, he's around thirty-seven, I guess. He's a minister.... Can you beat that? And not a hokus-pokus type minister, but a real live theological mastermind with his own church in Wyoming, a doctorate in theology. He's married with two kids.

"Ted, my surgeon brother, has three kids and a wife who will never need a bit of work from a plastic surgeon. Chris is a knockout. She's his surgical nurse."

"I wish I'd had brothers and sisters," she said, "but I understand why that wasn't possible. The way my dad had to travel was one thing, and he was kind of up there when he and Mom got married. He was over forty when I was born."

"You didn't now about any of the regular things kids grow up knowing about, did you? About fighting, games, fishing?"

She shook her head.

"How'd you figure you'd know enough to raise them?" he asked, nodding toward the boys.

"Well, first, I knew I wanted children, but I didn't know I'd get them. And second, I didn't know I'd be doing it alone," she said. "And I always had Jess. Do you see your family much?"

"I go to Denver whenever they're all going to be at my mom and dad's. They come here to ski, sometimes in large packs and sometimes in small groups. They're pretty neat people. There's one unique thing about my family. No one has ever had a girl. My mom had four boys, and my brothers had boys."

Now, she thought. Tell him right now.

"Do you think much about what kind of life you want them to have?" he asked her.

"I think about it constantly. I'd like them to have the kind of life you had," she said. Her voice was wistful and dreamy. "And maybe I'd give them just a smattering of what Jess and my dad gave me. I'm working on my own projects less so I can pay more attention to what they're doing. Every day I realize how much of the natural instinct for parenting I lack. Like that business about fighting. I never would have thought of something like that."

"They're pretty good guys," he said. "You must be doing something right. Want more?"

"You don't ask an unmarried woman if she wants children, John. It could get you into trouble. She could think you're discussing the future."

"Okay, okay, unfair question. So, you're working less. That was one of the things you said terrified you."

"When I said that, it was true. I just didn't know the reason. And the reason is simple—whenever I wasn't very busy working on something challenging, I noticed how lonely I was and how everyone else had friends and things to do. Or seemed to. I began to change that before leaving Los Angeles. I was in a women's group, did some volunteer work and generally learned how to make friends. Not the kind of friends you can only find hovering over microscopes and computer terminals, but friends who liked going to ball games, movies and the beach.

"The boys helped me do that. I met some of the other mothers in water-babies classes, tiny-tots gymnastics and finally preschool."

"What would it be like for you to just be a housewife?" he asked.

She laughed at him. "*Just* a housewife? This is 1990, buster. Talk like that will get you drawn and quartered."

"Okay, okay... What if you didn't have a full-time job besides being a mother? What would that be like?"

"I'm always going to do some work in addition to raising my family, John," she said. "When I was growing up and advancing past all the kids, sometimes feeling really arrogant and other times feeling really sorry for myself, Jess would always say something to me that maybe a lot of moms say to their kids. 'Your best is good enough, Leigh. But you must always do your best.' I'm exhilarated by work. I'm also exhilarated by my kids. Even though I knew I wanted kids, I wasn't prepared for how great having them would be. But I'm also capable of doing work I love and that can help other people."

"So you'll always work." It sounded a bit like an accusation.

"But maybe not in the same way, John. Maybe if I'm not alone and afraid to be without a huge professional commitment I'll work at a sane pace rather than in the frenzy I used to use to cover up all that was missing from my life. There was another thing my mother said when I was much older and the projects I worked on were enormously important to the world. 'I'd like you to remember one thing—if you have something special, you must respect it, and treat it with wisdom and compassion. It won't do the world any good for you to burn yourself out, but if you have something that will make the world better, give it if you can. If you're a gifted baker, make good bread for the community. If you're a gifted gardener, make the world beautiful. If you're a gifted scientist, make the world safer.'"

He whistled. "It would be pretty hard not to feel guilty about not working with something like that hanging over your head."

"She wasn't saying that to make me feel guilty. She and my dad had a very strong belief that you should use your skills to make every day good and add to rather than subtract from the world." Leigh added pensively, "Now one of my great gifts is Mitch and Ty, and Jess reminded me recently that doing my best with them will include sacrifice. Maybe it includes sacrificing that single-mindedness I gave my work. Jess has been talking a lot about love. You know, dating, men, maybe marrying again."

"I think Jess has it in for us. It hasn't escaped me that she's setting me up."

"I know. I'm sorry. But I am glad to spend a little time getting to know you again. And no matter what Jess does, we'll still just bide our time getting to know each other. Right?"

He just stared at her, then slowly moved his hand to cover hers. "Biding time with you has its high points . . . and its frustrations." He was just leaning toward her as if to kiss her when Ty yelled. He had a fish.

"Your bid, Jess. Are we playing bridge or what?"

Oooops. The mother of the bride was daydreaming, Jess thought. "Three hearts," Jess said, ignoring her partner's audible gasp. "I can do three hearts alone," Jess said, stubborn in her own defense.

"You're *going* to do it alone," Peg grumbled.

"She's in never-never land again. Plotting," Abby West observed.

"Any progress? Are we looking at silver patterns yet?" asked Peg, laying down her cards and looking hopefully at Jess.

It was unclear whether Peg was relentlessly curious about the John/Leigh romance being staged by the mother of the bride or whether she wanted a break from bridge. Peg hated bridge and only played to indulge the others.

Jess folded her hand and grinned. She had only been waiting to be asked. Thursday was bridge day for the widows' brigade. Monday—literary discussion group. Tuesday—mah-jongg. Wednesday—garden club. Friday—craft day for seniors. The only thing the women were really serious about was their kids.

Jess's three best friends had been keeping a close watch over the progress of Leigh and John's relationship. While none of the others had this exact problem, they all had the same general problem—grown-up kids who simply weren't as clever or sensible as their mothers. According to the mothers. And the majority of them were still unmarried. Jess at least had grandchildren.

"I think it's going great guns, so far. Since John is working on the yard all the time, I suggested to Leigh that she ask him about activities for the boys. He actually drove them to the community center to sign up for T-ball. Since then, they've spent quite a lot of time together. I wonder how she's keeping him at arm's length." She fanned her face with her hand. "You can almost feel the heat. But there are always two little boys between them."

"If this works, I want my Rebecca married to a doctor by Christmas," Kate, the most cynical in the group, put in.

"It isn't quite *that* simple," Jess argued. She had explained it all before, and it went like this:

Jess suspected but had not verified that John was the father of Leigh's children. She could be wrong, but it was doubtful. From the moment she learned that Leigh was pregnant and the children hadn't been sired by Leigh's estranged husband, Jess had been scouting for the lover who had somehow broken her daughter's heart.

Okay, okay... At first she was going to find him and kill him. But after she'd spent time helping Leigh cope with the divorce, her job change, moving and multiple pregnancy, she began to understand that it had probably been the other way around. Leigh was such a bungler when it came to romance that she'd probably broken the poor fool's heart. Jess had thought about demanding the name of the responsible man, but then she decided that what Leigh really needed was a specialist who could help her catch up socially with the rest of her age group. Otherwise, Jess's demands for the culprit's name would not have done much good. She might have gotten John as a son-in-law, but it would undoubtedly have been far too temporary.

While Leigh was carrying and birthing the twins—and seeing the therapist—she was also dropping hints about her Durango fling. "He's just a simple, semi-hardworking guy who hates the whole concept of me having a Ph.D. You wouldn't want to have me marry just any old ski bum, now would you?" she'd asked. "Oh, sure, he has a job, but until they form a ski patrol in L.A., he wouldn't budge from Durango. Besides, since this little accident occurred, he's gotten himself married... and he doesn't even know about the babies.''

After she had moved back to Durango, Jess called John out to do fix-it jobs at the house and watched him like a hawk. He never asked about her daughter, but she could see him scanning the place for pictures. She kept one old picture in a frame and moved it around the house to satisfy herself that John indeed seemed to look for it and relax around the eyes and mouth when he finally spotted it. She purposely did not mention her grandsons.... She was saving that for a time when she needed his reaction. Now she believed she had him cold.

Recently Leigh had herself paved the way for what would eventually become Jess's plan to get her daughter married to the father of her children. It was when Leigh said, ''I was always so smart, but so dumb about love. You know, Mom, I might not have picked the right guy, but I sure did love him a lot. And he's not a bad guy. In fact, he's a really down-deep good guy. He just couldn't accept *me*. I was too much.''

''Maybe he just didn't have a chance,'' Jess had said.

''And now it's too late.''

No way, thought the mother of the bride. It was never too late. For one thing, Jess knew that John was divorced, although she'd had to snoop to find out. And all she had to do was look at those little boys to see an obvious resemblance to their father. And knowing that Leigh had truly loved and wanted him and thought he was a good man . . . well, Jess was ready to have the invitations printed.

In her mind, the marriage was a go. Leigh, however, seemed reticent about returning to live with her mother; she was really dragging her heels. Scared, Jess decided. Well, who wouldn't be? But the twins were getting big; time had wings. They would start school next fall. So Jess made up a little, tiny, inconsequential heart problem. She didn't want to tell a *big* lie—just expedite her daughter's return before the boys were drafted into the military.

"It's nothing serious, darling," Jess had said, "and I don't want you to be alarmed. I just want to spend some time with my grandchildren before I die. This could be my last summer . . . or then again, perhaps I'll somehow drift on through many summers."

Jess had never done anything like it before. It had been Peg's idea, actually, and it had been fun.

Once Leigh was home, Jess had to get her back in close proximity to John, which had proved more difficult to arrange than she imagined. She enlisted the aid of the widows' brigade. It was Peg's idea to tell John about her heart condition, too, as the reason for Leigh's return. Peg really should be closely watched, Jess thought. Deceitful old thing. It was Kate's idea to get Leigh and John working on the same project together—the renovation of the yard. Jess couldn't have cared less about having a stupid gazebo, but there weren't many things she could think of that would take a while to finish. Abby's contribution was that Jess should drop very, very heavy hints that getting married to someone like John would make her old mother happy. "Old women," Abby said, "are expected to play matchmaker. Try to conceal that and they'll know something is up."

Now Leigh was home, working on the yard, watching John while *he* worked on the yard. And Leigh hadn't said a word. Not a *word!* But seeing them together—the two of them or the four of them—Jess was convinced they belonged together.

"I thought you said you could do three hearts alone," Peg said, drawing Jess back into the game. "Old liar."

"Don't you call me a liar. You're the one who told me to pretend to have a heart condition."

"I know. You ought to be ashamed of yourself. Do you do everything you're told?"

"I'm sorry, ladies. I cannot concentrate on anything while I'm worrying about that girl. All I want is her happiness. And I'd like her happiness in a hurry, I admit it."

"I'd like to get her married and out of here so we can get things back to normal," Kate said.

"Things have never been normal around here," Abby said.

"But I know that girl. I was married to her father," Jess went on. "She needs a simple, steady, reliable man like John. Believe me, I know. That's what her father needed—a stable, sensible, ordinary person who could keep track of that wonderful, wandering mind. Who would know that better than me?"

"Are we going to play bridge or what?"

Chapter Six

Leigh did a couple of weeks' worth of serious reading and writing while the yard continued to develop into Jess's idea of a backyard paradise. She always found a few minutes to spare to chat with John, and he became something of a fixture at their dinner table. Then he asked her to meet him again at their old haunt, the Steak House, and she found herself as giddy as a teenager over the prospect of more hugging and kissing. So *this* is why most teenagers couldn't concentrate on their math, she thought. To Jess she said, "I might be late."

"You like him, then?"

"I like him fine," Leigh replied. I'm absolutely wacko, she thought.

He met her at the front door of the restaurant. "I want to show you something," he said. "Do you feel safe enough to come to my house with me?"

"Are you going to behave yourself?" she asked.

"Maybe, maybe not. That's up to you."

She thought about it and decided that when she had first met him she was a fifteen-year-old emotionally, which meant she'd been thinking with her libido. Now she figured she was at least twenty years old emotionally and could add brains to her already breathless libido. She went.

John had a house in town that he'd been working on, part-time, for about three years. "I want you to see it. I want to show you how I think it'll shape up over the years."

"It's lovely," she said as they pulled up to the curb in front. It was quintessentially small-town, with its front porch and white picket fence. A family house, was her first thought. Her second thought was, there's no one here but us, and my brain is going out the window. But fear began to run away as John talked about his house.

"It's fifty-five years old. I knocked out the wall that separated the living room from the dining room to make more space. I'm working on a new kitchen, but since I don't do a lot of cooking for myself, it's been slow going. I'm a good cook, though. Did you know that?"

She hadn't.

He pulled her along. He opened the refrigerator door and withdrew a bottle of wine. "I plan to replace this fridge with a subzero one that has matching cabinetry. And a built-in microwave, new stove and, rather than this old-fashioned pantry, I'm going to build out into the back porch, put in a bay window and have a breakfast nook."

He planned more shelves than cupboards, and showed her a picture of a country French kitchen that seemed to have a spirit of good food and community. She began to envision it.

"The attic is unfinished," he went on, digging in a drawer for a corkscrew. "There are two bedrooms upstairs, and I'm going to open up the staircase, build a couple of dormer windows and an outdoor staircase to the yard. It's a small yard, but with a covered patio and some landscaping, it'll be beautiful. Come on," he said, abandoning the wine and taking her out the back door.

There was an old two-car garage with a peaked roof. "I'm going to enlarge the garage and build on a workshop. There'll be storage up top, the workshop out back, and separate garage doors." He led her back inside. "I'm going to tile where there's linoleum and refinish the hardwood floors. And the front porch—now it's small...." He poured two glasses of wine and handed her one. "Come on," he said, taking her back to the living room. He had a curved sofa that sat before an old-fashioned fireplace. No TV, but a fancy stereo unit. He pointed to the window, outside of which was the front porch. "I'm going to make it larger and screen it, and that will give me more space to enlarge the upstairs."

"It's wonderful," she said, sipping her wine. "How long have you been working on it?"

"A few years," he said. "I've been doing a little here and there, but I haven't done a lot of serious work yet. I can do a lot of the cabinet work myself, but for an addition I'll need a bona fide builder and a permit. I'm just getting serious about it. It has to be a lot larger than it is. I wasn't going to finish the attic, but now I'm going to make sure it will hold two bedrooms with a bathroom in between. I thought about fixing it up to sell it—and now I'm thinking of fixing it up to live in it. It's pretty messy, huh?''

"Just sawdust," she said. "I'm the messy one— I can have a completely finished house and still it's a disaster. I'm getting better, but I never had to do much of that myself while I was growing up. But now Jess is beginning to really get testy about my messiness.''

"Look at this," he said, leading her to the upstairs hall. It was a short hall with one bathroom between two bedrooms. Tacked to the wall were pictures torn from magazines of bedrooms, a bathroom, linen closets. The bathroom picture showed an old tub with feet, an antique linen cupboard and baskets holding rolled-up, multicolored towels. One bedroom picture showed a canopy bed of brushed pine, built-in dressers, and flowered wallpaper with a matching bedspread.

"Try to picture this in there," he said, pointing to the clawfoot tub and then indicating the open bathroom door. The room definitely resembled the picture. And the bedroom had the built-ins done, but the canopied bed was not yet there.

"It's lovely, John. You've already resurfaced these floors."

"That rug was my grandmother's," he said proudly.

"You're really an artist," she said. So much more than a handyman, more than a Mr. Fix-it. There was real skill and imagination in this. The house surprised her. She had never given that much thought to her surroundings. She had always lived well, but she had never put energy into creating her own space.

"The elementary school is in the neighborhood. There's a playground at the end of the block."

"When did you decide to make it larger?" she asked.

"About three weeks ago. Leigh..." he began, struggling with the right words. "We're nothing alike. Nothing. I'm not even sure we want the same things. But...I tried marrying someone just like me. Someone who just wanted to play all the time and wasn't worried about the future, about families. It was awful.... We were barely out of the wedding chapel before we were fighting. And what about you? You married yourself a genius who was so wrapped up in work he didn't have time for anything else in his life."

"What are you saying, John?"

"Well, I'm not very good at this." He laughed with some embarrassment. "I don't know how to say it. You've only been back a few weeks. This is hard. I want you in my life. I can't stand it when you're not in my life. I want to know if we can make it work. People put together different kinds of marriages now, different from how they were in the fifties and sixties. It used to be that you had to have the same goals, the same ambitions, or you just couldn't make it. We've talked about how you love your work and how I love to play... I wonder if it's possible, if we try to compromise, for us both to have what we want and each other, too."

"I'm a mother. When I look at the prospect of having a man in my life, I have to know if he's interested in being a father."

"I like your boys," he said.

Now. Tell him now.

"I don't know what kind of a father I'd be, but I know I wouldn't be a terrible one. I get along fine with kids. But I'm not going to lie to you—I wouldn't be hooking up with you just so I can have kids. It's you, Leigh. I never got over you. I might never get over you. I don't get along very well without you. I really regret that we lost each other before."

"We never had a real courtship," she said, but he was leaning toward her, his lips getting closer and closer. They stood just in front of the bedroom door.

"I'll court you till you die... I promise...." His lips touched hers lightly, as if just testing the water. "I could get a lot of work done on the house this summer, and put you and the kids in it.... You could vacuum sawdust when you're not saving the world with your ethics paper."

When he put his lips on hers and talked through his kiss, her legs turned to rubber and she felt that fierce longing that she had only known with John.

"John," she said, stalling, but she didn't move away from him, "have there been a lot of women?"

"You mean, do I sleep around?"

"I guess that's what I mean."

"No. After our breakup I did try to find someone who would help me forget you ... but I couldn't. And in the tradition of the decade, I played it very safe. It's a whole new ball game—you have to keep a photocopy of your sexual history in your ski jacket, along with a note from your doctor. I'm okay. Soft in the head, but okay."

"You love me," she said, tears beginning to rise to her eyes.

"Uh-huh, I do. And don't think I didn't try to find another way. After you left and my marriage went belly-up, I tried to change everything. I tried to read smart books, but all I got from that was a lot of sleep."

Her laugh bubbled out, but she moved closer into his embrace. He moved into the bedroom and put his wine on the built-in dresser. His arms tightened as he held her, rocking with her. She sat her glass beside his so she could hold him, then kissed him deeply. She didn't want to stop kissing, but he was talking.

"Then I tried to concentrate on business, because if I couldn't be smart, I'd be rich. I kept trying to find a way to deserve you, even if you were gone. But I couldn't stay interested in getting rich. This is all I am, Leigh. I'm Mr. Fix-it. It's what I want to be."

"And I went away to try to learn how to be 'regular.' My lessons were as hard as yours.... I had to learn to relax. I had to learn to think of ordinary things. There's nothing like a real ripe diaper pail to help you face reality."

"You love me," he said, burying his face in her neck.

"Uh-huh, I do," she said. "I always have. What are we going to do?"

"We got a second chance, babe. We're gonna try it. That's all we can do. Remember that last fight we had—the one where I said 'then just go'? Well, it's gonna take a much bigger fight than that to get me to let go of you again."

Now. Tell him now.

"About the boys..."

"Not now," he said. "They'll be fine if we can work this out. They like me."

"I think they're already nuts about you, John, and..."

But she couldn't keep talking and kissing at the same time. This was what she had dreamed of so many nights—waking up with that gasping, choking feeling that was a prelude to tears. She had truly thought there would never be a way to feel this again. Not with him. Not with anyone.

John covered her with kisses, his lips roving from her neck to her ear, from her chin to her fingertips. The only sound from Leigh was a deep, enormous sigh of recognition, of longing. The only difference between the way she had always wanted him and the way she wanted him now was the proximity. Her body was beginning to respond in that wonderful way; her nipples stood taut, and her insides gathered up in a tight, luscious knot, ready to explode. The warmth of his body against hers, the pressure of his hands on her back, her buttocks, her breasts, brought such intense joy that she forgot where she was, who she was.

"I used to think about kissing you again," he said, cradling her in his arms. "I thought about it at the weirdest times. I'm starting to believe that old myth that there's a perfect mate for every man...."

"Are you saying you want to marry me, John?"

"I don't want to be stupid, and I don't want to mess anything up. You've only been back a little while...but does it count as a proposal if I tell you I want to head in that direction?"

"I think so," she said, tasting his ear, his neck. She tugged his shirt out of his pants and ran the palms of her hands up his chest. His skin was hot and dry; his nipples were pointed little knobs.

His hands tugged her shirt out of her pants. His lips demanded of hers, and his breathing became labored. "I want you in the worst way. Can we? Is it okay?"

Details, details. She was going to faint if he didn't undress her right away.

"We can," she said.

"Do you use something? We don't want any accidents."

Damn. "Oh, John . . ." she sighed. "When I thought about coming back here . . . I thought you were *married*."

He chuckled against her neck. "You won't get out of it that easily," he said. "Turn around," he directed. She did; she would have stood on her head right now if that was what he wanted from her. He began undoing her long braid. "I figured you hadn't covered that," he said, digging his fingers into her hair and fanning it wide. "You never did think about the practical aspect of things, so I went to the drugstore."

"Hoping?" she asked.

He sighed from his toes. "I've been hoping since I saw you again. Am I rushing you?" he asked, turning her back to face him. She shook her head as he slowly lifted her shirt over her head and tossed it aside. "I can't get close enough to you. I can't leave you alone. Sue me." He reached around her and unsnapped her bra. "Ahhhh," he said. "You're so perfect."

She closed her eyes and leaned her head back while he touched her breasts with his mouth. At the same time he popped the snap on her jeans, and when he raised his head again he ripped off his shirt in one perfect, fluid motion. And held her. Skin against skin. The soft, hot press of bodies. She shuddered slightly in anticipation and ground her body into his. How she had longed to have this part of her life back.

"This isn't going to last long," he whispered, his voice jagged and raspy. "The next time will last longer...."

"I don't care," she said, her own voice strange to her. There was something, she remembered as she ditched her jeans and underwear, about feeling out of control that was so wonderfully alluring. She couldn't stop him any more than she could stop herself. Maybe if she didn't know how finely tuned their bodies were she could have controlled herself. But the feeling that she had no power over her desires made her head spin and her body tremble.

While kissing her, fondling her, touching her in the most delicious ways, he also undressed himself, lowered her to the rug and found the protection he had purchased. She said a tiny, guilty prayer of thanks that he was sensible, because she herself was positively brain dead from lust.

His hand moved down her belly, over her mound of curly yellow hair, and his fingers gently spread her to touch her most delicate, sensitive place.

She shook from within, her legs instinctively tightening over his hand, her hips instinctively arching upward. Her breath came in one giant gasp, which he covered with his mouth and tongue while he pressed his hand harder into her flesh. Slowly, slowly, she came back, her eyes closed, her breath becoming even. He rose above her and looked into her eyes.

"Well, love, I don't have to feel guilty if I can't spend a lot of time inside you. I'm on the edge myself."

She only nodded, flooded with heat and passion. She opened herself up so that he could press himself inside her, and then a new sensation filled her. She loved this; she loved *him*. He moved, slowly and evenly, picking up speed and moving faster, and she began again, that build and rise. And just as she felt him lunge within, it happened again. Again, she was drenched in pleasure, flooded with heat.

In a half-dazed state, stroking his back and massaging his shoulders, she remembered back...way back...to their first time. She'd had so little experience when John made love to her the first time. And it had been like this before—his touch alone could propel her into ecstasy. She recalled thinking, "Wow, this is great!" like a kid who'd just discovered chocolate.

Now, however, she already knew how great this was. This time there was something more she had to deal with, think about.

"John?" she began.

"Mmmmm?"

"John, about the boys..."

He kissed her lips. "I'm crazy about the boys, Leigh. I'll adopt them, play with them, be as good a dad as I can... whatever you want."

"But, John, I want to tell you about the boys."

"Not now, Leigh," he said, kissing her ear, her neck, her breast. "We have a lifetime to talk about the boys and their future siblings. Right now is for you and me. We have to be sure, in and out of bed, that we want each other. I learned a couple of things in the past few years. I learned that there's only one way to really deserve you. I'm going to accept you exactly as you are, not try to live up to your brilliance. If you just say that I'm what you want—you'll get just the me you see."

"That's the you I want," she whispered.

Chapter Seven

It was lunch break for the crew, and Leigh sat up on the redwood deck with a cup of decaf and a book. The landscaping and building was nearly done; most of the guys had gone to get some fast food, but John had stayed behind to play a little catch with the boys. He had also stayed because Jess had offered him a bowl of her famous vegetable soup and a garden salad. And because he was planning to make a life with Leigh and the boys, if it was possible. At the moment, it looked more than possible.

"Are you playing matchmaker?" Leigh had asked her mother the week before.

"Well, yes, I suppose I am. My grandsons need a man in their lives. Bring me someone you like better and I'll stop working on John."

"Just stop," Leigh had said.

And Jess had replied, "No."

Since Leigh knew there was no one in the universe better than John, she let her mother's interference go. But she didn't dare encourage her. Jess already talked about John more than Leigh did. Leigh was in complete agreement, but she didn't want to scare him away. And they had decided not to rush for one reason only—it was ridiculous to get married after being together for a little under two months. She wasn't entirely sure *why* it was ridiculous, but it certainly *seemed* that way.

The boys weren't very good ball players yet, but they sure loved it when John gave them any attention. They had begun climbing all over him whenever they saw him. When his truck pulled up, they ran to him. It took a very stern mother to see to it that he was left alone long enough to get a little work done during the day.

Spring was at its lushest, and Leigh had been home for two months plus a few days. The gazebo was half constructed, the flagstone garden paths coming along nicely, and the barbecue pit would support a few burgers and steaks in another week. Because the lot was huge and abundant with brush, trees and plants, it didn't really appear to be under construction. When the mess was cleared away, it would be stunning. Leigh was so glad to be here; she felt such a sense of renewal. She believed in her future in a way she never had before.

Each moment with John seemed to improve on the one before it. The interest he showed in the boys, seemingly both entertained and fascinated by them, was something she had only dared dream of. Since she hadn't really expected it to go even half so well, she was very pleased with herself.

Leigh remembered when a book had held her interest more than John did. It had frustrated him terribly, back when he didn't understand how she had learned to escape her feelings—and the feelings she had around John were enormous. Now, with her renewed sensitivity to what she felt, the book that could draw her attention away from John for a minute had not yet been written.

He had been so good about recreating their friendship on her terms. He had taken the boys to sign up for T-ball, gone with them all to get ice cream, and just last Saturday they had attended a movie. Jess invited him to lunch and dinner nearly every day and wasn't fooling him at all.

"Your mother is making me very nervous with this setup. She isn't fooling anyone," he said.

"I know," she replied.

I'm not as dumb about relationships as I claimed, Leigh thought. Years ago she had known she wanted this: a lover, a friend, partner, children. It was one of the critical impulses that had caused her to separate from Max, because he had made it clear that this could never happen with him.

Then there was something else, something frequently covered in paperback novels. Romance. On at least one and sometimes two nights each week Leigh would steal an evening to be alone with John. And while he didn't push her or try to make love to her again, their kissing sessions were simply magnificent, spattered with dialogue, tense with desire, lush with emotion...and they couldn't help themselves. What a lovely thing to not be able to help. She wanted him so badly she ached.

She had made a deal with herself—to be fair, she was going to be sure he knew about his sons before they resumed that part of their relationship. A stronger woman would have kept that deal. She had failed that once, at his house, but she was determined not to fail again. But as much as she longed for honesty between them, as much as she longed to make love to him again, she was still a bit terrified of telling him. She was afraid he would be angry that she hadn't done it sooner. Soon, she thought. Maybe tonight.

She watched as Mitch overthrew Ty with the ball, and John clapped and whooped; they were pretty small to throw so well. He turned to look at Leigh and made the thumbs-up sign; she waved and smiled.

She ached for him, but the last time they had become lovers before they became friends... before they came to terms with what they wanted. It had turned out that they had wanted different things, opposite things. This time she was trying to put first things first, to begin at the beginning and not at the end. This time they were talking, at least. Finding areas of agreement.

"I thought," John had said, "that I actually liked you before I loved you. But knowing that for sure is as important to me as it is to you." He had something that Leigh had never had herself—and hadn't given him credit for the last time around. Wisdom.

Things were good. They were getting reacquainted; they were friendly. They were being sensible, postponing their marriage for a few months, even if they had been unsuccessful in postponing their sexual relationship. They were so hot for each other that they had to watch even kissing, because within seconds they were panting, squirming, nearly dying of longing. Her cheeks grew pink when she thought about him. She wasn't sure she could just sit there on the deck watching him without getting all hot and bothered.

So much for wisdom.

She loved watching him. Whether he was bending his back over bricklaying or playing with the kids, his lithe strength was so appealing.

He stopped playing ball suddenly and straightened his spine. The ball that Ty had thrown his way hit him in the knee, and he didn't move.

"Hey, John!" she heard Ty call.

John looked at Leigh, astonishment written all over his face. He turned back to the boys and said something she couldn't hear, and then the boys began to toss the ball back and forth without him while he turned and slowly walked toward the deck. His brow was furrowed, but his mouth was slightly open. He finally stood before her and simply looked at her for a moment.

"John?"

"Five pounds . . . each?"

"What?"

"The kids . . . they were five pounds each. They were early."

"Yes. Well, actually, Ty was four-four . . . and Mitch was—"

"How early?"

"Almost two months. A little over six weeks."

He winced visibly. He shook his head, then seemed to try to refocus on her eyes. "They're mine," he said.

She felt that old snap of panic in her gut. There it was at last. A little later she was going to be glad this part was over. This wasn't the way she had planned it. She nodded rather lamely.

"Were you going to tell me? Ever?"

She swallowed once and looked over her shoulder to make sure her mother and the brigade couldn't hear. "That's the main reason I wanted to come back . . . even though I thought you were married. . . . I knew I had to tell you that they—"

"Damn!"

"John," she said pleadingly, "I didn't know you didn't know. Until we met at the Steak House and you couldn't understand why Max felt betrayed... All these years I thought when you heard about them you would instantly know it was you."

"Know? Know and not even *care?* How could you have thought that?"

"You were adamant! You didn't want a commitment or children. Later, when I came back, you seemed so oblivious to it all. Even when you knew about them, the impact seemed lost on you."

The look of pain that crossed his features was unmistakable. "You thought I was too stupid to figure it out."

"No." She shook her head. "No, I just didn't understand. I mean, sometimes I understood. When I came back here pregnant as a cow and found you were married, I understood that you never knew I was pregnant...."

"You didn't *tell* me!"

"I know...I know...I didn't want to tell you until my divorce was final because, frankly, I didn't think the divorce was going to precede the birth. I had made such a mess of things. Even though I hadn't been with my husband in over a year, I was still legally married and pregnant. My divorce did come through before they were born, and then I was too late. And—"

"Come on, come on... That was then. What about now?"

"Well, after thinking about it, I realized that you probably didn't know all the details of childbirth, of how twins usually come a little early, of—"

"But you didn't hurry to explain, did you?"

"Hey, John!" Mitch yelled.

"Practice, I said!" he shouted back, an angry tone in his voice. "Why didn't you tell me right away? *Right away!*"

"I don't know. I was afraid to. And I thought this was better."

"What?"

"Well..." she tried, her voice shaking. Hadn't she made a lot of sense to herself before, when she was figuring this out? "Since you didn't seem to realize they were your children, I thought I'd let you choose them. I tried a couple of times, then chickened out. But I thought we seemed to be headed in the same direction this time, wanting the same things and all. And I thought you might be a little upset at first, but I really thought you'd be happy to find out they're—"

"Good God," he said, shaking his head. "Don't you know there's a huge difference between accepting them because they're part of the deal and wanting them because... And you're going to do a study on ethics. Leigh, it isn't *ethical* to keep information like that a secret."

"I know, sort of. But that's what makes ethics confusing and complex. Being dishonest is unethical, unless it's the lesser evil. Like, is it more ethical not to name the father of my sons than to name someone who would hurt them?"

"Why would I hurt them?" he asked, aghast. "Haven't I been pretty good with them? Good to them? Without even knowing—"

"But I needed to know you again. What if you didn't want them?" she said, her voice so low he had to strain to hear. "What if you didn't want me? Or me with them?"

He only pursed his lips tighter. "Why couldn't you just tell me the truth? Why didn't you leave me a message that you were about to give birth? If not that, why didn't you write, call, something—to let me know I was a father?"

"I didn't want to bother you. You said you didn't want to be a father. I left because you said that wasn't in your game plan. You said, 'Go. We're too different anyway.'"

"Leigh," he said as patiently as he could, "men always say stuff like that. It doesn't mean that much. A guy says something like that, and then his wife gets pregnant and you'd think he invented pregnancy."

"I don't know anything about guys and what they say and what they mean."

He ran a hand through his hair and shook his head. "Leigh, Leigh, stop. Listen to me. What you did to me is really unfair. No matter what happened between us, they were mine. No matter what my marital status was or yours, for that matter—you should have told me I had children. This could have worked out all different. I missed all this time with them because you decided it was better this way. Leigh, I know I hurt your feelings when I said 'just go,' but I didn't take your *kids* away from you! Is there anything else you should tell me? Anything that you either assume I know, assume I don't know, or . . . anything?"

"What do you mean?"

"The kids are fine? Normal? No mysterious conditions or anything?"

"Of course not. I would tell you something like that."

"You didn't even tell me that—"

"Soup!" Jess cried from the back door. "Leigh, the girls and I have ours in the kitchen. Why don't you, John and the boys help yourselves while we go back to our game?"

Leigh and John didn't respond, only looked at each other. "Does she know?" he asked after a long moment.

"Sometimes I think she does, sometimes I'm sure she doesn't. She hounds me about getting married all the time—she decided I should marry someone like you, but I don't know how she could know you're their—" She shrugged. "Maybe you just seem the perfect type to be their stepfather."

"Stepfather," he muttered, the set of his mouth angry. "You really did it this time. I can't believe you didn't tell me. Was it some kind of test . . . to see if I was good enough?"

"Oh, John, no. Oh, please," she said, tears coming to her eyes.

"Sometimes you have no *sense*," he said.

"I know, I know, but I thought—"

"Stop it!" He looked away. Were those tears in his eyes? He shook his head again, trying to clear the fog away. "I gotta go, Leigh. Tell Jess thanks anyway, but I need a little time to think. Alone. Let me have that. Okay?"

"Could you just remember one thing?"

"Yeah, what?"

"It's not their fault."

Work on the yard progressed with lightning speed, but without the foreman. John remained conspicuously absent while the roof went on the gazebo and the last brick was laid in the barbecue pit.

"Where is that young man?" Jess asked her daughter. "I haven't seen him in almost a week."

"Six days," Leigh replied morosely.

"I hadn't realized," Jess, who realized each minute, lied. "And here I was getting the impression that he had taken a real interest in you and the boys. Or was it just my cooking?"

Leigh made no response. She gazed off into space, as she had been doing quite a lot lately.

"The boys really miss having him around," Jess said. "The other fellas are just as nice, but don't seem to take the personal interest in them that John did. I mean, signing them up for a T-ball team and everything. What a guy."

"What a guy," Leigh said. What a jerk, she thought. No matter how mad he was at her, he shouldn't let the boys down like this. Of course, the boys didn't know they'd been let down yet, but surely they would notice soon. . . .

"Tell me what you think of this invitation, Leigh," Jess said, handing her a calligraphic page.

You are cordially invited to the home of Mrs. Jessica Stewart Wainscott for an outdoor springtime celebration of food, libation, music and good cheer on the afternoon of Sunday, June 10. Two o'clock

The address and a request for an R.S.V.P. appeared at the bottom.

"Good heavens," Leigh said. "This is pretty fancy, isn't it? For a backyard barbecue?"

"Well, when you spend thousands revamping the backyard, you ought to do up the party right. Don't you think?"

"How many people are you inviting?"

"Everyone I've ever met."

"Oh. And are you having it catered, or did you get together a bunch of friends to potluck it?"

"Oh, catered. Naturally. I'm using Berkley's Bakery and Deli. They're fantastic."

"This is going to cost a fortune."

"I only plan to do this once."

"Well," Leigh said, handing the invitation back to her mother, "just so long as you don't wear yourself out and get sick."

"Don't be silly. I'm not even doing any of the work. Shouldn't we get you a new dress for the party?"

"A dress? You're planning on guests wearing dresses?"

"Mom," a small voice said from somewhere below. She looked down to see Ty, the blonde, staring up at her. "Wanna play catch some more?"

"Where's Mitchell?" Leigh asked.

"Over there. Waiting for us."

"Okay," she said, moving down to the backyard and holding out her hands. She didn't do this well; another character flaw. Ty fired the first one at her and she missed it, so naturally she had to chase it. "So, Mother," she called, glancing back to the deck where Jess stood, watching them. "It's only three weeks till your party. You think everything will be done?"

"It's almost done now," Jess said, watching as Leigh pitched the ball to Mitch, missing him by miles. Mitch complained loudly and ran after the ball. Two more bad throws followed. "I'm going to have Peg's son, the florist, bring out a bunch of fresh flower garlands to decorate the gazebo and put arrangements on long buffet tables," Jess said, wincing as a ball hit Leigh in the leg. Leigh made a noise of pain and threw the ball—aiming for Ty, getting closer to Mitch—and both boys whined their unhappiness.

"Mom," said Ty, "throw it under. Under. Like this." He moved his hand very patiently, trying to show her how to do it. It didn't work. Leigh's aim was actually worse than a four-year-old's. She grouped them closer together. With them standing just a few feet apart, she could get the ball to the right person.

"Mom, let's not play," Mitch said. "We'll practice a while and maybe you can play later. 'Kay?"

"That bad, huh?"

"This is for babies," Ty said. "When's John coming?"

"I don't know, guys. Pretty soon, I suppose."

"Did he say anything to you about being away for a while, Leigh? If I didn't know better I'd think he was avoiding us," Jess called.

"I don't know, Mother."

"Why don't you call him for me? Ask him to dinner. I really think that young man has a thing for you. I *know* he gets a kick out of the boys. Something must have happened to—"

"*Mother!* For Pete's sake!"

"Well, what the heck?" Jess defended herself. "He's a nice young man. I've known him for years, and I can tell the two of you like each other. Maybe if you—"

"Mother! Stop it!"

"I am only suggesting," Jess said, in her most patient, long suffering voice, "that I could turn this garden party into a wedding in a snap. Then I could have you and the boys settled and taken care of before I die.''

"You know something, Mom? I thought this was humorous for a couple of weeks, but it's quickly losing its appeal. Now, do me a favor, don't bring up John, marriage or death—in a humorous *or* serious vein—again. Understand?''

"Oh, Leigh," Jess sighed. "You're too young to be so old and crotchety.''

"Sometimes I actually think you're serious.''

"If you'd get serious, we'd be in business.''

"I give up!" Leigh shouted. "I can't take this anymore!''

"Heavens," Jess muttered. "Testy.''

It was Wednesday. The brigade was seated in the front room when Leigh came in.

"Mom, Mitch and Ty are in front of the TV in the loft. I want to run to the bookstore, but I won't be gone long. Can you keep an eye on them?''

"Sure," Abby answered for her.

"Yes," Jess said, glaring at her friend. "Buttinsky," she muttered.

"Thanks," Leigh said, fishing in her shoulder bag for her car keys. She went out the back door. When she got to the car, she realized she hadn't remembered her checkbook and went back.

"So I'm stuck with a stupid garden party when what I wanted was a wedding," Jess was saying in the next room.

"Well, at least you tried," Abby consoled. "Do you have any idea what happened?"

"Not a clue. One minute they seemed ready to steam themselves straight—I've never seen so many passionate glances between two people. The next thing I know—whoosh—John is gone and Leigh is depressed. Kids. They can't even get a simple marriage right."

"The printer can add *wedding* to the invitations, can't he?" Kate asked.

"I think we're past all that. I'm picking them up tomorrow, and the party's in two weeks. But I could sure get on the phone."

"Well," Peg said, "what if you fake a real heart attack and make Leigh's marriage to John your dying wish?"

"I feel guilty enough just faking a heart condition. Last time I had a physical the doctor asked me if I'd be an organ donor." Jess sighed. "I'm thinking of coming clean about the whole thing."

"That won't be necessary," Leigh said. She stood just inside the kitchen doorway. "Oh, Mom, how could you be so sneaky?"

"Leigh!" Jess had the good grace to slap a palm against her chest as though a coronary might be impending after all—but Leigh was unimpressed.

"Shame on you, Mom. As if my problems aren't tough enough."

"I was trying to help," Jess said.

"She was," said Peg, ever so earnest. "She honestly was!"

"Peg put her up to it," Kate tattled.

"Abby was the one who actually got the idea," Peg confided.

"Oh, stop it," Leigh said. "You're all giving new meaning to the term busybody." She shook her head. "Shame on you all."

"Leigh," Jess said. "I *am* sorry, darling. I'm ashamed of myself."

"What were you thinking of?"

"I was thinking that you and John are perfect for each other, and I got a little . . . a little . . ."

"Carried away," Peg said. "But it's mostly my fault, Leigh. I egged her on."

"Me too," said Abby.

"I warned her from the start," Kate said.

"You should all be grounded," Leigh said, exasperated. "No wonder he ran for his life."

"But why, Leigh?" Jess asked. "What happened?"

"Oh, forget that! I'd be a fool to give you any encouragement at all! I'll be out for a while longer. I want to take a little think-time. Watch the boys?"

"Of course, Leigh," Jess murmured. She just stared at the doorway until she could hear the sound of the car. Then she turned to her friends. ''When I figure out which one of you talked me into this . . .''

Chapter Eight

"Fishing," Leigh mumbled, driving along a narrow, mountainous road. It just figured.

She had gone to his nursery to ask where he was. There was no one there except a high-school girl whose only job it was to ring up sales. Then she drove to his house and found a note on the door. "Gone fishin'." She thought that sort of thing had gone out with Tom Sawyer. Then she spotted a truck with John's logo on the door. She followed it, and when it stopped she asked the driver if he had any idea where John usually fished. He gave her three possible locations.

The first two, reasonably close, had proved futile. It just figured that John had to go deep into the woods, down a long unpaved road to a mountain stream. Leigh half remembered a place like this where she had come with John years ago.

She might have remembered some of the details if she hadn't been so busy building up a good head of steam. She was a little tired of this childish behavior. His and hers both. But she was a little tired of feeling guilty about not always doing the right thing. Couldn't people occasionally make allowances for mistakes? When you told a person you were nearsighted they didn't turn around later and point out something far away, then yell at you if you couldn't see it.

And furthermore, how many times was she supposed to say she was sorry? For everything? And how much time did he need before he realized how much courage she'd had to work up to come back here, to the scene of the crime, so to speak, to face him and tell him the truth about his sons, even thinking he was married? He never gave her any credit because he was always finding some fault with her.

She rehearsed all those arguments right up to the point when she saw his truck in the clearing. Yes, this was a place she had come with him. And yes, he was fishing now as he had fished then. And perhaps he had been here for a while, because he had a tent set up and a camp fire in front of it. Maybe it was his plan to just become a woodsy recluse until she got frustrated enough to leave.

That was what had happened before when they couldn't communicate, so in one insane moment they threw away all the good things they had shared. Oh, if she had told him then, just told him then, maybe . . .

It made her cry to think about it. She hardly ever cried normally, but she had done more sniffling since coming back here than she had done in ten years. She jumped out of her car, heedless of the tears streaming down her cheeks, and walked toward him. He had turned and seen her drive in, but he observed her heated approach with apparent calm.

She advanced on him, feeling anything *but* calm herself.

"I don't know what you want from me," she said to him.

He walked toward her. Very slowly. His lack of emotion only fueled hers.

"Do you want me to beg? Is that it? I'm sorry. I messed everything up from the very beginning because I'm smart in some things and stupid in others. I never thought about protection because my husband and I did not make love. And I never thought about what would happen if I fell in love with someone because I never *had* fallen in love, even slightly.... Not in twenty-seven years! I actually thought some people got love and some people got brains.... I didn't know love made people brainless! And I didn't tell you about the babies because you had just gotten married and I thought you loved someone else. And then I didn't tell you because I just plain didn't know *how*. So what do you want from me, huh, John?"

He stared at her during her tirade. No expression whatsoever.

"Huh, John? What if they weren't yours, but really my dead ex-husband's kids? Wouldn't it be pretty apparent that they're crazy about you just the same? They are, you know. They ask when John's coming, and I don't know how to tell them that John's mad because he just found out he's their real, true daddy and he's upset. But not about being a dad, I don't think. About not being told sooner.''

She gave a sniffly kind of gulp and wiped impatiently at her tears. He just watched her face, his arms hanging loose at his sides.

''What more could I have done if I'd wanted to do things perfectly? I just wanted to come back to Durango, where you are, and somehow make it right with you. I never dreamed you would be divorced. I was prepared to find you happily married and the father of a bunch of little, tiny kids. I didn't know if I'd be very good at working things out, but I knew it was *right* that you know about your sons.'' Her tone changed. ''They're good boys, John. They're sweet, honest, lovable, precious, smart little boys. I thought you'd be so proud of them.

''I was so stunned to find you alone. I was so surprised to find you still had some feelings for me. Honest. I had never given myself credit for being able to have that kind of impact on a man...especially a man I was wildly in love with. And then to see that you couldn't help but have some feelings for them, too...well, I was beside myself with happiness. But I messed up one more thing by not telling you soon enough.''

She gulped and hiccuped, then wiped her nose on her sleeve. She hadn't cried like this in a long time. And there he stood, right smack in front of her, watching without saying anything.

"I'm *sorry,*" she nearly shrieked. "Before, when I walked away and got on with my life and had them alone, it was because I didn't know anything. And now I know some things. And if you think I'm going to let you have a temper tantrum and walk away from us just because you're mad, you're wrong! Because I think you love me, and I *know* I love you! So what do you want from me? Huh, John?"

His movement was so fast that she gasped. He put his arms around her waist and pulled her to him, covering her mouth with his. He kissed her all over her sticky, teary face and held her so tightly that she could hardly breathe. But who needed to breathe?

This isn't likely to solve anything, Leigh thought abstractly. But then her thoughts faded completely, because the sensation of his lips, the taste of his mouth and the hard press of his body against hers made her deliriously, if briefly happy. She held him; he held her. Then it occurred to her. *This* was what he wanted.

And so did she.

After that long, emotional speech, Leigh could only say, "Oh, John..." Actually, she cried it, but she wouldn't let go of him. She wouldn't let go again. And neither would he, apparently. He lifted her into his arms and carried her to his tent. Inside was an open sleeping bag upon which they were soon tumbling, kissing, hugging, and Leigh was still crying.

"Are we going to be able to figure this out?" She wept. "Ever?"

"I didn't come up here to figure it out, babe," he said, kissing her neck, her wet eyes, her ears. "It only took me about two minutes to remember that I want you ... and them. But I had to think about how to tell my folks that I have kids, that I'm going to marry their mother, that it was just a stupid misunderstanding by two stupid people ... one of whom just happens to be the genius daughter of a prize-winning scientist."

A laugh bubbled through her tears.

"No one would ever believe this. I may not be as smart as you are, but would you believe one of the reasons I was appointed head of the volunteer ski patrol is that I have this uncanny intuition and great common sense?"

Again a laugh bubbled through. "I love you," she said.

"I know. And I love you. And even though I was pretty mad at first, and even though I wish you'd told me sooner, I'm really glad you brought the boys here. I want to be their dad."

That made her really cry. "I was so afraid you wouldn't. You were pretty adamant about not wanting kids."

"That was just a guy thing. I don't know where it comes from. Men are afraid that if they act like they even condone the *idea* of having children, they'll be rushed into a Lamaze class. I'm sorry. I was beginning to worry that I might never have kids, to tell the truth."

"Oh!" she said, and slapped his arm.

He kissed her hard.

"You put me through all that and you wanted kids after all?" she asked him.

"We're going to have to adopt a new game plan, Leigh. No way we can make a marriage work if we can't talk to each other. We've been keeping all these things secret. I was jealous of Max before...and afraid you thought I wasn't smart enough to be in love with someone like you."

She smiled lamely. "And I was afraid you thought I was a weirdo. A freak."

He brushed her damp cheek with one knuckle. "You are weird. Are you going to marry me?"

"Yes."

"Are we going to consummate the engagement?"

"If you tell me you just happened to bring along birth control on your fishing trip, I'm going to become suspicious."

"I didn't."

"Well, it's too big a risk, then."

He looked down at her, grinning. "Even though you make some very good accidents, I think I'd like to plan the next batch."

Leigh sighed and embraced him. "I hope I'm not going to keep having them in batches," she said very earnestly.

Although they really couldn't tempt fate and take any more chances, they could lie in John's tent all afternoon, kissing, hugging, touching, telling tender little secrets to each other, and laughing at how close they had come to losing each other again. If they laughed about it, they could keep from crying.

It seemed to Leigh that the only time there was ever any confusion was when they were apart. Together, they did just fine. Apart, they started to rethink everything and realized how little sense it made for them to be wildly in love. She decided they had better get married and move in together before there was time for much more thinking.

And for John, well, he hadn't believed he would ever have a woman like Leigh love him this much. She was not only brilliant, but she was also kind, honest, good and loyal. She didn't think he wasn't living up to his potential. On the contrary, she told him she was proud of everything he did, his commitment to kids, to the community, to the environment.

After a few hours of uninterrupted time to talk and touch and kiss, it was pretty clear that they were headed in the same direction this time. And that there was no point in waiting. So Leigh told him about Jess.

"From what I overheard, she even made up her heart condition. She's been plotting with the widows' brigade to get us married. She was hoping that her garden party would end up being a wedding."

To her relief, John laughed. "It figures. She needs to be taught a lesson. If you're sure her heart's okay."

"I'm sure. Though it may be somewhat weakened if I'm away much longer. Thinking that you've been stuck with four-year-old twins could wreck an otherwise strong heart."

"I'm not sure that's punishment enough. But," he said, grinning, "it's a pretty good start."

John and Leigh took on the widows' brigade. The four women took their tongue-lashing quite well, considering that not one of them would take the blame singularly. They busily blamed each other. And they unanimously swore they had only had everyone's best interests at heart.

"You two make such a wonderful couple," Peg said. "And you seemed to need just a slight push...."

"We only want our children settled and happy," said Abby.

"And in a family setting, not this significant-other stuff the young people are doing nowadays," Kate said.

"We're sorry we interfered, but we did think you'd be happy together. Really," Jess added.

"But that's not your place, is it?" John lectured. "It happens that you're very lucky you didn't do some real damage. You're lucky because it turns out that Leigh and I like each other and plan to go on seeing each other. But when and if we decide to marry, it's going to be *our* decision. Understand?"

The four women nodded with choreographed precision.

"And," added Leigh, "especially since there are children involved, this isn't going to be a snap courtship. John and I have done lots of talking about the kind of family life we have in mind as individuals. We're not going to rush into anything with the boys' futures at stake. We're going to be sure our values are similar and our goals can mesh. We're very different, you know. Understand?"

Four nods.

"From this point on, you are not to involve yourselves in any romantic notions that concern anyone other than yourselves."

Four sets of eyes rolled. As if any of them wanted any kind of romantic notions. Ha.

"And you will not make any plans for anyone else. If you're curious about something, you will kindly ask the question and take the answer, which might be 'none of your business.' Understood?"

"Yes, dear," Jess said. "But before you get yourself all in a lather about this, it was all well meant. And if it *had* ended in a wedding, we would all have been thrilled. But since it's not—so be it. I wouldn't hurt you for the world."

"But you have to let me live my own life, make my own mistakes, my own plans for the future," Leigh said. "I know I've needed your help before, Mom, but this time you went overboard."

"And now you'll be lucky to get invited to the wedding, if there is one," John warned. "You four are troublemakers. Are you going to behave?"

Oh, they'd behave. They promised.

When John and Leigh left them, he said, "I'd give anything to be a fly on the wall right now."

"They're just going to blame each other," Leigh predicted. "You think our plan is going to work?"

"It's fail-safe. Trust me."

And she did. Completely.

Chapter Nine

Jess mailed her garden party invitations without sulking. She and Leigh made up and spoke no more about interference; the widows' brigade got to put in their two-cents' worth about the party, and the yard was finished a week before the event. Leigh suggested having a string quartet play some music and chose the colors of the garlands and buffet table centerpieces. She visited the caterer with her mother and helped Jess pick out a lovely floral dress to wear.

When Leigh was sure her mother had a handle on everything and could spare her, she requested some baby-sitting. She wanted to fly to Denver for a couple of days; she needed access to the University of Colorado library for some of her research, and Jess said she could keep the boys.

"I'm a nervous wreck," Leigh told John.

"Me too. But it's going to be okay. I don't even think they'll yell. My mother will be relieved, and my dad will be secretly very proud."

"We could have thrown Jess a bone and told her she was right about that much—that you are the boys' father."

"I'm afraid it might give her the wrong kind of power," John said.

They were standing on the sidewalk in front of a modest, suburban house that belonged to John's parents. Leigh could imagine the activity that must have swelled within the walls of this small, two-story house during the years Mrs. McElroy was raising four boys. Leigh had never been accused of being psychic, but she felt that she would find love and acceptance here, despite her fears.

"Shall we?" he asked.

"Wait. What did you tell them? Exactly?"

"That I want them to meet the girl I'm going to marry."

"And what did your mother say?"

"She said, 'again?' "

"Oh, boy. I don't know if I can walk."

"Come on. Chicken."

"What else did you say?" she demanded.

"I said, 'This is different. I've been in love with this woman for years, and my marriage was on the rebound, but we've got it together now, and it's right.' Well, something like that."

"We do have it together now, don't we, John? It *is* right."

He kissed her, quick and efficient, and grinned that magnetic grin of his. "Right. Never more right."

Inside the McElroy house was a gathering that Leigh could never have prepared herself for. John couldn't have, either, for that matter. The entire McElroy clan had gathered under one roof to meet

and greet the newest addition. They had all hidden their cars down the block and in the garage.
There was the aroma of roast beef in the air and a
lot of noise in the living room. And right after
Jeanette McElroy opened the door and greeted her
son, they all yelled, "Surprise."

Minister Mike was the only one who'd had to fly
into town for this gathering. He and his wife and
kids were staying with Ted and Chris and their
clan. Bob had taken time off, and Judy had come
over early to help prepare an enormous meal.
Leigh was hugged and welcomed by each and
every one of them.

"We thought you should have a look at what
you're really getting into," Bob said. "This is no
quiet little family."

"It probably knocks you out to see this many of
us, but don't worry that we'll all converge on
Durango at once. We'll give you a couple of weeks
of wedded bliss before we do that," Mike said.

"There's a genetic problem in the family that
you should know about going in," Chris advised.
"This family hasn't produced a girl in genera-
tions, and we're counting on you to be the first."

"How did you dare do this?" John wanted to
know. "I mean, it's not as though this is my first
time around the matrimonial block. Or Leigh's,
for that matter."

"Easy," Jeanette said. "I knew in my heart you
had finally found your wife. The sound in your

voice . . . I've heard that sound four times now,'' she said, glancing around at her other sons.

It wasn't until the beef was sliced, the many kids settled in the dining room and the adults gathered in the living room at a long, portable dining table, that someone ventured the hope that John and Leigh planned on having a large family. The conversation slowly ground to a halt as the question hung in the air unanswered. Mouths slowly closed, eyes slowly turned toward John and Leigh.

"Ah," John said, "that's one of the reasons we decided to come out and see you personally. It's . . . ah . . . well, we've already gotten a start on that."

Silence was heavy around the table. It was the minister who broke the ice. "That happens. We're delighted you've decided to get married. Double congratulations." The family concurred, slowly coming to terms with this announcement, raising wineglasses one at a time, congratulating, finally laughing and toasting.

"Well . . ." John began. "Actually, Leigh isn't pregnant. Um, we have a set of twins . . . who are about . . . um . . . four years old."

Again silence reigned. Everyone knew when John had gotten married and divorced. When had there been time to father twins in all that confusion? Even the minister couldn't think of anything to say. Jeanette McElroy's mouth stood open. Leigh's cheeks were on fire. Robert Mc-Elroy frowned at his son.

"Four?" someone whispered.

"Twins?"

"That's a start, I'd say."

"Well . . . as a matter of fact . . . they're boys," Leigh said, watching the stunned faces turn to regard one another in total shock.

It was Chris who burst into laughter. "You might know. Boys!"

"I can explain. . . ." Leigh began, but they were recovering, laughing and slapping each other on the backs.

"Quadruple congratulations."

"We're mighty pleased you're getting married!"

"No rush, of course, but we do have a minister at the table!"

"Where have you been hiding them?"

"What's the hurry?"

It was Robert Sr. who spoke the only reasonable words. "We'll hear that explanation later. For right now, there are two things we need to take care of. One—when's the wedding? And two—when can we see our kids?"

Our kids. It had a wonderful sound to it. Leigh realized she hadn't known just how smart she really was in choosing the right guy. Not only was John too good to be true, but his family was terrific. One of the things she wanted for her kids was siblings, cousins, grandparents, and a life filled with love and noise and people.

They were a hard group to keep down; the racket went on and on. So did the conversation. Leigh learned a lot about John's family, all their various careers and their children's activities. And they learned about her. Ted was familiar with some of her father's medical research and went on to regale them with tales of his brilliance and breakthroughs. By early evening Leigh was both relieved and exhausted. Most of the children had quieted down, the sun was setting, and those adults not involved in cleaning up were seated in the living room with coffee. There was an after-glow of peace and acceptance.

Leigh offered to get the coffeepot for refills and went through the swinging door into the kitchen. There she found Mike giving his mother a com-forting hug while Jeanette seemed to be having a little cry. Leigh was stopped in her tracks. And so were they. They broke apart to regard her, and Jeanette turned away, fishing for a tissue in her pocket.

"Oh, Leigh," Mike said.

"I've made you cry, haven't I? Because of the boys...and because of..."

"No, Leigh," Mike said, moving toward her to give her a hug of support. "You'll find we're not the kind of people who do a lot of looking back.

You don't have to worry about that. We keep our eyes cast forward."

"John had a hard time forgiving me for keeping the boys' paternity from him. I was confused.... He had just gotten married, and I guess I—"

"No, dearest, no. Whatever your reasons, I don't blame you and I won't ask. I'm happy, Leigh," Jeanette said with a sniff. "I'm delighted to hear I'm a grandmother again, but it's more than that. It's John. I've worried about him having such a hard time finding what he wants—finding the right person to share his life with. I know it's old-fashioned, but all I really ever wanted for my boys was for them to have the kind of family life that would fulfill them."

"It isn't too hard to see that my brother is a new man," Mike said. "We've all hoped he would find the kind of special happiness that we've found. And now he has."

"Thank you," she said. "Thank you for letting me in."

"Leigh, we didn't do you a good turn by 'letting' you into the family. We're honored to have you. And I mean that sincerely."

June tenth was a bright, glorious day. Leigh and Jess got up early; there was a great deal to do. The house had to be straightened, though it had already been thoroughly cleaned. The boys had to get their first bath of the day and their first set of clean clothes.

The first to arrive was the florist, who came at nine in the morning to begin decorating the gazebo and tables. Leigh met his truck, and shook his hand, and he passed her a little bag, which she carried off to her room.

Next the caterers arrived in two vans and began to unload their supplies—food, serving trays, punch bowls, linen and other accessories—into the kitchen. Leigh whispered with the caterers for a moment.

"What is it?" Jess demanded. "What's the matter?"

"Nothing's the matter, Mom." Leigh laughed. "I just asked them to get the tables ready but not to put the food out until the guests start to arrive. We don't want to poison anyone with spoiled potato salad."

"Oh. Of course not."

Next the string quartet arrived to set up their instruments and chairs in the gazebo, though they would leave and come back later to play.

And then John arrived. "John!" Jess said, surprised. "You're early! The party doesn't start until two!"

"I know, I'm sorry. I just wanted to see the backyard all finished, set up and ready to go. Unfortunately I can't come to the party after all."

"Oh, no," Jess said. "I won't hear of it! You're not working, are you?"

"No, but as it happens, some of my family is in town, and I'm going to have to spend the weekend with them."

"Well, bring them!"

"Oh, Jess, I couldn't. It isn't just some of them, it's a lot of them. I have a big family. They do this sort of thing sometimes. My mom and dad decided to drive down, and my brother and his wife decided to come along, and another brother was planning a long weekend with his kids and . . . this sort of thing happens with my family. They don't necessarily do it on purpose, but they tend to flock. You couldn't ask that many—"

"But I could! Bring them!"

"Are you sure?"

Leigh came into the room. "Oh, Mom, maybe John could just stop by for a few minutes later and—"

"Don't be silly. Bring them all. Half the town's coming. Well, not half, but a grand showing. It would give your family a chance to meet Leigh." They both glared at her. "Oops. Well, if your family happens to be here when my daughter happens to—oh don't scowl. I don't know what came over me."

"Well, can I see the yard anyway?" he asked.

"Sure you can, John." Leigh laughed. And she took him through the kitchen and down the stairs from the deck, and let him get an eyeful.

Next it was time for Mitch and Ty's second bath and second set of clean clothes. Seems they had been remodeling their fort out in the far back of the yard. The fort had a dirt floor and there was a lot of moss to make grass stains. Leigh welcomed a chance to give them another bath and spend some time with them, sharing a secret or two. During the bath they did a lot of whispering, giggling and splashing.

Finally it was one-thirty. The food was ready to be put out, the flowers decorated the tables and structures, the quartet had arrived, and Jess and Leigh stood together on the deck to look everything over. It was a lovely sight; peach-colored ribbons were woven through the carnation and rose garlands. Exotic centerpieces adorned the twelve-foot-long tables. Silver serving dishes shone against the linen tablecloths. And the sun was bright and warm.

"It's beautiful, Mom," Leigh said. "It would have made a good wedding chapel."

Jess turned to her daughter. "Sweetheart, I hope you truly forgive me for being such a busybody. I've never done anything like that before, and I swear I never will again."

Leigh kissed her cheek. "I know. I'm just grateful you don't have a heart condition, and I *am* glad to be back here. You were right. This is the perfect place to raise the boys.''

"I thought I was doing a good thing."

"It was very sneaky of you."

"If I've hampered anything...if I've caused you and John to delay making plans just because I'm such a buttinski..."

"Now, Mom, didn't we decide you weren't going to have any more to say about that? You have to butt out."

"Yes, yes, but may I ask one question?"

"One."

"Didn't I pick out *exactly* the right man for you and the boys?"

"Mom..."

"Well...?"

Leigh relented and smiled. "Yes, you did pretty well. And I hope you never try anything like that again. Oh, look, people are coming! And I'm not ready!"

"Well, hurry up. I'll greet them."

Leigh went into the house and sent out the boys. The first to arrive were the coconspirators, Abby, Kate and Peg. Next came Tom Meadows, bringing flowers for each widow and a lovely bunch for Leigh. Next the pastor and his wife, the golf pro, the local librarian, the town council. John arrived with his entire family, who took up three cars. Not surprisingly, the boys ran to him and seemed to be inclined to stick to him like glue. He introduced them to his entire family. Then the butcher, the baker and the owner of a gift shop. Then the Literacy Council and the Friends of the Library. Nearly fifty people were standing around the backyard with cups of punch before Leigh found her way down the redwood steps.

She wore a long peach-colored dress, nothing too fancy, but Jess had no idea where the dress had come from. And Leigh had brushed out her long blond hair and pinned it back with baby's breath. "Look at her," Jess said half to herself.

Tom Meadows cleared his throat. "Are you sure your heart is up to this?"

"Up to what?" Jess asked as Tom began to walk toward Leigh, taking her the bouquet.

John moved quickly toward the gazebo where his brother Mike magically produced a small, black leather book. John said something to the quartet, who stopped playing midsong and began again, a tune that had a very familiar sound.

Jess and Leigh's eyes met across the yard. Jess's mouth was hanging slightly open, and Leigh's lips curved in a smile. She blew her mother a kiss just before she accepted the bouquet and looped her arm through Tom's. And then, to the melody of "The Wedding March," Tom led Leigh toward the gazebo where John and the two little boys waited. John stooped to say something to them, and they laughed and nodded. Then he stood up to greet Leigh.

An idea began to take shape in Jess's mind. His family had just happened to flock to town. And she had never before seen John in a tie. He wasn't wearing a tux or a suit, of course. But he had on a white-on-white shirt with a peach-colored tie that matched Leigh's dress. It took a moment to sink in. She just couldn't believe what was happening.

"Dearly Beloved," Mike began.

Jess nearly swayed against Peg, and Kate came up on her other side. Abby joined Kate, and the four women stood, not six feet behind Leigh, struck speechless for the first time in all their lives. "He's a minister!" Jess whispered. "I can't believe it!"

Finally, after a few introductory remarks about being gathered in the presence of God in the event of Holy Matrimony, Mike looked over the heads of the bride and groom and said, "Who gives this woman to be wed?"

Peg held hands with Jess, who held hands with Kate, who held hands with Abby. They looked at one another and grinned through the hint of tears. And then all four hands went up in the air, and with a laugh they said, "We do!"

And they did.

When the bride and groom finally sealed their vows with a kiss, a cheer went up through the yard. The hugging that followed was too complex to keep track of, but families were united, children were passed around, glasses were filled with champagne that Jess had not ordered, and confusion of the most lovely sort reigned.

"You sneaks," Jess said.

"We had good teachers," John informed them.

"You're lucky I *don't* have a bad heart."

"But did you get what you wanted?"

"Well...I did.... But I wanted to be in *charge*."

It turned out that very few people other than Jess were surprised, because Leigh had found a guest list and charged Tom and his receptionist with the duty of informing most of the guests by phone that a surprise wedding would be taking place. Although it was requested that there be no gifts, it seemed that some people just wouldn't be denied the privilege and went to their cars to retrieve presents. There were many toasts to the newlyweds, and finally John proposed one.

"I'd like to propose a toast to my mother-in-law," he said.

"Hear, hear," everyone chanted.

"Jess, I love you, but we'll take it from here."

And she raised her glass and drank.

It was quite late on Saturday night. The caterers had cleaned up, the kitchen sparkled, the music had died, and even the widows had gone home. The house was quiet, and only a few lamps were lit. Jess held her grandsons on her lap; they were heavy and big and smelled of shampoo and fabric softener.

"Gramma, what's a honeymoon?"

"It's when the new husband and wife go away to be alone and get to know each other in private. Quietly. Without any grammas or little boys or anyone."

"Doesn't Mommy already know John?"

"Yes, but they still like to be alone together because they love each other. And then they'll come back home and be with us."

"And John will be our dad?"

"And John will be your dad."

"And take us to T-ball and fishing?"

"Yes, and more things. From now on."

"But what are they *doing?*" Ty demanded.

"Fishing?" Mitch asked.

She squeezed them tightly and laughed. "Oh, I don't know if they're fishing. I bet they're hugging and kissing, playing lovey-dovey and saying 'I love you' a lot."

"Bllllkkkk," said Mitch.

"For two days?" asked Ty.

"What's the 'moon' part?" asked Mitch.

"I'm glad we didn't have to go," Ty said.

"Why do they have to play lovey-dovey?"

"Just to get in the habit, I guess," Jess said. So they can be friends and lovers for life. Nice habit. Who says Mother doesn't know best?

* * * * *

Robyn Carr

I was accidentally married in 1971. I say accidentally because I was nearly twenty and not smart enough to know what a good guy I was getting. Also, had I known he would move me nineteen times in nineteen years, I might have given it a second thought. I still ponder whether any man has enough sex appeal to sustain his allure through that much packing. I do happen to know a man, however, who has enough humor, loyalty, compassion and caginess to get a woman to do that much following.

Some of those nineteen moves have been from apartments into houses, from houses into better houses, but ten of them actually crossed state lines. That kind of business can involve some loneliness. Meeting people can feel scary; learning the new streets and highways can be heart stopping. But I always had a couple of constants in my life: my husband and children, and my writing.

I've been writing for fifteen years now, mostly fiction. Since my oldest child is sixteen, the kids have never known me any other way. They are impressed by what I do only when they think it will impress one of their teachers. What impresses me about my own writing is not my ability to do it but the consistent happiness it still brings me. I consider it difficult yet fulfilling. It is surprisingly tiring yet energizing. And it packs and moves well, waits for me, is always there and is the longest-lasting vice I've ever maintained.

My husband works long hours; my kids are in every activity they can pack into a day. I have a lot of time on my hands. I write and read and amuse myself by doing laundry at the speed of light, preparing boring dinners that can be eaten at a variety of times on the same night, and doing a few light chores that keep us from being shut down by the health department. It is as close to the perfect life as I think I'll ever get.

So This is Love

**CHERYL
REAVIS**

A Note from Cheryl Reavis

What can I tell you about mothers? There is my own sweet mama, of course. The one who tirelessly made up stories for me because I wanted them to come out of her head and not out of a book. The one who gamely sang ninety-nine verses of "Close Your Sleepy Eyes, My Little Buckeroo" because I was in my Roy Rogers phase and cowgirls couldn't possibly go to sleep to anything else. The one who still surprises me with homemade yeast rolls just because I like them.

I was sixteen years old when I first really understood that there were people around me who were not so fortunate, people who didn't have storytelling and lullaby-singing and bread-baking mothers, people who desperately needed mothering but who were, for whatever reason, denied. And people who, if they were very lucky, sometimes found a substitute.

My grandmother had died after a long and painful illness. It was the custom then that the body lie in state at home, in a room bared of all its furniture and filled with sprays of carnations and mums and gladioli. People came and went all day long, bringing food and words of sympathy and their memories, people whose faces, after a time, became one long blur.

But everyone who was there remembers when *she* arrived. I never heard her called anything but Sal, and she was a pretty young woman, known not just by her nickname, but by the worst of Southern euphemisms for a female of loose morals and ill repute. She was rough, wild. She got into fights. She hadn't been "raised." She always wore tight sweaters and tighter rolled-up jeans, and she swore out loud and smoked cigarettes and drank whiskey in public. The men loved her, and she had, well before Hollywood celebrities made it more a fashion than a sin, an illegitimate child or two. Fortunately, though all the conversation in my grandmother's house stopped when Sal arrived, my mother and my aunts kept their composure, not one of them swooning like Aunt Pitty-Pat in *Gone With the Wind*.

It would be a gross understatement to say that Sal was out of place there. Everyone knew it. Even she knew it. But she still came, holding her head high, dressed for the first time in anyone's memory in "decent" clothes—a subdued, dark gray dress and a lighter gray wool coat. She even carried gloves and wore a hat. And she said goodbye to my grandmother, gently stroking her cheek and patting her hand, not caring who saw her cry. She said and did all the right things, embarrassing no one, reverting to her old militant self only briefly when she discovered the flowers she'd ordered hadn't arrived yet. The next day, she came to the funeral service, and apparently no longer trusting the hired help, she got the flowers she'd sent out of the funeral home panel truck herself, carrying them directly to the front of the church and placing them just so at my grandmother's feet.

It wasn't until later that I learned why all this had come about, that Sal and my grandmother had worked side by side in the cotton mill and that my grandmother had always been kind. And it wasn't until later that I saw the card that accompanied those flowers. There were a few words scrawled on it in an uneven, childish hand: "For 'Mama,' " it said. "I love you. Sal."

It has been my joy to have known many kinds of mothers since, but it was then that I understood the need for mothering is great and that because of that need, lives are changed and sometimes one enters the state of motherhood entirely by the back door. These "second" mothers, as well as the "real" ones, were on my mind when I began to write my Mother's Day story.

Cheryl Reavis

Chapter One

*W*hispering.

Someone was whispering—and she wasn't dreaming. The bedroom window was slightly open, and Jessica Markham could hear the voice distinctly. Though she didn't recognize actual words, she knew it was a person speaking and not the wind or distant traffic or anything else she would have liked to attribute the sound to.

She opened her eyes; the whispering stopped. She sat up in bed so she could see the clock. It was six-thirty in the morning. Who would be whispering on her front porch at six-thirty in the morning?

She eased out of bed and walked barefoot into the long hallway that ran through the middle of the house, listening intently as she made her way to the front door. She wished that she had the handgun her co-workers at the bank insisted a woman living alone needed. When she'd lived in the city, she'd felt that she'd *had* to keep a gun, but not here in Silk Hope. Silk Hope was no more than two intersecting roads in the North Carolina Piedmont. There was no crime here to speak of, and that was one of the reasons she'd come home. She nearly smiled at the irony. All the time she'd lived away, she'd had a small automatic pistol within reach, and she'd never needed it. Now that she had come home and she felt safe enough to sell the thing, she had prowlers.

It was nearly daylight. The bare wooden floor in the hallway was old and scarred and cold against her bare feet. She could see the lace window curtain in the big, old-fashioned front parlor to her left billowing outward. She shivered in the draft. Last night, it had been hot and humid enough to leave the windows open, but this morning she would have been happy to have a fire in the wood stove. "Blackberry winter," her mother would have called it—that time in May the weather suddenly turned cool and wild blackberries bloomed.

How cold had it gotten during the night? she wondered. Cold enough to hurt the peach crop? She pushed the thought aside. Peaches were no longer her concern.

She reached the front door, standing off to the side so she could peer out unobserved. She could see no one, no movement, nothing. Perhaps she had been dreaming, after all. After a moment or two of intense listening, she put her hand on the doorknob and turned it, refusing to cower in the house over something she may have only dreamed or imagined. The door was warped, and it made a loud scraping sound as she pulled it back. The screen door wasn't latched, so she quickly hooked it before stepping closer to try to see both ends of the porch.

No one was there.

She looked down. Just to the left of the front door, a small, burning white candle flickered in the brisk morning breeze. Two candles, she could see now, flanking what looked like a small pile of leaves and nuts and some kind of long sticks. She looked out across the long yard toward the pecan trees and the crape myrtles between the house and the road. Nothing stirred. No one was around. She quickly closed the door, her heart pounding.

Who was doing this? What did it mean? She had no enemies. Her upbringing had been typically southern. She was respectful of her elders, kind to animals and small children, and even if she weren't, she hadn't been *back* long enough to offend anyone.

She closed her eyes and tried to think of what to do. She needed help with this, and only one name came to mind. *Jacob.* But she couldn't call him— wouldn't call him. The abrupt ending of their budding relationship nearly four months ago had been entirely his doing. She still didn't know what had happened. Something she'd said? Some major flaw in her character she'd unwittingly revealed? She had thought that they liked each other. She had liked him certainly—and his son, Thomas. One minute people were beginning to think of her and Jacob Brenner as a couple; the next minute she was alone, with nothing she could call to mind to comfort herself but the last thing he'd said to her. "I'll call you." She was the one who was supposed to have been so sophisticated from big-city living, and she felt like such a fool for not recognizing his departing comment for what it was—a time-honored euphemism for goodbye, an empty, token gesture on the part of a restless male so that he could disengage himself with as little aggravation as possible. She'd been stupid enough to believe him, so much so that when several days went by and he hadn't telephoned, she called him. She still cringed at the memory of it. She, so friendly and unsuspecting, and Jacob, so distant and cool, until it suddenly dawned on her that she'd been abruptly and unceremoniously dumped.

The only problem was that she missed him. She missed the winter walks with him over the orchards he coaxed so hard into making a profit every year. She missed their talks about growing peaches and growing a teenage son, both of which she knew about only vicariously. She missed the teasing banter with what she had thought was an interested male. And she missed his kisses. *Kiss*. Only *one,* on the last night they'd been together. If she really thought about it, she could still feel it, still feel the cold of that starry January night and the warmth of his body and his hands, still taste the sweetness of his mouth, still smell the clean soap-and-water scent of his skin—

Who am I kidding? she thought.

It wasn't trying to remember that was difficult; it was trying *not* to. She had left Silk Hope eighteen years ago. She had gone to college "up North," as the people in the community would have put it, and after she'd graduated, she'd stayed there. She'd had a good job; she'd met a lot of interesting men, several of whom had been her lovers and none of whom she'd ultimately wanted to marry. She'd sold securities and real-estate investment packages and she'd reached a point in her life when she never expected to marry anyone. She never expected to come home again, either—until her brother, the world traveler, started making noises about selling the home place instead of having to bother with renting it out to strangers.

Suddenly she didn't want to lose her roots. She didn't want to have to deal with the competitive, cutthroat world of high finance and live with a gun without knowing that she still had a place in Silk Hope whenever she wanted it—*her* place, the place where she'd grown up dreaming dreams and making plans for her life. Suddenly feeling burned-out and used up, she bought the big old house with the pecan trees and the hammock and the crape myrtles in the yard herself. She came home, and incredibly, she was quite happy to be here. She took an undemanding job as an investment counselor at a bank in nearby Siler City, and she met Jacob Brenner.

Jacob was one of the bank's lesser clients and a peach-grower extraordinaire. All those years away from here and all those relationships with what anyone would have termed successful men, and she hadn't felt about any of them the way she felt about him. She smiled a bit to herself. Jacob and his peaches. Everyone in and around Silk Hope knew that the real money was in raising chickens, but he was undeterred. He didn't like chickens. He liked a rolling field full of peach trees blooming in the spring, and rich, ripe fruit in July and August.

"Ain't no money in peaches, Jake," the old men who hung out in Silk Hope's only store felt obliged to point out every time he came in.

"Yeah," he'd tell them with that quiet smile he had. "But they smell good."

His sudden departure had hurt. It still hurt, but at the moment, she had a more pressing problem. She walked purposefully through the house to the telephone.

"Where is it?" the deputy asked before she had the chance to find out his name. She had hoped that Sonny Cook would come. She had gone to high school with Sonny. Her school image had been one of stability and levelheadedness, and he would have been the deputy least likely to think she was entirely crazy for calling the sheriff's department. She didn't recognize this one. She only recognized that he was very businesslike and very young, and that he seemed to think this was a big to-do over nothing. He kept looking at her—for some sign of hysteria, she supposed. She wondered which would give her complaint more credence—hysterics or the lack of them.

"It's on the front porch. I'm sorry to ruin your Sunday morning," she said, leading the way.

"It goes with the job. What time did you find it?"

"About six-thirty this morning."

"Do you usually get up that early?"

"No. Well, yes, on weekdays. But not on Sunday. I heard whispering. That's what woke me."

He made no comment, and she had the distinct feeling she'd just lowered her credibility a notch or two.

"See?" she said of the candles and the leaf pile when they reached the front porch.

He stepped up onto the porch. "Did you touch anything?"

"I blew the candles out. That's all."

"Probably some kid's prank," he said, stooping down to get a closer look. He gingerly pushed one of the candles.

"This isn't the first time. Well, it's the first time for this, but there was another thing—"

He picked up one of the leaves and smelled it. "Kids watch too much television, and they—"

"What?" Jessica said, when he frowned. "What?"

"I'm going to bag this stuff," he said, pulling out some Ziploc plastic bags from his back pocket.

"What is it?"

"Well, I'm not sure. The sticks are some kind of incense, I think. I'll check to see if I can find out about the other stuff. You said there was another thing?" He wasn't looking at her, and the off-hand way he asked the question made her a little nervous.

"Yes. There was a bamboo pole on Valentine's Day."

"Valentine's Day?"

"Yes, Valentine's Day. February the four-teenth," she said pointedly, because he sounded as if he didn't believe her.

"I know when it is," he said. "What about the pole?"

"It was just ... bamboo. Long, like a fishing pole. It was stuck up in the backyard. It had bells on it."

"Bells?"

"Yes, bells," she answered, wishing he wouldn't keep repeating what she said. She could feel his incredulity growing. "Little round brass bells. Like the ones little girls used to wear on their shoe strings in grammar school," she continued with a patience she didn't begin to feel. "A dozen or so of them. And a circle of braided thorns and some kind of little figures made out of clay."

"What kind of figures?"

"Roughly human, I guess. Head, arms and legs."

"Why didn't you call us then?"

"I thought what you thought—it was just some kind of prank. For all I knew it was some kid's weird fishing gear."

"Sticking up in your backyard?"

"There's a farm pond just down the road. I thought my yard might be on the way—a shortcut or something—and for some reason someone left their things behind. Kids do crazy things, even if they don't watch television," she said, giving him all the reasons she'd given herself that morning back in February.

"Do you still have it?"

"No. I left it in the yard and one morning it was gone."

He stood up. "I'll get back to you on this. In the meantime, maybe you ought to keep your doors locked." He walked toward his car. "You don't have any disgruntled boyfriends or anything like that?" he suddenly turned and asked.

"No," she said evenly, wishing she'd never exercised her right as a Chatham County taxpayer and called the sheriff's department. "I don't suppose anyone else has reported anything like this."

"Nope," he said, getting into his car. "You're the only one."

Chapter Two

*Y*ou're the only one.

Jacob Brenner sat on the back steps staring at nothing. He'd been up all night, keeping vigil against the possibility of a frost. His eyes burned from the lack of sleep, his head ached, and all he could think about was Jessica Markham. Not the money he stood to lose if the peach trees were damaged, not the money he already owed or the money he'd had to spend these past four months to keep his family and his honor. Just her.

You're the only one, he thought again. The only one he wanted to talk with, to laugh with, to make love with. They had nothing in common, and he would have been the first to admit it. He stubbornly grew peaches, even though it was generally recognized that the real peach-growing region was sixty miles farther south. It was all he did and all he'd ever wanted to do. He didn't know about securities and real-estate investments, and Jessica didn't know a damn thing about what it took to get a decent peach crop. It hadn't mattered. It hadn't mattered that he wore a baseball cap and worked twenty hours a day and smelled of sweat and got his hands dirty, or that *she* was the one with the briefcase and the three-piece suit.

The first time he met Jessica Markham, she'd looked directly into his eyes and she'd taken his breath away—when he'd thought he'd learned to live with loneliness. He was thirty-eight years old and he was as gun-shy of personal relationships and commitment as any one man could get. He had no reason to believe in love—at first sight or any other way. He'd been married at nineteen, divorced at twenty-four. The divorce had been entirely his fault. For three of the five years he'd been married, he'd been with the Third Marines in Vietnam, trying desperately to stay alive and to stay sane, and trying to hold his neglected marriage together long-distance. He'd managed one of the three—he'd returned physically intact—but he'd been only marginally successful with the other two. He came home to his young, unhappy wife silent and sleepless and brooding. There was such a dearth of emotion in him then that he couldn't talk, couldn't laugh, couldn't feel. It was more than their already strained relationship could bear, and he went from thinking he'd die if his wife ever left him to being immensely relieved when she'd gone. He still remembered what he'd been like then—completely, totally empty of everything but his own private guilt. The guilt was his; he'd earned it, and he let himself wallow in it. He had nothing to give anyone, and he wanted nothing in return. It had taken him a long time to get better of that affliction, if indeed he had.

Until he met Jessica, the only really good thing in his life had been his son, Thomas, who had been born out of the misery of two people who had been married too young and had been unaffected by it somehow. He was kind and cheerful, and he had lived with Jacob since he was ten. At sixteen, he worked in the orchards as hard as any grown man, but with the arrival of a letter at least four months ago from the Vietnam Veterans of America Foundation, he had suddenly had to face the fact that his father was disappointingly human.

Jacob could blame the letter for his estrangement from Thomas but not for his estrangement from Jessica. He had felt panicked by the rush of feeling Jessica elicited in him, and he had been afraid of having the same thing happen again: He was truly afraid of caring about a woman and still being so locked-up inside that he could do nothing but watch the love die. He was having a hell of a time of it now. He had more family troubles than he could handle. He'd tried to convince himself that he shouldn't get involved with Jessica, and the present upheaval in the family had only served to underscore the correctness of his decision. But he couldn't get her out of his mind.

He went to bed thinking about her, got up thinking about her, and carried her around with him all day long in between. He thought about the only time he'd kissed her, about the way she smelled and the way she leaned into him, her mouth as eager, as needy as his. He missed her and he couldn't stop missing her.

He sighed heavily, suddenly remembering Thomas's teasing the first time the two of them encountered Jessica at the bank. The loan officer hadn't been there that day, and Jessica had met with him instead. He remembered what she was wearing—an expensive-looking navy-blue suit and a white silky blouse with a gold pin on her lapel— a rose. Her dark hair had been pulled back in some kind of gold clasp at her nape, and she'd looked coolly efficient and incredibly beautiful, so beautiful that he'd worried that she'd glance up and see the "hubba-hubba" facial expressions and hand signals his son kept giving him.

In spite of Thomas's embarrassing gestures, he'd stayed much longer than he'd intended. He'd kept asking her questions that had nothing to do with peach growing and bank loans, incredibly unsubtle questions, the kind he hadn't asked a woman since he'd been Thomas's age.

"You got the hots for her, huh, Dad?" Thomas asked the moment they were out the bank door, causing an elderly lady on her way in to raise both eyebrows. "You do, don't you?" he persisted, holding the door for the old woman and then boxing him on the arm with his fist while he grinned a happy grin of discovery a mile wide.

"Will you quit!" Jacob said, because Thomas was still grinning and trying to punch him on the arm as they crossed the parking lot. "*No*, I don't have the hots for her."

"You don't have the hots for who?" Thomas asked innocently, the grin even wider because he'd laid a trap and Jacob had walked right into it.

"For whoever you're talking about."

"You know who I'm talking about—Miss Jessica in the bank. See here?" he said, pointing to the side of his face where a few errant whiskers tried to sprout. "Singe marks from the heat. I can probably go a whole lot longer without shaving."

"You don't shave but twice a year now," Jacob said, but Thomas wasn't listening. He was dramatically holding up both hands.

"I mean, you looked at her, and then she looked at you, and then there was some more looking.... I didn't know you had it in you, Dad. I mean the way you checked her out. Really cool, Dad. I have to tell you I am *impressed*. You going to ask her for a date?"

"No."

"You going to call her?"

"No."

"Why not?"

"She knows I have a teenage lunatic for a son," he said pointedly.

"Yeah, but you got the hots for her, right? Right? *Right?* You can tell me, Dad. Come on, tell me. You got the hots for her. Tell me, tell me—you got the hots for her, right?''

Jacob suddenly grinned. ''Yes!'' he said in exasperation.

''Hot dang, that's my daddy!'' Thomas hooted. ''Can he pick 'em or what!'' He pulled Jacob's ball cap down over his eyes and gave him a bear hug, while Jacob tried to get into the truck before someone had them arrested.

Thinking about that day, Jacob smiled, but then the smile faded as the memory of it gave way to the reality of the present. He could hear Thomas moving around in the kitchen behind him. Eating again, more than likely. The boy hadn't spoken to him once today—or yesterday—that he remembered. But at least he was here. He didn't have a damn thing to say, but he'd come back home of his own accord.

Jacob sighed again, this time thinking of the money he'd had to spend on airfare in the last four months. First there had been the cost of plane tickets from Ho Chi Minh City to here, and then he'd immediately had to fly to Seattle to bring Thomas home again. He looked around as Thomas came to the screen door.

''*She's* been looking for you,'' he said, his face carefully neutral regardless of his tone of voice.

''Where is she now?''

Thomas gave an elaborate shrug of uninformed indifference.

"She has a name, Thomas."

"Yeah, well, I can't pronounce it."

"You could if you tried."

"What do I need a name for? I'm not planning on talking to her."

"I thought you were teaching her to drive. I finally got the car and the truck running for you."

"She knows how to drive. It's not breaking the law that's the hard part. She thinks you can drive all over the road."

"Then you teach her what the laws are! I don't have time to do it."

"Yeah, well, maybe *I* don't have the time, either!"

"Make the time, damn it!" Jacob yelled, losing his temper. "See if you can't be good for something around here!"

He didn't mean it; Thomas was the best help he had. But he said it anyway. That was what the situation had come to. Now he was stooping to getting at his son when it was himself that he was angry with.

He didn't know what to do about that, either.

"I'm going to the store," he said, getting up and walking off toward the truck. "You teach her to drive!"

"What does she need to learn to drive for?" Thomas yelled after him. "The only place she goes to is church!"

"You heard me!" Jacob yelled over his shoulder. He got into the truck and drove out the driveway too fast, before he said or did anything else he knew he'd regret.

He had to go past Jessica's house to get to the crossroads and Silk Hope Service. It was only a community store to him, but she loved it, loved a place where she could buy a real fountain soft drink—or chicken wire and a handful of nuts and bolts if she needed them. As always, he was tempted to turn in when he neared the long shaded driveway that led to her back door. He did slow down a bit, looking at the house and the neatly trimmed yard she mowed herself. He hadn't seen her since the night he'd kissed her. In January. Four long months without seeing her, talking to her. It occurred to him how hungry he was just for a glimpse of her.

But her car was gone. She seemed to be gone a lot lately, a fact that added to his misery. He didn't know what he expected. He'd deliberately made her think that their relationship had run its course, and whatever she was doing these days was none of his business.

He drove on down the rural road, past the scattered houses and soybean fields and fenced pastureland, past Silk Hope School and the redbrick building that was a combination fire department, Ruritan Club and community meeting hall. At the crossroads that was Silk Hope in its entirety, he pulled across the macadamized road and into the dirt parking lot of the only convenience store between here and Siler City. It was crowded with people on their way home from church.

He got out of the truck and went inside, though he had no real idea what he wanted to buy. Time, he supposed, so that he didn't make matters worse at home. And milk and bread. A household with a teenage boy in it always needed milk and bread.

He entered the store, speaking to the customers he knew as he worked his way around them to the bread rack. Jessica was just paying at the cash register, and he didn't hesitate, pushing his way back through the crowd to follow her out.

"Jessica," he called, but she didn't stop until she reached her car. She turned and faced him, standing with her hand on the doorhandle.

"Jacob," she said quietly, looking frankly into his eyes the way she always did. She was clearly waiting for him to say something, but he hadn't intended to talk to her. He'd only blindly followed the impulse to be with her, even if it were just for a few seconds out in front of Silk Hope Service.

"You look...very nice," he said, knowing how stupid it sounded. It was the only thing that came to mind. That and the knowledge that he didn't mean "nice" at all. He mean "beautiful." She looked so beautiful.

She smiled and lifted the door handle. "I do the best I can, Jacob," she said dryly.

"Jessica," he said to keep her from getting into the car. "I—"

"What?" she asked, waiting.

He looked away, over her head, over the top of the car to the gas pumps, and then back at her again. "I want you to know it wasn't you. It was me. I—"

She didn't pretend not to know what he was talking about. But, to his surprise, she suddenly balled her right hand into a fist and hit him on the upper arm. Hard.

He didn't flinch, but he wanted to. He stared into her eyes, holding her gaze. She wouldn't look away, and neither did he.

"Ow," he said finally, and she tried to fight down a smile.

"So," he said after a moment. "Do I get to know what that was for?"

She shifted her bag of groceries. "It was for what was coming, Jacob. The part where you tell me I'm too good for you and I'm better off without you."

"You are," he said, catching her hand when she would have socked him again. He was glad of even this opportunity to touch her, and he let his thumb caress hers. "But," he went on, "*but* I was kind of hoping you'd overlook it."

She didn't say anything.

"I've missed you," he offered.

"I've been right here," she parried.

"I told you. It wasn't you. It was never you."

She pulled her hand away and pulled open the car door. "Since I was the only other person around, you'll forgive me if I don't believe you."

"Jessica—"

"Don't jerk me around, Jacob. Last January, I was playing for keeps. I admit it. I don't know what *you* were doing. I don't know what you're doing now." She got into the car. "And I really don't care," she said before she slammed the door shut.

He stood in the dirt parking lot and watched her drive off.

Chapter Three

Thomas tried to hang on to his anger, but with Jacob gone, it rapidly dissipated. His feelings were hurt, and there was nothing he could do to make things better. He was more miserable than he'd ever been in his whole life, and he was stuck with it. He'd tried going to his mother in Seattle, and what a bust that had been. His mother had a brand-new husband, and she'd called Jacob to come and get *his* son so fast it had made Thomas's head swim. Dear old Mom couldn't afford him, she'd said. Too bad she wasn't more like Jacob. Whether or not Jacob could afford a child was the last thing he considered.

Thomas turned at a noise behind him. So. *She* was back from wherever it was she'd gone. She was always disappearing, always creeping up on him again. *Ho Xuan Huong.* What kind of name was *Ho Xuan Huong*?

He exhaled sharply. He knew what kind of name it was; she'd told him. *Her* mother had given her the name of a Vietnamese poetess who was strong and whose work was bitter and sarcastic and vulgar. Like Joan Rivers, she'd told him.

Thomas didn't know how she knew about Joan Rivers, and he didn't ask. He didn't have to ask anything. She seemed to consider it her duty to tell him everything about herself whether he wanted to know or not.

"He's unhappy again," she said now of Jacob.

"Yeah, and we both know whose fault that is," Thomas said, finding his sarcasm easily, no matter how much deference she showed him.

"Not all me," she answered. Her English was very good, but sometimes she left out parts of it. "*You* ran away to Seattle."

"I came back home, didn't I?"

"So did I."

"You popped up out of nowhere, uninvited. This wasn't your home."

"It is now," she said stubbornly.

"Jake didn't even know he had you."

"He knows now," she insisted. "If he didn't know, I wouldn't be here."

Thomas had nothing to say to that. It was one thing to discover that your old man had the hots for the investment counselor at the bank. It was something else again to find out that he'd shacked up with a Vietnamese interpreter when he wasn't much older than Thomas was now and to have his bastard daughter come home to roost. As far as Thomas knew, Jacob hadn't tried to deny for one minute that she was his. And not only had he not denied it, but he'd gone halfway around the world to get her with money they didn't have to spare. And Jacob expected *him* to take care of her. To

take her into Siler City to St. Julia's Catholic
Church every time she wanted to go. To introduce
her to his friends. Well, he hadn't seen Jacob introducing Ho Xuan Huong to any of *his* friends,
and he'd bet that not one person in all of Silk
Hope knew about his Vietnamese bastard. Not
that Thomas blamed him. It wasn't the kind of
thing a person went around telling, and Jacob was
a quiet man.

That was one of the first things Thomas's
mother had wanted to know when he'd arrived in
Seattle—if Jacob still went for days without talking. He didn't, but then he wasn't one to hold a big
conversation, either. Except with Jessica Markham. Man, Thomas thought. His father, for once
not thinking about damned peaches, scoping a
beautiful woman for no other reason than he'd
liked her looks. That really had been something to
see. And his old man was really good at it, too.
Had to have always been good at it, or else
Thomas wouldn't have a Vietnamese half sister in
the kitchen with him now.

He glanced at her. When it came down to it, he
supposed that she looked more American than
Vietnamese. She had round eyes that looked a lot
like his own blue-gray ones. Her skin was darker
than his and her hair was black and straight, but
still he could see the American and the Jacob
Brenner in her. She was much smaller than
Thomas, though they were less than a year apart

in age. What was he supposed to say to people when it did get out about her? That they were twins?

He sighed at the hopelessness of the situation. She sometimes forgot how to talk, and she didn't know what to wear, and she cooked weird food for them. Sometimes life was just too much for an ordinary mortal.

"I don't know how you found us in the first place," he complained out loud, because he felt driven to have the last word.

"I prayed," she said simply. "To the Vietnam Veterans of America Foundation. To the Pearl S. Buck Foundation. To Buddha. To Confucius. To my ancestors and the God of the Hearth and the Jade Emperor. And to St. Joan of Arc and Sun Yat-sen of China and St. Victor Hugo of France—"

"St. Victor Hugo?" Thomas interrupted. "Jesus, Mary and Joseph," he said, rolling his eyes.

"Them, too," she said, unperturbed. "Thomas?"

"What?" he said, his sarcasm still intact. But his sarcasm seemed to have no effect on her.

"I picked my American name," she said, obviously pleased.

"What American name?"

"Our father says I can be a Brenner. Huong Brenner isn't good."

"You can say that again," he said under his breath.

"You want to know what name I pick?" She hovered behind him, not too close but close enough to get on his nerves.

"No," he assured her.

"But you gave it to me."

"*I* gave it to you?" he said incredulously. He'd called her a lot of things since she'd come here, to her face and behind her back, but absolutely none of them made a good match with Brenner.

"What name?" he asked in spite of himself.

"Now I'm Heidi. Heidi Brenner."

"*Heidi?*" he repeated. "You want to be called *Heidi?*"

"I like Heidi," she said, serene as ever.

"Look. When I called you Heidi, it was because—"

"Yes, I know," she said quickly. "Because you hate me."

Thomas stared at her, taken aback by the casual way she'd said it, as if she had expected no less from him and she bore him no ill will because of it.

"I don't . . . hate you," he said after a moment, realizing for the first time that it just might be true. He was embarrassed by her, disappointed in his father, upset with his mother, and terribly put upon, but he didn't hate her. "I called you Heidi because you were hiding bread in your room like crazy when you first got here.''

"It's hard to trust things in this place. I don't like to go hungry, Thomas."

"Well, who would?" he said, defensive because he'd led a good life here with their father in the United States and she'd grown up in the streets of Ho Chi Minh City, in a terrible place called "The Amerasian Children's Market." She still had nightmares. Sometimes he and Jacob both would sit up with her, he grudgingly, but doing it anyway because he felt it was a family matter and Jacob shouldn't be left to cope with everything alone. The last nightmare had been because she couldn't remember the names of the cigarettes she and her mother had sold. The cigarettes were the difference between eating and starving, and she'd woken up desperate because she couldn't remember the names, didn't know where to find them or what to ask for. And she had to have the cigarettes, or she and her mother would die.

"Gauloises," she kept whispering. *"Gauloises,* and Jet and Hero and ... and ... What are they? What are they?"

Jacob helped her, because he still remembered the street vendors with their portable wooden boxes filled with cigarettes. "Scott. Capstan."

"Yes, yes! Scott and Capstan. Thank you, Father."

"When I called you Heidi," Thomas said now in an effort to explain, "I was being...a smart ass."

"Yes," she quietly agreed. "A smart ass. But I read the book. I got it from the sisters at St. Julia's. I feel lost sometimes like Heidi. It's a good name for me. You will call me that?" It was more a question than a command.

They stared at each other across the kitchen until Thomas finally shrugged. "It's no big deal. You can call yourself whatever you want. You want to be Heidi, then be Heidi."

"Thank you, Thomas."

"Hey! You don't need my permission. This is America."

"Yes. America."

She turned to go, and he found suddenly that he didn't want her to.

"So. Are you still hiding bread in your room or not?" he asked, careful to keep his voice nonchalant, as if he didn't care in the least whether or not she answered.

She gave him a smile, a very small one. "Sometimes."

"Yeah, well, me, too. Only I'm partial to Doritos."

"Do I know Doritos?"

"I hope not. I might never get any."

"I don't eat big, Thomas."

"Yeah, but you *hide* big."

He went back to what he was doing before he had that altercation with Jacob—covering the last of the bread he'd toasted with a heavy layer of peanut butter and apple jelly.

"Thomas?" the new Heidi said.

"What?" he said wearily in case she thought he wanted her to hang around and talk permanently. He poured himself a large glass of milk.

"When it comes to pass, then I'll go."

"When what comes to pass?" he said without looking at her.

"I can't leave in the middle."

"In the middle of what?"

"Today is Mother's Day, isn't it?"

Thomas looked up and frowned. "What are you talking about?"

"Mother's Day. When you get a mother."

"You *don't* get a mother," he said with his mouth full. "You do something for the one you've got. I sent a card to mine in Seattle. Your mother is dead now, so you'd just think about her, remember her. Stuff like that."

"You *don't* get a mother?" she repeated, her voice sounding a bit strange.

"No."

She was very close suddenly, and she put her hand on his arm. "Thomas, are you sure? That's truth? You wouldn't give me the...the...store?"

"The business," Thomas corrected. "No, I'm not giving you the business. Well, what did you think it was?"

"I thought you look for mother," she said worriedly. "We had a Groundhog Day since I come here. On Groundhog Day you look for a groundhog. I didn't have a mother so I—" She broke off, as the significance of his statement only just hit her. "Oh, Thomas!" she said, bouncing up and down. "Oh, Thomas!"

"What? What?" he said, growing alarmed.

"Thomas!" She had her fingers over her mouth and she was still bouncing.

"What?"

She seemed to be searching for the words to tell him, but she couldn't find them. "Thomas!" she cried finally. *"Oops!"*

"Okay," Thomas said, trying not to panic. "Okay, let's see if I understand this. You—" He didn't understand anything. And if he lived to be a hundred, he hoped he never heard the fateful word "oops" coming from her lips again. "Why did you pick Jessica Markham, for God's sake!" he cried. "Our old man is crazy about Jessica Markham!"

"I know that, Thomas," Heidi said, her bottom lip trembling. "When I first come here, you and Jacob fight, like today. You said he wasn't going to see Jessica Markham anymore because of me. And Jacob said it *wasn't* because of me. It was because he didn't do good with marrying. And you said the way this house was filling up with his strays, he must have been doing good at *something*. You remember?''

"I remember, I remember."

"And then I saw how he looked at Jessica—"

"You met Jessica?"

"No. No, she doesn't see me. When Jake took me to St. Julia's last time, she was coming out of the bank. I asked him who the beautiful lady was because he looked at her and his face was so sad. And he said 'Jessica Markham.' Who else would I pick?'' she asked earnestly.

"Who else? *Who else?* Jake is going to have a hissy!''

"Is that a bad thing?''

"Oh, no, heck, that's not a bad thing. The *bad* thing is that he's going to think *I* had something to do with this! I'm supposed to be looking after you! I'm supposed to be keeping you straight and keeping you out of trouble. Teach you to drive, for God's sake!'' He stopped yelling long enough to take a breath. "Okay. Okay, so tell me. What did you do?''

"Which time?''

"*Which time?* Oh, my God! Just...just start at the beginning, okay? Just start there and tell me.''

"Are you sure, Thomas? You look ... upset.''

"I look upset? If you think this is upset, you wait till you see Jake. Go on. Tell me."

"Well . . ."

"Go on."

"The month was . . ." She thought hard. "February!"

"February? February! You've been calling up water spirits and stuff like that since *February?*"

"I didn't call up water spirits."

"Well, thank God for that."

"I used a *cay neu.*"

"A *cay neu,*" he repeated, hoping it wasn't as bad as it sounded.

"Yes," she affirmed. "Exactly."

"And?" he shouted.

"And . . . and nothing! It was *Tet.* The New Year. I wanted to guide all the good spirits to her home—not the water spirits—and keep the bad spirits away. Until I could think what to do next."

"Well, why not?" Thomas said, throwing up his hands. "Did she see it? Did Jessica see this *cay neu?*"

"It was very . . . seeable, Thomas."

"Yeah, I was afraid of that. And what did it look like?"

She told him in detail. "When *Tet* was over, I took it back again."

"Were *you* seeable? Did she see you take it?"

"No."

"You're sure?"

"Yes. I waited until she left for the bank."

"How the devil did you get there!"

"I drove the truck."

"You can't drive, Heidi!"

"I *can* drive, Thomas," she said, a bit indignant. "I just don't know where to do it."

Thomas sat shaking his head. "And you didn't do anything else until today?"

She shook her head, wiping at her eyes. "Just prayed. To—"

"I know the prayer list," Thomas interrupted. "And you picked today because it's Mother's Day."

She nodded.

"Okay," he said carefully. "What did you do?"

"I don't want to tell you."

"Better me than Jake," he warned her.

She didn't say anything.

"I'm waiting," Thomas prompted.

"I . . . betrothed Jessica to Jacob," she said in a rush.

"You what?"

"Betrothed Jessica to Jacob?"

"That's what I thought you said. And just how did we do that?" he asked, his sarcasm firmly in place again.

"*You* weren't there. *I* did it," she corrected him.

"Yeah, and you just remember to say that when Jake finds out. So *how* did you betroth Jessica to Jake?"

"I used the front place for a family altar."

"What front place?"

"The place. The thing like out there." She pointed.

"The porch. The front porch?"

"Yes. Exactly."

"And?"

"And I made the offering. Now I'm Jacob's oldest living relative. There is no father, no mother, so I had to do it. It should be his father and mother going to see her father, but that couldn't work."

"How, Heidi? How did you do it?"

"With betel leaves and areca nuts and sticks of incense."

"Where did you get the betel leaves and whatever nuts!"

"Areca. Areca nuts. From the Asian Food Store in Siler City. That wasn't hard. Incense was hard. Not many places get incense around here, but I kept looking."

"Just tell me what you did with that stuff?" Thomas said.

"I put it on her porch. With candles. So St. Victor Hugo and St. Joan of Arc and Sun Yat-sen could find her."

"She didn't see you?"

"No."

"You just put that stuff on her porch."

"Yes. And I prayed."

"Well, that doesn't seem too bad."

"There is the other thing," Heidi said.

"What other thing?" Thomas knew better than to ask, but he asked anyway. "No, don't tell me."

"Okay," Heidi said, clearly agreeable to leaving him in the dark.

He took a deep breath to brace himself. "No. I can take it. I'm a strong healthy male. Tell me."

Jacob heard Thomas yelling the moment he got out of the truck. And if he wasn't mistaken, Huong was yelling right along with him. It didn't sound like an argument exactly, more like some kind of two-part howl of distress. He left the truck door open, bounding up the back steps to get inside.

"What the hell is going on in here?" he yelled over the noise.

"Oops!" his children cried when they saw him, both of them still in unison.

Chapter Four

"Don't you ever yell like that again!" Thomas whispered fiercely the moment Jacob left the kitchen. And it was no easy task getting him to go. Thomas had never been able to fool Jacob in his life, but because his father clearly had something else on his mind, he was apparently willing to put off this one time with Thomas's assurances that he and Huong were merely practicing for Huong's first baseball game. A stroke of genius on Thomas's part, if he did say so himself. Jacob Brenner loved baseball.

"I don't start the yelling!" Heidi whispered back, indignant. "Why did you yell like that, Thomas? I thought something awful happened."

"Something awful did happen! You dug up Jessica's ancestors!"

"I don't dig up anybody! I was just telling about how it is in Vietnam—digging up the bones and taking special care of them—so you'll know how important ancestors are. Ancestors can help you, Thomas. You think I'm crazy enough to go around digging up American people?"

"Yes!" Thomas cried.

Heidi's eyes welled and her bottom lip began to tremble again.

"Now don't go crying, you hear me?" he said, trying to sound tough enough to make her stop. It didn't work. A great splash of tears suddenly rolled down one cheek.

"Jeez, Heidi, don't. If Jake comes back and sees you..." He patted her awkwardly on the back, looking all the while for Jacob's return from outside. He didn't see him, and he let his exasperation take over. "Well, what was I supposed to think? You were talking about digging up people and washing bones!"

"I didn't mean I did it to Jessica's ancestors!" she cried, wiping her eyes with the backs of her hands.

"Then what did you do?"

"Nothing!" she cried. "Much," she added.

"Oh, jeez," Thomas said, collapsing in a chair at the kitchen table. He sat holding his head in his hands. He had no idea what he'd done to deserve this. After a moment, he lifted his head and looked at his half sister. She was no longer crying, at least, but she looked no less worried.

"Define much," he said bravely, and she shrugged.

"Just...pulling out weeds. Putting in flowers."

"Where, Heidi? *Where?*"

"At the burial place. When you come out of Siler City, where you turn to come down the road to Silk Hope. That burial place."

The burial place would have been more accurate, Thomas thought. She seemed to be bracing herself in case he started yelling again.

"Okay?" she asked when he didn't.

"I don't know," he said truthfully.

"It was only just the Markham burial places," she said earnestly. "Well, there was one 'Jessica,' because I forgot which way the names go in America. In Vietnam, it's last name first with the first name last, but here, it's first name first. Very confusing."

Thomas slid down in his chair and stared up at the ceiling.

"Thomas?" she said.

He didn't answer; he only groaned.

"Thomas?" she said again.

"What?" he asked wearily.

"Are we in trouble?"

"*We?* No, *we* are not in trouble. *You* are in trouble. You, Heidi. *You.*"

"Oh," she said meekly.

He glanced at her. She stood in the middle of the room with her head bowed. He sighed heavily. So far, this had been one hell of a morning.

"Thomas?" Heidi said, looking up at him.

"What?" he answered, as weary as ever.

"In America, do the brothers help the sisters with their troubles?"

He stared at her for a moment before he answered. "Well, I don't know how else you're going to get out of it." He stood up. "We're going to have to clean up Jessica's porch, undo everything."

"Undo?" she asked worriedly. "We can't undo, Thomas. It's very bad luck. Very bad."

"Heidi, we can't leave all this stuff you've done! We've got to get it before Jessica sees it and calls the police."

"Police?"

"Yes, police! We have to get that stuff before we end up on the six o'clock news for practicing satanic rituals."

"Satan?" Heidi said in alarm. "He's not on the list, Thomas."

"Yeah, well, you know what Jessica's going to think, don't you?"

"Not . . . exactly."

"Heidi," he said, trying not to lose patience. "Jessica isn't going to know about areca nut and betel leaf offerings. She's going to think she's being stalked by some blood-crazed cult or something, and it's not going to help Jake any if she finds out the cult's only got two members, is it?"

"Two?" she said, still worried.

He pointed toward her chest and then his. "Guilt by association," he said ominously.

"Oh," she said in dismay.

"Right. 'Oh.' Let's go."

"Now?"

"Yes, now! We'll tell Jake we're going for driving lessons." he headed for the door, but she didn't follow.

"Heidi!" he said in exasperation.

"I have to tell the God of the Hearth," she said in a rush, heading for the fireplace in the living room. "I have to tell him everything we're doing now is because you're ignorant—"

"Thanks a lot!"

"—so he can explain it to the Jade Emperor."

"Heidi—"

"I have to do this, Thomas!"

He waited while she respectfully knelt in front of the fireplace, rolling his eyes upward but keeping quiet while she made her explanations on his behalf. A few hours ago, his life was reasonably normal—brand-new illegitimate half sister or not. Now he was waiting until a hearth god got the official version of the latest turn of events so he could go undo his father and Jessica Markham's leaf and nut betrothal. If, mind you, *if* St. Victor Hugo and Joan of Arc and the Chinese guy didn't get in the way.

"Let's go," he said when she stood up again. "Hurry. And if we run into Jake, I'll do the talking."

"Why?" she said, falling into step with him, letting him rush her toward the back door.

"Because if he says 'Where are you two going?' I don't want you telling him we're off to get him unbetrothed."

"I don't think we can get him unbetrothed, Thomas. I think we can only get him bad luck."

"There's bad luck and there's bad luck," he said philosophically, pushing the screen door open ahead of her. "Understand?"

"No," she said with a sigh. "But I trust you to do what is best."

"Well, better late than never, I guess. From now on, you don't do anything without talking to me first. Head for the truck."

"Father's at the truck," she whispered over her shoulder.

He shooed her along anyway. "We'll just have to bluff it out."

Jacob stood watching his children drive away, wondering how it was that he'd left two reasonably sensible young people at home while he went to Silk Hope this morning, and ever since he'd come back, he'd felt as if he were trapped in an old Laurel and Hardy movie. Neither Huong nor Thomas had any guile whatsoever, and while he had no idea what they were up to, he was reasonably certain it had nothing to do with driving lessons. They were in too big of a hurry, for one thing, and Thomas nearly died when he thought Huong was actually going to get behind the wheel.

He exhaled sharply and shook his head. He trusted Thomas, and whatever was going on, he was going to do his best to stay out of it, because his daughter and his son seemed to be communicating with each other finally. On what level, he couldn't imagine. He was going to try not to worry about the circumstances. He had enough to worry about. Peaches. Money.

Jessica.

Now what? was the question that kept running around in his mind. Jessica had made it clear that she didn't want anything to do with him, and he could accept that—except for one small problem. He didn't believe her. When he'd looked into her eyes, he could literally *feel* that something that always passed between them when they were together. He'd felt it the first day they met. And he felt it again today. It wasn't merely that he was a man and she was a more than attractive woman. It was more that she was *the* woman, a fact he could no longer deny no matter how hard he tried or how long he stayed away.

He smiled to himself and rubbed his upper arm. He had been less than considerate of her, and she'd let him know it. And she had looked so pretty today, fist and all. But it was obvious to him that she hadn't been pining away for him these past few months. She looked fine. Healthy. Happy.

Soft. Soft dark hair and soft brown eyes and soft full breasts. He wanted to put his face against her neck and hair. He wanted to lie somewhere with her face-to-face, skin to skin. He wanted to make love with her. He wanted to live with her, to have her in his life every day, to work hard for her and to come home tired and hungry and have her look up and be glad to see him. He could imagine it if he tried. It wouldn't matter that he'd be wearing his jeans and his T-shirt and his Braves ball cap or that she'd be wearing that navy-blue suit and carrying her briefcase under her arm. The two of them would still be happy and in love with each other.

Jessica!

It had been all he could do to keep his hands off her.

"Ah, hell!" he said out loud.

He walked toward the orchard, trying to take his mind off his troubles by putting it on the flourishing trees. When he'd come back from Vietnam, this orchard had been his salvation, but for once, he couldn't hide from his feelings by becoming preoccupied with fruit trees. His mind ignored the peach trees entirely, remembering instead the walks through the orchard with Jessica, cold, crisp afternoon walks that were made special somehow just because she was there. She'd wanted to come with him, wanted to see what he did to his peach trees and why. Once, it had been so cold that she'd

slipped her hand into his jacket pocket as they
walked along. And, God, how much it had pleased
him knowing that she felt comfortable enough
with him to do that, to let him keep her hand
warm. He'd been like some half-grown boy no
older than Thomas, crazily happy just to be with
her.

So damned happy—

His mind abruptly cut to the other women he'd
cared about in his life. To Thomas's mother, who
had asked more from him than he could give. And
to Huong's mother, who had asked for nothing.
Neither of them had been better off for knowing
him, and what did he have to offer a woman like
Jessica but himself and his troubled family? He'd
already ruined the possibility of the two of them
being together. *He* had ruined it, because he had
been on the verge of loving her and they had come
to the point of becoming intimate or becoming
nothing. In his panic, he'd chosen the latter.

He couldn't blame his loneliness now on the
situation with Huong. Jessica didn't even know
about this new daughter of his. He sighed heavily.
He was doing the best he could, not in just trying
to keep his family together, but in attempting to
forge an entirely new one by accepting his responsibility for Huong and trying not to completely
alienate Thomas. He had asked a lot of Thomas,
but he'd known of no other way to handle it than
to simply tell the boy the situation and leave the

rest up to him. It hadn't been easy to trust that Thomas would eventually accept Huong or Jacob's human frailties, but for a change, it appeared as if that trust might just have been well placed.

He pulled down a peach tree twig to inspect it, but he didn't really see it. It occurred to him suddenly that he owed Jessica the same kind of trust he'd shown his son, if he cared about her. Maybe she cared about him, too, but in any event, he couldn't just pop back into her life without explanation and expect her to welcome him with open arms. He was going to have to sit down with her and *tell* her what he'd felt when he stopped seeing her and what he felt now. He'd have to let her decide whether or not she wanted any part of him. He'd tell her, the way he had told Thomas, and he'd hope for the best.

He looked around him at the expanse of orderly planted trees, his mood much improved now that he'd decided on a course of action. The sun was shining brightly, the robins were singing. And all he had to do now was get Jessica to stand still long enough to listen to him.

He suddenly smiled again, thinking of his children.

Oops!

What the hell did that mean?

Chapter Five

Jessica heard the whispering again—while she was sitting in her father's wingchair in the living room, trying to unravel the mishmash of conflicting emotions Jacob Brenner's reappearance had elicited. The window was cracked; the lace curtain billowed outward from time to time, and she *heard* it.

But by the time she'd gotten to the front door and dragged it open, there was nothing, not even the leaves and nuts and candles this time. The porch, the front yard were forlornly empty. She stood holding the screen door open, peering in every direction and feeling ridiculous that she'd been so certain when now she wasn't sure at all. She wasn't sure about anything—except that Jacob Brenner made her knees week when he looked at her, much less touched her, and that perhaps she was losing her mind.

She closed her eyes for a moment, then went back inside. She had to get herself in hand. She had a dinner guest coming, and given the peculiarities of the morning, she was preoccupied at best. During the time she'd spent in her father's favorite chair staring into space, she had made few inroads into deciding what Jacob had been about this morning, and no inroads at all into why she should care. The only truth that stood out plainly was that she *did* care. Something was worrying Jacob. She saw it in his eyes just before she'd let her injured feelings take precedence and she'd closed herself off from everything he'd said or wanted to say. She was so exasperated with Jacob Brenner. Now, *now,* when Charlie Hilton from the bank was coming to dinner, Jacob had decided to engage her in conversation in front of half of Silk Hope. She had been able to feel the speculation going on behind the roll-out windows of Silk Hope Service, the clusters of interested heads trying to see.

Jake's out there talking to Jessie. What do you reckon that *means?*

What indeed?

She'd invited Charlie to take her mind off Jacob in the first place. Jacob had been on her mind only moderately when she'd issued the invitation. Now, after this morning, she could think of nothing else but him—about what he'd said and the way he'd looked, about the feel of his warm hand on hers. It had been all she could do not to fall all over herself—all over *him*—just because she'd run into him unexpectedly and he'd deigned to talk to her. It made her angry just thinking about it. She'd wanted to punch him much harder than she had. She'd lived in the big city; she had enough experience with the misogynists of the world to

know how to handle herself. But when she'd
looked into his eyes, her heart had pounded like a
silly teenager's. She'd wanted to put her arms
around him, to pick up exactly where they'd left
off that cold, starry night in January.

She made a noise of exasperation and walked
back through the house. Where was her pride? In
Jacob Brenner's hip pocket apparently. She certainly didn't seem to have it anymore.

She glanced at the clock, calculating the time
she had before she needed to start dinner. She
liked Charlie Hilton. He was younger than she
was, and he'd been asking her out since she came
to work at the bank—not because he wanted to go
out with her, she suspected, but because he was
new in the investment business and he wanted the
benefit of her years of experience. In any event,
they got along well together. She just wished she
hadn't decided to invite him this particular evening.

As she came into the kitchen, she caught a
glimpse of someone walking past the dining-room
windows toward the back door. Charlie—four
hours early—with a half-open briefcase under his
arm.

"Jess!" he said brightly when she opened the
door. "I know I'm early, but I want to make you
a deal."

"What kind of deal, Charlie?" She smiled because she was hoping for a rain check.

"You go over these accounts with me and I'll take you into Siler City later and buy you dinner. Price is no object. What do you say?"

She looked at the bulging briefcase. Reviewing investment packages for the rest of the afternoon was *not* what she had in mind. She wanted to get to the cemetery to visit her mother's grave. She wanted to worry some more about Jacob Brenner. "Charlie, it's Sunday. It's Mother's Day. Shouldn't you be off somewhere making your mother happy?"

"I already did that. Jess, I need your help. Desperately. The bigwigs have given me all these new accounts to look after. You know these people better than I do. I need your input so I don't mess up." He pushed his very fashionable eyeglasses up on his nose with his free hand.

"Charlie—"

"Please! *Please!*" he said earnestly, clearly about to get down on his knees since the situation seemed to require it.

"Get up, you idiot," she said, laughing. Charlie wasn't the least bit suited to handling investments or the investors, but he worked hard and she did like him.

"Get up, you idiot," he repeated hopefully. "Does that mean you'll help me?"

"Yes, I'll help you. Come in."

"Oh, thank you, thank you, Jess. You'll never regret it," he said, trying to squeeze in the door past her and not hit her with the briefcase. "Kitchen table all right?"

"Fine. Do you want something to drink?"

"I thought you'd never ask. Anything you've got is fine with me. Iced tea, coffee, water—" he rolled his eyes "—Demon rum . . ."

"I think you'd better stick with iced tea. If I'm going to do this, I want you to remember what I've told you."

He already had his jacket off and his tie loosened, and he was about to roll up his sleeves. "Right. Whatever you say. You are a wonderful woman, Jessica Markham."

"Yes," she said agreeably, going to get the iced tea. Only a wonderful woman would have a date with a younger man that involved his briefcase.

"This is going to be a piece of cake," he assured her.

But, unfortunately, it was more like a ton of bricks. Charlie, who was a whiz with figures, couldn't remember the first thing about individual people. Finally, in desperation, Jessica adjourned them outside to sit on the brick patio by the back door, hoping that a change of scenery and a little fresh air would help. The patio was shaded but dappled in sunlight, and it was sheltered from the still chilly "blackberry winter" wind. She already had her pots of blooming red geraniums out and lining the brick perimeter. The patio had a beautiful view of the surrounding countryside, pastoral and uninhabited and greening. It really was a pleasant and peaceful place to be in, but it soon became apparent that the migration didn't help Charlie in the least. He sat slumped on the glider with his arm thrown over his eyes, and she sat in a wooden yard chair across from him.

"I told you to take notes," she said in exasperation.

"I can remember it, Jess."

"No, Charlie, you can't."

"I can. I'm just—"

"All right. Tell me about Godwin."

"Godwin. Godwin," he repeated, clearly straining hard to try to get some shred of information to wander to the forefront. Absolutely nothing came to him.

"Godwin doesn't like to be told anything," Jessica said for the hundredth time. "Unless he asks for it. So you keep your mouth shut. You don't suggest anything, because if you do, he'd do exactly the opposite whether it's a bad idea or not. He'll do the opposite and if he loses money on it, you'll lose him as a client. You sit tight and you wait until he asks for your opinion. *When* he asks, *then* you tell him. Until that time, you make sure you know everything about every stock and bond he has in the market and you just give him specific information about how they're doing. And don't fake it because he won't ask you anything he doesn't already know himself. But don't tell him what to do. Got it?''

''I got it,'' he said from under his arm.

''Good. Then tell me.''

He looked at her. ''Tell you what?''

''What I just told you, knucklehead!'' she said, reaching out to take a swipe at him with the file folder she was holding. Charlie caught her wrist, pulling her out of her chair and scattering papers everywhere, both of them laughing. She was off balance and ended up piling into the glider with him, catching a glimpse of something out of the corner of her eye as she did.

She looked sharply around. Jacob stood at the corner of the patio.

Jacob Brenner had never felt more like a fool in his life. He knew he should say something, but absolutely nothing came to mind—except what Thomas and Huong would have said.

Oops!

Jessica was seeing something else. The realization came quick and hard. He should have anticipated that, and he should have called her first. He should have seen the strange car parked behind the row of crape myrtle bushes before he got this far. He should have waited for Thomas and Huong to come back with the truck. It was noisy enough to have alerted Jessica and her whatever-he-was that they weren't alone. He should have done *any-*

thing but let himself become so caught up in what he wanted that he failed to use good sense.

"I'm sorry, Jessica," he said finally. "I didn't mean to intrude. I'll come back another time."

He turned to go, but she got up from the glider and walked toward him. "No, wait. You aren't intruding. Do you know . . . ?"

"Charles Hilton," Charlie said, standing up and extending his hand. "You're Jack Brenner, right? You've got a farm loan with us at the bank." He pumped Jacob's hand vigorously and shot a triumphant look toward Jessica that Jacob didn't begin to understand. "So. Jack! How are you doing?"

"Jacob, Charlie. It's *Jacob* Brenner," Jessica said.

"I'm doing fine," Jacob told him, taking his hand back. At the moment, that certainly wasn't the truth, but what the hell, he thought.

"Is there someting I can do for you, Jacob?" Jessica asked, her eyes trying to probe his.

Yes! he thought, deciding to let her look into him deep and long. *You can dump this banker. You can come walking with me. You can let me talk to you and hold you and love you!*

But he said, "Nothing that won't keep. I'll come by again when you're not so . . . busy. Nice to meet you, Charles," he added, lying again. He turned and walked away, not realizing that Jessica was following him.

"Jacob!" she called when he reached the white-and-beige '76 Buick he'd come in. The car was old, not like the silver foreign model behind the crape myrtles *Charles* drove. Old and damnably quiet. He stood for a moment before he turned around.

"What's wrong?" she said when he looked at her.

He smiled a smile he didn't feel. "Nothing. I'll be seeing you, Jessica."

"Jacob Brenner!" she said when he opened the car door. "You are making me crazy! You know that!"

"You make me crazy, too, Jess," he said quietly, his eyes holding hers.

She stared back at him, her lips parted. The sun was shining on her dark hair; the wind lifted a strand and blew it across her face. He reached out without thinking to brush it away, deliberately letting his fingers graze the warm softness of her cheek. He was certain she had no idea how attractive she was at that moment.

"Jacob," she protested, but she didn't move away. She stood still, letting him tuck the errant strand of hair behind her ear, her eyes searching his face. "I don't know what you want."

"You," he answered simply. "I want you." She might as well know why he was pushing his way back into her life again, especially since Charles was standing at the edge of the patio looking on. But he didn't wait for her to respond to his bold declaration of intent. He didn't have the nerve for that, not with an audience.

He got into the car and slammed the door, leaving her standing while he started the engine and backed out the long driveway to the road.

"Is he mad, do you think?" Heidi whispered.

"No," Thomas whispered back, watching Jacob head out into the orchards. Jacob was too far away to hear him, but he whispered anyway.

"But he's not talking, Thomas. Ever since we came back, he doesn't even ask us about the driving lessons. He doesn't say anything!"

"That's how I know he's not mad. If he was mad, you'd hear about it—exactly what, when, where and why. Believe me."

"What's wrong with him then?"

"How the heck should I know? Maybe he saw that dude in the silver BMW at Jessica's. That'd be enough to depress him."

Heidi worriedly nodded her head, and Thomas sighed. What with having to leave the truck parked by the road and trying to sneak up on Jessica's front porch without her seeing them when her house was out in the middle of an open field, and then finding all of Heidi's ritual betel leaves and areca nuts gone, his nerves were shot to hell. They had just made it out of Jessica's yard and back to the truck when that overly helpful big shot driving a silver BMW stopped and asked them what they were doing parked on the side of the road. Thomas had said that the engine was running hot, and he wished he hadn't. He could live with lying to Jacob when it was for his own good, but he absolutely hated lying to strangers. It was taking an unfair advantage somehow. He should have said that they were just changing drivers. That would have been a little closer to the truth.

"What do you think Jessica did with all the betrothal things, Thomas?" Heidi asked worriedly. "You think she gives them to the police?"

"Nope. I think she gives them to the *FBI*. With our luck, who else would she give them to?"

"Oh, Thomas—"

The back door suddenly slammed, and they both fell silent, sitting quietly at the kitchen table, waiting for Jacob.

He came in and went directly to the kitchen sink, pushing his ball cap back on his head and letting the tap run a long time before he got himself a big glass of water. They both sat and watched him drink it.

He gave them a quizzical look when he sat the glass down, but didn't say anything—then. He went out the door again, but he came back almost immediately.

"The Ruritans are having their big hamburger and hot dog supper at the Fire Department next Saturday," he said. "I want you ready to go at six o'clock sharp, both of you. It's time we introduced Huong to everybody."

Chapter Six

Jessica kept waiting for the telephone to ring. A mere two encounters with Jacob Brenner after four months of nothing, and she was back to square one—waiting for the damned phone to ring! Between fearfully anticipating the return of candle-bearing prowlers and hoping for a Jacob Brenner telephone call, she was exhausted. She had gone to dinner with Charlie after Jacob left on Sunday afternoon, but she had gone firmly believing that Jacob would be back to talk to her. He didn't come back, not Sunday night and not the rest of the week. Every evening, pretending that she was going about her business in a normal fashion, she'd waited, and every evening she'd been disappointed. She slept fitfully; her appetite was gone, and every time someone came into the bank she couldn't keep from looking up hopefully like a lovestruck schoolgirl.

But she had no intention of making the same mistake she'd made last time. She would *not* call him no matter how much passively waiting went against her nature.

You. I want you.

How could he say something like that and then not come by to see her, not even call?

Because he was Jacob Brenner, she thought in exasperation, and she certainly should have remembered that. She had already learned the hard way that he was unpredictable. Some people marked the passage of time in minutes or hours. Others, in days or weeks. Clearly, Jacob thought of time in months, years, centuries. If he thought of it at all.

Late Saturday afternoon, she remembered her commitment to help with the Ruritan hamburger and hot dog supper. The civic club's suppers were a famous and frequent event in Silk Hope to raise money for college scholarships for local high-school seniors. She had agreed to help knowing that Jacob would likely be there, but that was before the craziness of last Sunday.

She hesitated only a moment before she decided to go. She had things she wanted to say to Jacob that she didn't want to say in front of all of Silk Hope, but she got dressed anyway.

Jacob waited in the trunk for Huong and Thomas, drumming his fingers on the steering wheel in an effort not to lose patience. He had thought when he came out that both his children were ready and dutifully following in his wake. It quickly became apparent that that was not the case.

He studied his hands on the steering wheel for a moment. He'd had to work a long time to get them clean, and they still looked exactly like what they were—rough, battered, workingman's hands. And yet, with Jessica, he'd never felt he had to make any kind of apology for them, never felt uncomfortable. It was only with her friend Charles the Banker, that he'd felt the need to wipe his hand on his clothes before he offered it in a handshake.

Were they lovers?

If they were, he had no one to blame but himself, but he still didn't want to think about it. *If* they were, he'd made an even bigger fool of himself by telling Jessica that he wanted her. And he hadn't even said for what. She could be thinking that he meant anything—if she thought about it at all. If things were serious between her and the banker, she probably hadn't given his impulsive announcement even a moment's consideration.

He should have made the time somewhere to talk to her, he thought, sighing heavily. This had been no easy week; everything had gone wrong in the orchard. He'd had to replace a hundred trees that should have lasted at least seven years and didn't. He'd had to stay awake to battle the threat of frost nearly every night. The rest of the time he'd been pressed to repair sprayers and fertilizers that had suddenly gone from aging to inoperable. He'd had no time to see Jessica, unless she would have been willing to drop by the orchard sometime between midnight and seven in the morning. Seeing her Sunday afternoon with the sunlight on her hair, it had seemed the right thing to do—to just *tell* what he was feeling for her, but likely as not, he'd only made everything worse. Still, there was that one encouraging thing she'd said—that in January she'd been playing for keeps.

He looked up suddenly because Thomas was standing at the truck window.

"What?" he said, silently congratulating himself because he hadn't said *Now what?* The troubles of the week had left him little tolerance for the now decidedly peculiar behavior of his son and daughter. He still had no idea what was going on with the two of them, and coward that he was, he didn't want to try to find out.

"You better come talk to her, Dad," Thomas said without prelude.

"Why?"

"She's crying."

Jacob frowned. "Why is she crying? I thought everything was okay."

"Yeah, well," Thomas said unhelpfully, stepping back so he could open the truck door.

"You two didn't get into an argument, did you?"

"No, we didn't get into an argument," Thomas said testily. "How come you always think everything is *my* fault?"

"Probably because you're the only other person here. Where is she?"

"She's sitting on the front porch steps. Make her stop crying, Dad. She's going to ruin everything."

Jacob almost smiled. "Everything" in this instance was hair and makeup. It had been incredible to him that Thomas had suddenly turned teen fashion consultant, advising his sister about her hair and picking out what he considered the right color of eyeshadow and lipstick. He'd even donated the money for everything—the cosmetics, the haircut *and* a new blouse and short set, withdrawing the cash from the holy of holies, his "Porsche Fund"—with the understanding that when Huong got a job, she'd pay him back. And he'd gotten all stiff necked and indignant when Jacob would have praised him for it, insisting that he'd only done it to keep from being embarrassed. He'd insisted, but it wasn't the truth. Huong had been miserable ever since she found out about having to go to the Ruritan supper, and clearly Thomas had done everything he knew to do to make it easier for her. A failed gesture, it now appeared.

Jacob walked through the house, looking for Huong as he went in case she'd come back inside. The house was spotless, all her doing because she was determined not to be a burden to him. He understood her need to feel useful, but he'd tried his best to convince her that this was her home now, that she wasn't here on trial. He looked into her bedroom as he passed the door, but she wasn't there. She was still sitting on the front steps, her back to him as he opened the screen door. She didn't look at him when he sat down on the steps beside her. She really was very pretty, Jacob thought, pretty in the pink short set Thomas had steered her toward and the merest hint of pink lipstick and eyeshadow he'd suggested. She looked like any pretty American teenager, except for the stain of tears down her cheeks.

"Huong—"

"I'm trying not to cry," she said quickly, giving him only the briefest of glances. She wiped her eyes with the backs of her hands. "It's just that . . . I'm so . . . happy."

"Yeah, I can see that," Jacob said, taking his handkerchief out of his pocket and giving it to her, fully aware that his even having one was yet another earmark of a workingman. Bankers didn't need handkerchiefs, not the kind that were meant to be used. Their hands stayed clean, and the most they needed were "pocket silks." "Here. Wipe your eyes. I know it's hard for you, but I thought we'd settled all this. You have to meet people sometime, you know."

"I know, Father. It's just—"

"Just what?" he asked when she didn't go on. "We can talk about this. You can tell me."

She answered him, but he didn't hear what she said.

"What?" he asked.

She turned to look at him. "My mother wanted this for me—to come here and find you. It was what she . . . lived for."

"Yes," he agreed.

"But I don't want to be your . . ."

He waited, watching her gather her courage, not knowing what she was about to say.

"I don't want to be your . . . shame," she said finally. Her voice trembled, but she didn't look away.

"I see," he said, surprised at the tension in him because he'd half expected her to say *daughter. I don't want to be your daughter.* She was so quiet and shy, and he'd been so insistent that she stop hiding at home.

But he did understand. He'd had long talks with the sisters at St. Julia's and with the counselors from the Vietnam Veterans of America Foundation. He knew the ridicule and abuse she had endured because her father was an American soldier, the "child of the dust" label she'd borne.

"The way I was your shame," he said quietly. "In Vietnam."

She looked at him in surprise. "You weren't—" she protested, but then she let it go, bowing her head.

He reached out and put his hand on top of her head. "What you went through in the Children's Market because of me was much worse than I'll

ever have to go through here because of you.
You're not my shame. You're my daughter. You're
mine, and I don't want you to think that you're
any less to me than Thomas."

"Thomas is a son."

"You're both my children."

She looked up at him. "You loved his mother.
My mother was . . ."

The memory of a young Vietnamese woman in
a long, white silk dress suddenly came into his
mind. The memory was vivid and painful, and he
looked out across the yard, feeling the fear and
misery and loneliness of that time as if it were
yesterday. He'd thought that he couldn't actually
remember her face, but he saw it now amid a rush
of fractured images that fell into his consciousness like shattered glass—himself in muddy Marine fatigues, the dead, the dying, the wet heat and
smell of Vietnam, James Taylor singing "Carolina in My Mind," and the softly whispered
French of the young Vietnamese woman named
Ho Thi Lan.

Il y a longtemps que je t'aime, Jacob.

He looked back at Huong. It was hard for him
to say what he felt, but for this unhappy child of
his and for the young woman in the white silk
dress, he would have to try. He took a deep breath
to push the pain of remembering aside. "Your
mother was one of the kindest people I've ever
known. She was beautiful and gentle and I'm glad

that you're more like her than me. I won't ever forget her. She was an important part of my life. She loved me, and she suffered for it. I'm very sorry about that, but I'm not sorry about you."

He could see the relief spread over her face, a relief he knew was mirrored on his own, because for once in his life he thought he'd said the right thing.

"Thank you, Father," she said, dabbing her eyes again with his handkerchief, this time more careful of the pink eye shadow. "I can be very brave, Father. Truly, I can."

"Huong, if this is too painful for you, you don't have to—"

"Hey!" Thomas said from the doorway behind them. "Are we going or not? Everything'll be gone before we get there!"

Jacob smiled. "I think your brother's hungry again," he said to her.

She managed a smile in return. "What a surprise," she said drolly. "I guess now we go feed the bottomless hole."

"Pit," Thomas said, holding up one finger. "That's *pit*."

Thomas noted as soon as they got out of the truck at the Silk Hope Community Center that he'd been wrong to worry about all the food being gone. From the number of cars parked along the road, a hundred people must have been inside the

building, but there were still plenty of hot dogs
and hamburgers cooking. And they smelled *wonderful*. Three big charcoal grills stood on the cement driveway out in front of the double doors,
where faithful Ruritans flipped and singed meat
patties and wieners nonstop. Several rows of long
tables had been set up inside the building for people who wanted to stay and sit down to eat, and
Thomas's personal favorite, the dessert table, still
held plenty of chocolate cakes and apple and
peach pies. He took another deep breath to savor
the aroma of charcoaling meat. Absolutely wonderful!

But he didn't let himself get so carried away
with the prospect of a good feed that he failed to
note two other things as well. One was the look his
father and Jessica Markham exchanged the minute they saw each other, and the other was the
presence of big Sonny Cook, the sheriff's deputy.
Jessica and Jacob stared at each other across the
open room, their eyes locking just as she plunged
both her plastic-gloved hands into the huge stain-
less-steel pan of chopped onions, and Sonny stood
talking to a whole crowd of people by the tubs of
ice and soft drinks, all of whom, for a change,
seemed to be listening to him.

And no wonder, Thomas thought. The words,
"heathen occult practices," "devil worshipers,"
and "Jessica Markham" floated out over the
clamor of people trying to get fed. Jessica looked

around sharply at the sound of her name, leaving a woman in an orange-and-white dress still holding her hot dog out for extra onions, and Heidi stopped dead in front of him. He had no doubt at all that if he hadn't been directly behind her, she would have turned and bolted.

"Keep going," he insisted without moving his lips. If the you-know-what was about to hit the fan, he wasn't going down with an empty stomach. He pushed Heidi forward, expecting Jacob to go talk to Jessica. It was obvious that he wanted to. Thomas could almost feel the longing that passed between them.

But Jacob didn't go. He bent down to Heidi instead.

"It's going to be okay," he said to her in his ignorance. "You follow Thomas. He'll show you what to do."

She nodded dutifully, and Jacob walked away, but she reached out to grab Thomas by the arm, because Jacob wasn't going to talk to Jessica after all. He was going to go talk to Sonny Cook.

"Thomas!" she squeaked in a whisper. "We don't want him to find out about the areca nuts at Jessica's, do we?"

"Of course not!" he whispered back. "How long do you think it would take him to find out who around here even knows what they are?"

"Oh, Thomas, it was wrong to undo. Look how things are going! Jessica doesn't even say hello to

Father, and she has such kind eyes. She would make a beautiful mother. Thomas, do something!''

Do something?

He wanted to "do something," all right. He wanted a hamburger, maybe two or three. And a hot dog hiding in a big pile of onions. Chocolate cake. Apple pie. He looked longingly at the food line and gave a little whimper. Oh, the pain of it!

"Just do what I do," he said, still whispering.

"You aren't doing anything."

"I know that, don't I? That's what I mean. Be cool! We'll just stroll over there and get Jake and tell him we want him to come and eat with us."

"Stroll?"

"Walk like we're not the heathen occult devil worshipers Sonny is talking about!"

"Oh," Heidi said, clearly bewildered. "I don't even know what a heathen occult devil worshiper is."

"And I don't have time to explain it to you now! Come on, before Jake gets an earful!"

At Thomas's urging, she came along, hurrying to catch up with Jacob, but the worried expression on her face would have stopped a truck.

"What's the matter?" Jacob said the moment he saw it.

"Oh, nothing, Father," Heidi said quickly. Too quickly. "We were just worrying about your, um, ear," she finished lamely.

"My—?"

"Stomach!" Thomas injected. "She means stomach! Come on, Dad! Let's eat!"

"You two go on ahead," Jacob said, his look going from one to the other as if he knew there was more to this than met the eye, if he could only figure out what it was. "I want to hear what Sonny's saying."

Thomas sidled closer to whisper into one of the ears Heidi claimed to be concerned about. "Ah, it's a matter of money, Dad."

"You've got money."

"Not enough for both of us. I'm hungry, Dad. *Really* hungry."

"Me, too," Heidi assured him.

Thomas knew they were laying it on thick, but desperation left no time for polish. "And you really ought to talk to Jessica, Dad," he added, his desperation mounting. "She keeps looking at you."

"Thomas—"

"Ah-ha!" Thomas said loudly, because, incredibly, Jessica walked up at this most opportune moment. "Look who's here, Dad! Well!" he babbled on. "Let's eat! You eaten yet, Jessica?"

"No—" she managed to get out before he interrupted.

"I thought not! This way, Dad! Just come along with us! You, too, Jessica?" he said, taking her by the arm.

"Thomas!" Jacob said.

"Yeah, Dad?" Thomas answered with as much innocence as he could muster.

"The next time we work out in the sun all day, I want you to be sure you wear a hat."

"Yeah, Dad. Right. Wear a hat. I'll do that very thing."

"You want to turn Jessica loose now?"

"What? Oh! Sorry, Jessica."

"And do you want knock it off?"

"Knock it off? I don't know what you mean, Dad."

"Now?" Jacob added pointedly.

Thomas was about to continue his protest, but Jacob put his hand on Heidi's shoulder.

"Jessica," he said. "I'd like you to meet my daughter."

Yes, Jessica thought, faltering for a moment, then looking into the girl's eyes. She was amazed by the lack of surprise she felt after the initial shock. She could easily see how much this young girl resembled Jacob. She was amazed, too, that in spite of this sudden announcement, her previous annoyance with him had all but dissipated. Glancing at him, she realized that she needed to make some response, and she smiled.

"Welcome to Silk Hope," she said, extending her hand to the girl. "I've lived away from here for a long time, so I'm getting used to it, too."

"Is it strange here sometimes for you, too, then?" the girl asked shyly.

"Very strange," Jessica answered, glancing again at Jacob. The grateful look he gave her was nearly more than she could bear. She stared back at him, wondering what he had expected. Deliberate unkindness on her part? She was annoyed with him for popping in and out of her life, but not enough to take it out on his children, even the one she didn't know about. "Huong?" she said, repeating the girl's name. "Is that right?"

"Exactly right, Miss Jessica, the way you say it."

"Please. Just call me Jessica."

"Jessica," she repeated tentatively.

"Here," Jacob said, handing Thomas some money.

"What's this for?" Thomas wondered.

"Thomas, are you trying to gaslight me or what? You just said you needed money."

"Oh, yeah, Dad. I did."

"Well?" Jacob said.

"Well, what, Dad?"

"I thought the two of you were hungry. Take the money and go use it!"

"Oh! Okay, Dad. How much change you want back?"

"As much as I can get. I think I'm going to need it for your treatment."

"Aw, Dad," Thomas said, poking his father once on the upper arm. "You coming, too?"

"In a minute," Jacob said pointedly.

He hesitated, but his sister took his arm.

"Let's go now, Thomas. Very nice to be meeting you," she said politely to Jessica. "Father, I will try to keep him from eating your supper, too."

Jacob smiled. "You do that, but you've got your work cut out for you."

"She's very pretty," Jessica said as Jacob watched Huong lead Thomas away.

"Yes," Jacob agreed.

They stood awkwardly, Jessica no longer knowing what she wanted to say to him now that she had the opportunity. Jacob Brenner was a handsome man with quietly sad eyes and a warm, gentle touch she'd missed more than she had been willing to admit. If she didn't remember that starry January night, if she didn't feel such longing when she looked at him, she wouldn't be having this difficulty letting him know the emotional turmoil he'd caused her all week. But he had a daughter suddenly; nothing else seemed to matter, and she waited for him to elaborate.

He didn't. He simply looked at her, and she had the distinct feeling that if all these people hadn't been standing around, he would have reached out for her. She thought that she had never in her life seen a man so in need of comfort, and it was all she could do not to give it. She wanted to put her arms around him. Unhappily she realized that she didn't even have to understand why he was hurting. It was enough just to know that he was in need.

"Jacob, you keep disappearing," she said, some remnant of her injured pride resurfacing because she'd waited all week to talk to him. It was obvious that they had a great deal to talk about. "I thought you'd died."

He almost smiled. "No. A hundred peach trees."

She frowned. "What?"

"A hundred peach trees died."

"I see. And that kept you too occupied to pick up the telephone," she suggested.

"No."

"No?"

"I could have made the time, but I didn't. I thought maybe you needed time to think."

"I might, Jacob, if I knew what I needed to think about. Let's not beat around the bush, okay? What did you mean?"

"When?"

"You know when!" she said. "When you said you wanted me."

"What did you mean when you said you were playing for keeps?"

"*I* asked first," she said, and he smiled and took her arm.

"I think we'd better get into line so all the people who are trying to hear this conversation can go on about their business."

Jessica looked around her. They were indeed drawing an even bigger crowd of none-too-subtle eavesdroppers. "Jacob," she whispered as he moved her toward the food tables. "I want to know what you meant."

"I meant exactly what you think I meant, Jess. I meant that and everything else."

"Everything else?"

"Everything else," he repeated.

"Just like that. Out of the clear blue when I haven't seen you in months."

"Yeah. You want a hot dog or a hamburger?"

She made an impatient gesture toward the hot dogs. "Jacob, this doesn't make any sense to me."

"Me, either, Jess."

"Jacob—"

"Take the hot dog, Jess. Don't hold up the line."

"Is Huong the reason you stopped seeing me in January?" she persisted.

"No."

"No?" she said incredulously, fully aware of how willing she would have been to accept the sudden arrival of his daughter as an excuse for his abrupt withdrawal.

"I found out about her after we stopped seeing each other."

"Well, what then? You had an extra wife nobody knew about?"

"I was never married to Huong's mother," he said, calmly moving down the line with his plate. He looked up at her.

"Why not?" she asked. "Apparently the relationship was of some import. Or did you plan to marry her now?"

"Huong's mother is dead, Jess. She died in Vietnam last winter without knowing that Huong had found me. I hadn't seen or heard from her since I was there seventeen years ago."

"Was that her doing or yours?"

"Jess . . ."

She sighed heavily. "Never mind. I think I know the answer. You're a hard man to pin down, Jacob. I don't know it if helps to know you've always been that way or not."

"Jessica, wait," he said when she turned to go.

"You were right," she said over her shoulder as she walked away. "I do need to think."

"I'll come by later."

"No," she said, stopping to look back at him. "I won't be there."

"You going out with the banker?"

"Jacob," she said in exasperation. "You can't just stroll back into my life and expect me to answer questions like that."

"Maybe we should just forget the whole thing, then."

She looked into his eyes for a long moment before she answered. "Maybe we should."

Chapter Seven

Jacob worked all of Monday in the orchard fertilizing trees, but he wasn't thinking about peaches—again.

Maybe we should just forget the whole thing, then.

The phrase kept repeating in his head, and he couldn't stop it. What a stupid, *stupid* thing for him to have said, particularly when he already knew that forgetting Jessica Markham was beyond him.

God. He could hear himself saying it. He knew that he should have had more sense; what little of his relationship with Jessica that remained was precarious at best.

Maybe we should just forget the whole thing, then.

He certainly hadn't meant it. He would like to pretend that he had no idea how this rash suggestion of his had come about, but he couldn't manage that, either. He'd looked into Jessica's eyes and seen the disappointment there, and he'd let himself panic. There was a little comfort in thinking that if she didn't care for him, he couldn't disappoint her, but there was no comfort at all in the fact that for all his big plans to tell Jessica what he was feeling, once again, he'd made everything worse. She'd left him standing in the hot dog and hamburger line, and he'd spent the rest of the evening fielding pointed questions from half of Silk Hope about whether or not he and Jessica had had a fight.

He had been able to say in all truthfulness that no, he and Jessica hadn't had a fight. Hell, he couldn't get her to stand still long enough to fight, but the people of Silk Hope were still so interested in the possibility that they hardly took note of Huong. This first family outing had accomplished nothing in the way of introducing her to the community. He supposed that they all thought she was simply a friend of Thomas. And thanks to the drama that surrounded his own attempt to pursue Jessica, Huong was going to have to make her debut as a member of the Brenner family all over again. He didn't want to even think about the speculation the announcement that she was his daughter would precipitate after Jessica's abrupt departure from the Ruritan supper. Huong already thought everything was her fault, and the last thing she needed was to hear some chance remark that she was responsible for his breakup with Jessica.

He still had more than half of the fertilizer spikes to put out, and the sky was becoming increasingly cloudy. He worked on the orchard, looking toward the house from time to time, expecting Thomas to come out to help as soon as he came in from school so they could get the trees fertilized before it rained.

But the Buick wasn't parked in the yard, and as far as he could tell, Thomas hadn't come home yet.

After a while, he walked back to the house to ask Huong if she knew anything about any side trips Thomas might be making on his way home, but he couldn't find her, either.

He wasn't surprised not to find her. She frequently went off on her own, but Thomas should have been here by now. He walked outside again and stared down the road. The wind was picking up, and the sky to the southwest darkening. He could smell the rain coming.

The Buick was unreliable at best, and he abruptly decided to ride to Silk Hope on the chance that Thomas was stranded someplace along the road. He walked back to the orchard to get the truck, looking up at the threatening sky as he pulled the tarp over the rest of the fertilizer spikes in the truck bed. The sky was taking on a yellow cast. High wind, hail, he thought grimly. Just what he needed.

He got into the truck and drove toward Silk Hope, past the lone chimney in the middle of a plowed field that was all that remained of an old burned-down farmhouse, past the fenced pastureland, and past the sandy driveway that led into

Jessica's house. Surprisingly she was home from the bank already—or perhaps she hadn't gone in to work at all. The clothesline next to the house was full of towels and sheets and quilts, and he saw her immediately, running to get them in ahead of the rain. The wind whipped the pecan trees and the crape myrtle bushes that stood in her front yard, and the first raindrops splashed against the windshield of the truck. It took only seconds for them to become a downpour.

He abruptly stopped in the middle of the road, then backed up so he could turn into the driveway.

Jessica struggled to get a quilt off the line, but it tangled in the wind as the rain came harder. She looked around sharply at Jacob's arrival. Jacob with his ever-present Braves ball cap. Jacob with his unfathomable intent.

She was startled to see him, but she didn't say anything, letting him help if that was what he wanted to do. She didn't let her mind dwell on the why of his being there, only on the fact that she was glad to see him. Too glad if she told the truth about it. She glanced at him from time to time, but he was engrossed in getting the half dozen quilts she'd hung on the line to air out, sticking clothespins into his shirt pockets as he went along.

He loaded her arms down with the quilts so she could go on inside while he brought in the last few towels and sheets. They were both soaked by the time they reached the back door. Jessica led the way into the house, dumping the quilts on the top of the washing machine in the small alcove between the kitchen and the back porch. She turned around to take the towels and sheets out of his arms, giving him one towel back so that he could wipe the rain off his face.

She stood watching him, trying not to let herself be affected by his nearness. She was cold; it was all she could do to keep from shivering. Her wet T-shirt stuck to her breasts, a fact that he didn't fail to notice. She should have stepped away from him then, but she didn't. She stood there, letting him appreciate the fact that she was a woman and perhaps letting him have his regrets.

Abruptly she reached out to take the towel from him to wipe her own face and arms. "I didn't expect to see you again," she said. "I thought you wanted to forget this whole thing."

The rain came harder, splattering loudly on the brick patio, and he looked around out the screen door behind him. "Sometimes I say really stupid things," he said when he looked back at her.

"There's hail in that," she said of the rain, careful not to look into his eyes. "Shouldn't you be worrying about your peach trees?" She knew that ordinarily he would have been home, pacing back and forth until the storm was over as if he could, by sheer force of will, keep any damage away from his trees.

"One thing at a time, Jess."

She could feel his eyes, how intently he still looked at her. She was so aware of it that she began to gather up towels that had slid off the pile on the washing machine onto the floor. She didn't know what to say to him. She didn't know what he was doing here; she didn't know what he wanted. She only knew what *she* wanted.

Him. She wanted him. She didn't want to think about the months he'd stayed away. She didn't want to think about his newfound daughter. She just wanted to be close to him, because she cared about him and she'd missed him and because he was a beautiful man to her.

"You didn't go to work at the bank today?" he asked after a time.

She still didn't look at him. "No. I'm taking a few vacation days." That was the truth, though it implied that she'd planned this hiatus from her job. In actuality she hadn't. The truth of the matter was that she was tired—tired of worrying about his intentions, tired of trying to figure out the answers to questions she was too proud to ask, tired of listening for prowlers leaving leaves and candles and bamboo poles on her doorstep.

She could feel him move closer.

"Oh. Well, that's good. I'm glad you're not sick or anything. I was out looking for Thomas when I saw you bringing in clothes."

"He was here earlier," she said. "He said he was going to Siler City." She didn't mention that Thomas had seemed as harassed as he had been at the Ruritan supper, as if there were a hundred other things he should have been doing rather than stopping to talk. She supposed his agitation was some sort of teenage phase.

She glanced at Jacob in time to see him frown. "What was he doing here?"

"Nothing. I was working in the yard. He just stopped long enough to say hello," she said, folding towels that were too wet to fold as if it were a matter of life and death. She could hear him give a soft sigh.

"Well, I guess I'll be going," he offered. He hesitated, then turned to leave.

"Jacob," she said when he got as far as the back door.

"Yeah?" He stood awkwardly, as if he didn't quite know what to do with his hands. Open the door? Reach for her?

She let her eyes just graze his. "Thank you. For helping me bring the clothes in."

"You're welcome, Jess," he said quietly.

She could feel him waiting, and she understood perfectly what he was waiting for. He'd almost but not quite told her that he hadn't meant what he said at the Ruritan supper, and now, based on that meager development and with no encouragement from him whatsoever, she was supposed to make some kind of decision where he was concerned.

She closed her eyes for a moment. Lord, he was an infuriating man. And relentlessly honorable and responsible, even if he did have a penchant for disappearing.

I'd like you to meet my daughter.

No excuses and no explanations—except that Huong wasn't the reason he'd gone away in the first place.

What then? she wanted to ask him now, but she couldn't bring herself to say anything more.

He opened the screen door.

"Jacob?" she said before he went outside.

"Yeah, Jess?"

She looked at him this time, letting herself bear the full brunt of his sad, sad eyes. She pursed her lips to say something—anything—but nothing came.

Why was this so hard! she thought in desperation.

Because she was afraid. Because she didn't want to make a bigger fool of herself than she already had. Because she really cared about him. She pressed her lips together in a tight line.

"Tell me not to go," he suggested in a whisper, and she gave a short laugh in spite of herself.

"Jacob," she tried again, staring into his eyes. "Don't . . . go," she managed.

He didn't remember crossing the room to get to her, but he must have. He was holding her tightly, letting her cling to him as hard as she wanted. He closed his eyes against the wave of emotions that threatened to overwhelm him. He wasn't used to physical closeness, and the feel and the scent of her body, the desperate need she elicited in him were nearly more than he could bear. But he savored all of it, everything, the fear and the joy and the intense desire, feeling more alive than he had in a long time.

He wanted her. He stroked her back, lifted her wet hair off her neck, his hands trembling. He pressed a small kiss against her cheek, her ear, and her arms tightened around him.

"I missed you, Jess," he said. "Every day, every day."

"I've been here. I told you that. Jacob—"

His mouth found hers, cutting off her next words. God, he loved the way she tasted, loved the way her lips parted under his. "What?" he murmured with all the absentmindedness of a man whose burning need was *not* for conversation but who felt he should still be polite. "What?"

She leaned back to look at him, her dark eyes searching his, her lips still parted and her breath as ragged as his. She abruptly reached up and snatched his Braves baseball cap, tossing it away and cupping his face in both hands.

"Never mind," she said as she kissed his mouth. "It's too late now."

It was too late, Jacob thought. Yes, they had a great deal to talk about, to get settled, but the time for that wasn't now, and he gladly let himself be swept away by the passion that swirled between them. He pulled her wet T-shirt out of her jeans so that he could touch her bare skin, her breasts, and lifted her off the floor to carry her into the downstairs bedroom.

Into her bed.

He had fantasized a thousand times what it would be like to make love with her in this bed. He wasn't disappointed. She was neither bold nor shy. She was warm and loving and beautiful, and the soft sighs she gave when he touched her made him forget everything else. And he did touch. Every part of her. With his mouth. With his hands. Her skin was incredibly smooth under his hands, and let his exploration of her drive them both to the brink.

When he thrust himself inside her, his name was a whisper on her lips that he could see but not hear. She wanted to look into his eyes. She wanted to know. And he let her.

See what I am. Take what I am.

Jessica!

* * *

The storm was over. Outside. Inside. Jessica lay with her eyes closed, not moving. For four months, she'd pretended that she hadn't really wanted him in her life. Lying with him now, warm and languid in the aftermath of their lovemaking, she knew beyond a doubt that it wasn't true.

Oh, Jacob, is there more to us than this?

She was afraid to ask him. She wanted there to be more, but even if there wasn't, she told herself that she had no regrets. She'd wanted him, and she'd taken him willingly to her bed.

He kissed her closed eyes, and after a moment, he rolled away from her. She expected that he would want them both to return to their discrete selves, separate, still estranged, but he gathered her up and brought her close to him.

"I love you, Jessica," he said, and she felt the sudden sting of tears behind her eyes. That was the last thing she thought he would say, and she turned to him, pressing her face into his neck.

"Did you hear me?" he asked.

"I heard you. I didn't think—" She leaned back to look at him, searching for some sign that he meant it. She couldn't tell, and so she asked. "Jacob, are you sure?"

"I'm afraid so," he said, his solemnness matching her own. She could see the mischief in his eyes, and if he was about to tease her, she really *would* cry. She wanted to be happy that he'd said he loved her, but everything was so complicated!

He smiled and brushed her rain-damp hair back from her face. "I can't help it, Jess. It's one of those things, like hail storms and wind damage."

"Jacob," she began, making herself look into his eyes. "I . . . love you, too. But you're going to have to make me understand what went wrong before. If it wasn't Huong—"

"It wasn't, Jess. It was me. I couldn't—" He rolled onto his back and looked up at the ceiling.

"Couldn't what?" she insisted.

He closed his eyes for a moment before he answered. "Couldn't take the chance," he said, looking at her now. "I couldn't take the chance on letting you in my life. I didn't want to get hurt. I didn't want to hurt you because maybe I can't give you what you need."

"Now you've changed your mind?"

"Yes."

"Why? We could both still get hurt."

"I don't know why." He reached up to touch her face. "I'm still scared, but I don't want to miss this chance with you. I'm not much of a bargain, Jess. I'm in debt. I've got a ready-made family. God knows it's full of problems."

"Because of Huong?"

"No. Because I felt sorry enough for myself when I was a twenty-one-year-old Marine to take advantage of a young Vietnamese girl who cared about me. She was an interpreter for the base. She spoke French and perfect English. She came from a wealthy family, and she was so...serene. I'd never met anyone like her before. All the officers were after her—she was beautiful—but her family was strict, and she wouldn't have anything to do with any of them. I used to talk to her sometimes when she came to the base. About everything—her family, mine. She knew I was married. I wasn't looking for anything from her. She was just so easy to talk to. I guess that's why she listened to me, because I wasn't after her like the others. But in the end I took everything she had to give and I didn't—''

He broke off suddenly, as if telling her this was more painful than he'd bargained for. Jessica pressed closer to him and waited.

''It's been hard on Thomas,'' he said after a moment. ''Huong's sweet and good, but she's illegitimate and she's half-Vietnamese. He's upset about that and he's disappointed in me. He ran away when she first came, back to his mother in Seattle. But she'd just remarried and she made it clear that she didn't want him underfoot. He thinks both his parents have let him down, and he's miserable. *Everybody's* miserable most of the time, Jess, and I don't know what to do about it because the bottom line is Huong's *my* kid. I can't *not* take care of her.''

The telephone rang, and Jessica had to reach across him to answer it.

"It's for you," she said, giving it to him.

He frowned. "Nobody knows I'm here."

"They do now," she suggested, and he gave one of his quiet half smiles.

"Yeah?" he said into the receiver. "What? What for? No, no, I'll be there. No, I appreciate your looking for me." He handed the receiver back to her and immediately began looking for his clothes. "Damn it all!"

"What's wrong?" Jessica said, her alarm growing.

"Thomas," Jacob said, dragging his jeans on. "He's in jail."

Chapter Eight

Jacob was lucky, he supposed, that Thomas had only been detained and not formally charged. He had thought that Thomas had settled down, that he and Huong were getting along better. My God, what kind of father was he that he hadn't seen this coming?

He knew the answer to that well enough. He was the kind who had had his mind entirely on other things. Even now, with his son in jail, he hadn't wanted to leave Jessica. The memory of her soft, warm body made him give a sharp sigh. He'd wanted to stay as long as she'd let him. He'd wanted to hold her, to make love to her again.

Damn it all!

"You want to tell me what is going on?" he said the moment the sergeant brought Thomas out. Thomas looked properly contrite, but Jacob still wanted to whack him. "What the hell were you doing hanging out in a graveyard?"

"Nothing, Dad!" Thomas insisted, his eyes wide with an innocence that Jacob would have sworn wasn't feigned.

"Yeah, right! Thomas, they don't pick you up and put you in jail for 'nothing!' You were supposed to be in school. Where do I sign?'' he asked the sergeant.

"I was in school, Dad. For a while."

The sergeant pointed to a line on the printed form. "They'll be bringing the other one out in just a minute, Mr. Brenner."

"What other one?" Jacob said.

The sergeant looked at his clipboard. "A Heidi—"

"I don't know any 'Heidi,'" Jacob interrupted.

"Uh, Dad?" Thomas said.

"The information she gives is that she resides at—"

"I don't know anybody named 'Heidi,'" Jacob repeated.

"Dad? Dad?" Thomas persisted, pulling at his sleeve.

"Whatever you say, Mr. Brenner," the sergeant said.

"Dad!"

"What!" Jacob snapped at Thomas. He was absolutely not in the mood for any teenage boy's insouciance.

"That's, uh—" Thomas made a little gesture with one hand "—Huong."

"What is?" Jacob said, his voice deadly.

"Um, Heidi?"

"You had Huong with you!" Jacob yelled. "My God, don't tell me the two of you are using aliases!"

"Yeah. I mean, no, Dad! See, she just wanted to be called Heidi instead of Huong because you said she could be a Brenner and she thinks Huong Brenner sounds kind of weird. Well, I do, too, you know, when you think about it. And, hey! This is America. You can be called anything you want, right? No problem! I figured if she wants to be called Heidi, she can be called Heidi. That's the way we do things over here. Didn't she tell you?" he asked. "I guess not, huh?" he immediately decided.

"Thomas!"

"Now, Dad, this isn't *my* fault. I didn't have anything to do with this 'Heidi' business!"

"We'll get into that later."

"Mr. Brenner!" the sergeant interrupted. "Do you or don't you know the subject in question?"

Jacob gave a sharp sigh. "Huong—*Heidi* Brenner is my daughter."

"You're sure?" the sergeant asked, looking at him over the top of his glasses.

"No!" Jacob snapped again, glaring at Thomas. "I've got teenage children. What the hell do *I* know?"

Jessica thought that Jacob had come back when someone knocked at the back door. It was raining again, and she hurried through the house to let him in.

Sonny Cook stood on the doorstep, looking rather ridiculous in his yellow sheriff's department rain slicker. He looked like a giant, well-fed canary. It was *not* becoming to a man his size.

"Sonny," she said, opening the door. "Come in."

He grinned the same grin he'd had when he was fifteen. "Hey, Jessie. How you doing? You haven't had any more trouble out here, have you?"

"I'm okay, Sonny. No more prowlers as far as I know. Is this an official visit?"

"Well, sort of. I just wanted to tell you something. The lab report's not back on those leaves and things you had on your porch, but I was wondering if you had any dealing with any foreigners at the bank. You didn't *not* give somebody a loan or something like that, did you?"

"Foreigners? No. I don't have anything to do with loans. I do investments."

"You didn't go and lose anybody's nest egg?"

"No," she said, laughing. "Not yet anyway. Why?"

"You know anything about déjà vu?"

She frowned. "I know what it is."

"Well, good. I just wanted you to know I got a bad case of it when I opened that bag of stuff from off your porch."

"Sonny, I don't understand."

"Déjà vu, Jessie. Man, when I took a whiff of what was in that bag, I swear I was right back in Nam like it was yesterday. They're a superstitious people over there, Jessie. I've known them to use all kinds of spells and things to get rid of—"

"But you thought it was some kind of cult. Isn't that what you said at the Ruritan supper?"

"No, that was before I smelled that stuff, Jessie. Tell you the truth, if you haven't offended some Vietnamese someplace, I don't know *who* would be doing it."

Jessica stopped listening. The nuts and leaves and candles were part of some kind of Vietnamese ritual?

"What?" she said when she realized Sonny had asked her something.

"I said if you think of anybody from the bank or from where you lived before that might be doing this, will you let me know?"

"Yes. Yes, I will."

"I'm not wanting to worry you, Jessie, but I just didn't think I ought not say something to you about it. You know what I mean—just to be on the safe side. Now you keep your doors locked, hear?"

She heard, but she didn't think there was much need to keep her doors locked, not now that she knew who had left those things on her porch.

Huong.

Of course, it had to be Huong. She had only just found her father, only just become part of his family. She had to feel that her new place here was precarious. She would be afraid, threatened by anyone strange coming into Jacob's life.

Jessica sighed heavily. Now what? She'd only just begun to try to work things out with Jacob, and their relationship had a serious problem he probably didn't even know about.

She had no idea what she should do; she only knew that she wasn't going to sit here and wring her hands. She'd had enough of that of late. Jacob hadn't been gone very long. She might have the chance now to talk to Huong before Jacob came back with the errant Thomas.

She said her token goodbyes to Sonny and began looking for her purse. In a quick pass through the dining room she caught sight of herself in the mirror on her mother's sideboard. Her hair was still disheveled, her eyes worried now instead of soft with the love she felt for Jacob Brenner.

"Oh, Jacob," she whispered before hurrying outside to the car.

As she backed out the driveway past the front of the house, she suddenly slammed on brakes. She got out of the car, leaving the motor running and running through the rain onto the porch. A burned-out candle stood in the center of a pile of nuts and sticks and leaves.

Chapter Nine

There was a fallow field between Jacob's house and the paved road. Jessica drove carefully down the bumpy driveway to the grove of trees where the house itself stood. It was still raining, and she waited in the car for a moment, looking for some activity in the house or the outbuildings surrounding it.

She couldn't see anything, no lights, nothing. After a moment, she got out of the car. She knocked vigorously at both the back and front doors, but if Huong was in the house, she was choosing not to answer.

Jessica stood impatiently on the front porch. Now what? she thought. She could wait, but she didn't know what kind of trouble Thomas was in. Nothing serious, she suspected; he was a nice boy. But if Jacob and Thomas came back soon, she didn't want to add to an already difficult situation by confronting Huong, even if ''confronting'' was a bit strong for what she had in mind. She just wanted to talk to the girl. She just wanted to reassure her that her relationship with her father wasn't in jeopardy regardless of the feelings Jessica might have for him.

But the decision to go or to stay was taken out of her hands. Jacob's truck was coming up the long driveway from the road.

She stood waiting on the porch while a subdued Huong and Thomas got out and trudged toward the house. She could see immediately how upset they all were, Jacob, in particular. And she was only going to add to his difficulties.

"Jess?" he said as he stepped up on the porch out of the rain. "What's wrong?" He held out his hand, and even though she didn't touch him, the memory of their lovemaking came suddenly into her mind. She still felt close to him; she loved him, but she pushed the memory of what it was like to lie in his arms aside. She didn't want to lie to him. If she—if *they*—had a problem and if he loved her, he needed to know about it.

"I need to talk to Huong, Jacob."

She glanced at Huong and Thomas; they both looked as miserable as she felt.

"Huong?" he said, clearly puzzled.

"About these," she said, holding up the paper bag she had with her.

"What is this?" he asked, reaching to take the leaves she removed from the bag out of her hand.

"I knew it!" Thomas burst out. "You did put it back! I tried to get to Jessica's porch to see, but she was in the yard."

"It's wrong to undo, Thomas!" Huong cried. "It's very bad luck! I told you!"

"What are you two talking about?" Jacob said. "What is this stuff?"

"I'll tell him," Thomas said.

"No," Huong protested. "It's for me to say—"

"No, *I'll* do it! You aren't going to make him understand about the Jade Emperor and Victor Hugo and the Pearl S. Buck Foundation!"

"The what?" Jacob said.

"She didn't mean anything wrong, Dad!"

"Thomas, be quiet!" Jacob shouted. "Go inside, both of you." He held the door open to let his children precede him. Jessica hesitated, but he reached out to put his hand on her shoulder and bring her into the house.

"We're going to sit down at the kitchen table," he said to Huong and Thomas. "You two are going to talk, and Jessica and I are going to listen."

"Dad," Thomas began. "It's not what you think."

"Son, you are pushing your luck with me, you know that, don't you? I don't think anything yet."

"I just want you to let *me* tell you."

"Thomas, it's not for you to be saying this," Huong insisted. "It's me. I was wrong about the

Mother's Day. I don't want you to have a... a...hissy, Father.''

"Too late now," Thomas said under his breath. "Dad," he said out loud. "It's...she thought you looked for a mother on Mother's Day, and she always covers all the bases. That's the way she gets things done.''

"What bases?" Jacob cried.

"Well," Thomas said thoughtfully. "At least three religions, I guess. Maybe four, I'm not sure. And there's an international foundation," he added, counting that one on his thumb, "and a government agency. Now, I don't know where the *cay neu* fits—"

"The what?"

"The *cay neu?*"

"Thomas, I don't know what you're talking about!"

"Dad, I'm trying to tell you!"

Jacob threw up both hands. "Sit down. Everybody. Jessica, I have no idea what the hell is going on here." He waited until everyone was seated. "All right. Tell me this. What were the two of you doing prowling around in the graveyard?"

"That was because I made her undo Jessica's ancestors, Dad!" Thomas insisted as if anyone with any sense at all could see that.

"Thomas!"

"Could I say something?" Jessica interrupted. "I think maybe I understand this."

"I betrothed you and Jessica, Father," Huong said suddenly, her voice very small.

"You what?" Jessica and Jacob said in unison.

"Exactly what *I* said," Thomas noted.

"I'm sorry, Father."

"Huong," Jacob said. "I told you before. You can talk to me. *We* can talk. I want you to start at the beginning."

She glanced at Thomas. "Can Thomas help?"

"Thomas is *not* a help, but if I need him to explain anything, I'll ask him," Jacob said pointedly, because Thomas was about to comment again.

Huong took a small breath and looked from her father to Jessica and back again. "I wanted you to be happy, Father."

"Is having to go get the two of you out of jail supposed to make me happy?"

She looked up at him. "You don't understand."

"No, I don't. You tell me everything so I will."

"This is a big thing to tell, Father."

"I have plenty of time."

She was silent for a moment, then she took a deep breath. "You were very...not happy, Father," she said quietly. "And I got the holiday wrong."

"Go on," Jacob prompted.

"I know the holidays in Vietnam but I don't know the Groundhog Day and the Mother's Day here. On *Tet*—February," she added, struggling with the word, "I put out the *cay neu* for Jessica to keep her safe for you."

"For me? How did you know about Jessica?"

"I heard you and Thomas fight. I heard what Thomas said—that you can't see Jessica anymore because of me."

"That wasn't true, Huong. I told Thomas that—"

"I know. I heard what you said, too. But you weren't happy, Father. I thought Jessica could make you happy, but you don't go back to her. You stay here all the time and work. When you go to Silk Hope or to Siler City, you always look for her when we pass her house. Your face is sad if you don't see her. Your face is sadder if you do. I thought you needed help, like I did when I was still in Vietnam and my mother died. It took many prayers to get me here, Father, but it happened. So I started the many prayers it might take for you and Jessica. I put the *cay neu* out to keep the bad spirits away. And there was the Groundhog Day. The television said all those people were looking for the groundhog that day, so I thought it would be all right to look for a mother on Mother's Day, to pick Jessica because you love her." She stopped and sighed.

"Go on," Jacob prompted.

"Thomas explained you *don't* look for a mother then the way you look for a groundhog on the Groundhog's Day. Thomas said you honor the mother you've got. I don't know how I thought I was understanding the Mother's Day when I don't even know what a groundhog is, but it was too late when I found out the truth because I already did it."

"What did you do?"

"I made the offering on Jessica's front place."

"Porch," Thomas supplied, and Jacob gave him a hard look.

"Yes," Huong said, glancing at Jessica. "On Jessica's porch I made the offering for a betrothal, because I'm your oldest living relative."

"What were *you* doing all this time?" Jacob suddenly asked Thomas.

"Me?" Thomas said, startled. "Nothing, Dad."

"Thomas explained *after,* Father. I don't tell him about these things until I find out I messed up the Mother's Day. Thomas said Jessica would be afraid because she wouldn't know what the offering was for. She wouldn't know betel leaves and areca nuts and everything, so we had to undo it quick. We had to undo *everything* so people wouldn't think there were heathen...occult... devil...worshipers running around loose. But the offering was gone off the front place when we got there and it was too late. We got the ancestors undone, but Thomas must be right because at the Ruritan supper, Sonny Cook was talking about the...heathen...occult people in Chatham County."

"Sonny knows what you did?" Jacob asked. He looked at Jessica, and she shook her head, "What about the graveyard today?"

"It's bad to undo, Father. I put everything back—flowers and things. I just wanted Jessica's ancestors to know that we still needed their help. But Thomas was worried, I guess."

Jacob glanced at his son, who rolled his eyes upward at the gross understatement of his angst.

"And then the deputy came," she added. "And you know what happened then."

"I see," Jacob said after a moment.

"You do?" Thomas said incredulously.

"Amazing, isn't it?" Jacob said. "I want you two to go on about your business now. I want to talk to Jessica."

"That's it, Dad? No yelling? No nothing?"

"No, that's not it! I have to think about this for a while. The two of you should have come to me when you knew you were in trouble. In the meantime, I suggest you get out of here and stop push-ing your luck.''

''You got it, Dad!'' Thomas said, clearly re-lieved. ''Come on, Heidi, you heard the man.''

But Huong held back. ''Jessica. I want to say, please, that I didn't mean to make you afraid.''

''I understand that,'' Jessica said.

''You won't be angry with my father?''

''No, Huong. I won't.''

''Good,'' she said. ''Father? There is one thing now.''

''What?'' Jacob said.

''You will get to calling me Heidi?''

Jacob was about to say something but seemed to think better of it. ''I'll try.''

''Good,'' she said, following Thomas out.

''Talk about pushing your luck,'' Thomas said to her.

After a moment, the blare of the stereo came from a room at the back of the house.

Jessica looked at Jacob across the table. He sighed heavily and shook his head. ''I don't know what to say, Jess. I heard part of what Sonny was telling the crowd at the Ruritan supper—about the candles and the pile of nuts and leaves. I didn't realize it was *your* porch he was talking about. You must have been worried to death.''

''Well, I didn't know the part about my ancestors.''

"Why didn't you tell me about all this?"

"Jacob, we had other things to talk about. I didn't realize it was probably Huong until after you left this afternoon." She told him about Sonny's visit.

"I appreciate your not saying anything to him about her. I'll tell him myself, if you don't mind. Ah, hell, Jess, I wouldn't blame you if you ran for your life. I should be angry with her and Thomas, but . . ." He gave another heavy sigh.

"I was worried when I thought Huong wanted to keep me away from you. Now that I know it's the other way around, it's . . . okay."

"Is it?" he asked, his eyes searching hers.

"Yes," she assured him. He looked so miserable that she brought her chair around so she could sit next to him. She leaned against him and put her arms around him to give him a small kiss on the cheek.

He rested his head on her shoulder. "My kids are going to drive me crazy," she thought he said.

"Well, maybe not," she reassured him.

"I knew something was going on, but I didn't ask. How the hell am I going to explain the Jade Emperor and Victor Hugo to Sonny Cook?"

"Just tell him we got betrothed. Twice," she suggested, and he gave a short laugh.

"I think I will tell him that. With three religions, an international foundation and whatever else was mixed up in this betrothal, it might be easier to stick with it than to try to get out of it.''

He leaned back to look into her eyes.

He's doing it again, she thought. An almost proposal to go with the almost apology he'd given her earlier.

''People will talk,'' she reminded him, because the community was already entirely too interested in the outcome of their relationship and because she wanted him to say what he really wanted.

''I can take it,'' he assured her. He gave an off-hand shrug. ''So. Do you want to get married?''

''Why would I want to do that?'' she asked, deciding that she really ought to play just a little hard to get.

He smiled, and his eyes held hers. He reached up to touch her cheek, his thumb lightly brushing over her lips. ''Because I love you, Jess. And you love me.'' He brought her face close to his, his mouth ever so gently pressing against hers. ''Don't you?'' he murmured, the kiss becoming deep and probing and long. It made her knees weak. It made her fully appreciative of the fact that she was sitting down. It made her forget that there were two other people in the house.

''Don't you?'' he insisted, his mouth finding hers again.

''Yes!'' she admitted, hugging him hard. If she did, she did, and there was nothing she could do about it. When they were together like this, there was nothing she wanted to do about it.

"Hey," he said, reaching into his shirt pocket, his eyes filled with mischief. "You want your clothespins back?"

"Nope," she assured him. "My clothespins are your clothespins."

Epilogue

Jessica woke up late, roused from sleep by downstairs noises. She didn't ordinarily spend the night in the upstairs bedroom, and it took her a moment to decide where she was and why she could smell the delicious aroma of brewing coffee.

"Ah, yes," she remembered. Huong was in the house and already hard at work to get the both of them ready.

She turned over to look at the small travel clock she'd brought upstairs with her. She still had a little time, and she closed her eyes, not to sleep again but to enjoy the quiet of the May Sunday morning. She could hear the birds singing outside her window, and Huong was humming something that sounded like "Blessed Assurance" downstairs in the kitchen.

Jessica gave a contented sigh. It had taken a great deal of pain and worry to get her life into the peaceful order it was in now, and she wanted to savor it. Twice betrothed or not, she hadn't let herself be hurried into a wedding. It wasn't that she didn't love Jacob. She did, and she didn't doubt that he loved her in return. But she knew that he'd needed to resolve the problems associated with one major upheaval in his life before he entangled himself in another. With the discovery of his Vietnamese daughter, the chaotic feelings he'd worked so hard to keep buried since he'd come back from Vietnam had resurfaced.

During Thomas's Christmas break from school, she, Thomas and Huong had gone with Jacob to the Vietnam Memorial in Washington. It was the last place in the world she'd expected him to want to go.

The day was cold; the trees winter bare. The sun was shining at the memorial site, but a sharp wind cut across the Mall. Jacob took her hand as they walked toward the long black marble wall that seemed to be a part of the earth itself. His fingers were warm around hers, and she held on to them, a dull ache pounding in her heart because she was so afraid of losing him.

But she hadn't been disappointed. It was as if seeing the Wall, touching the names of fallen friends, had validated his own experience so that he could finally deal with it. In the weeks that followed, he found a support group for Vietnam veterans on his own, and he went regularly, taking her with him when he was ready for her to know what had happened to him.

Jessica looked at the travel clock again and got quickly out of bed. She didn't want to be late. She had had a long, hard journey to get to this particular day, and she didn't want anything to spoil it.

She was at last getting married. Today, Mother's Day. It was perhaps not the most traditional day for a wedding, but for her, it was the most appropriate. There was no "blackberry winter" this year; the day was warm and bright with sunshine, but there were betel leaves and candles and areca nuts on the front porch again.

She showered quickly, and when she came out, she found a breakfast tray waiting. She smiled. Huong was still working hard to make sure everything turned out all right.

She ate quickly and got dressed. She had a few minutes to spare. She could hear the guests arriving, and she walked to the front window in time to see Thomas in his new suit and tie and pink carnation boutonniere out directing cars. She watched until he went back inside again. Both of Jacob's children were certainly doing their part.

Someone was coming quickly up the back stairs, and she looked at herself in the dresser mirror one last time.

"Jessica?" Huong said tentatively at the bedroom door. "Are you ready now? Oh, you look so beautiful!"

"Thank you, Huong," Jessica said. "So do you." Neither she nor Jacob had adjusted to calling her "Heidi," but she didn't seem to mind.

"The reverend is here. It's time to come downstairs. Wait till you see Father in his suit. He looks so handsome, like a real hunk."

"Wait," Jessica said as Huong turned to go. "I want to tell you something."

"Yes?"

"I just wanted to say thank you—for everything. For the breakfast. For all the prayers. I don't know if Jacob and I would have made it without you."

Huong smiled, and how much of Jacob Jessica could see in her. "Thomas helped me get the offering ready for today."

"Did he?" Jessica said, smiling in return, wondering how well Thomas had gotten on with the hearth god.

"Oh, yes. So you don't have to worry. Everything is done to make for your good luck and happiness. And I wasn't wrong, you see? Sometimes you do get a mother on Mother's Day, only it takes longer than you think. Will you hurry, please? Father is so nervous and Thomas says his collar is too tight. He might crack."

"Croak," Jessica said, laughing, because she'd heard the threat all the way upstairs.

"That, too, I think," Huong said. "Hurry, Jessica!"

Jessica hurried, pausing for a moment at the head of the stairs. The house was full of the people of Silk Hope, people who had known her all her life and who came now to wish her and Jacob well. She smiled at them as she went down the stairs with Huong, and when she reached the bottom, she hugged a beaming if choking Thomas.

Jacob stood waiting by the doorway to the living room, freshly barbered, freshly shaved, and like Thomas, dressed in a new suit.

Lord, she thought. He *was* handsome, incredibly so today. He smiled at her as she took his proffered arm. His eyes were still sad, but the haunted look was gone.

"The peach trees are looking good," he whispered as they were about to walk toward the minister, because it was the last thing that might have put a damper on the day. "You are so beautiful. I love you, Jess," he added loudly enough to make the guests closest at hand smile and give a round of applause.

"I love you," she responded, lifting her mouth to be kissed.

"Jake! Jessie!" the minister chided. "Now cut that out! Come on over here and let's get you two married!"

Jessica laughed and squeezed Jacob's arm. It was the best offer she'd ever had, and it was a beautiful, beautiful Mother's Day.

* * * * *

Cheryl Reavis

It always surprises me to hear writers say they "fell" into the writing profession by accident, that they had no idea they could write or even that they wanted to. I can't remember when I didn't think I was a writer, regardless of the fact that I had no expertise. I certainly didn't know any writers. I had no role models. None of my friends tried to scribble animal stories in their Blue Horse writing tablets. None of them thought a five-year diary or a box of blank stationery was the most wonderful gift in the world. None of them had a reading fervor and spent all their pocket money on *Wonder Woman* comic books instead of chocolate candy and a fountain cherry Coke. The ideas were always there inside my head, the stories, the words, the characters—all those things that begged to be written down. I can recall vividly my first failure. I was perhaps eight or nine. I had read *Black Beauty,* and I came away from it completely convinced that I, too, could write such a story. I couldn't. I couldn't even begin, and what I remember most about the experience is my complete surprise.

I think of myself now as a late bloomer, but actually I began my writing career at exactly the right time. When I had a wealth of life and death experiences from public-health nursing—my "other" career. When I was old enough to know what my weaknesses were and resistant enough not to let anyone make me conform. When I was secure enough to be undaunted by the criticisms of writing professors who didn't know half as much about human nature as I did and to take what I needed from them and disregard the rest. Did I say that I had to *learn* how to write? I did. It wasn't enough for me to simply have a head full of stories and ideas. I also had to know how to get them down. So when I was in my thirties, I set about learning how to do just that. I went to creative-writing classes and critiquing groups. I joined writing clubs, subscribed to writing magazines, read how-to writing books. I even found a phrase to live by. *En écrivant on apprend à écrire.* By writing you learn to write.

I learned the mechanics. And, in considerably more time than it took me to learn to be a nurse, I became a published writer. "Overnight" success stories are terribly glamorous, I suppose, but I did it the hard way, and the journey from Blue Horse writing tablets to worldwide contemporary romance fiction was quite a trip.

I still don't know what it is that makes me want to neglect husband and son, family and friends, and constantly take one of those determined jaunts into a world of my own. I only know that I do, and what's more, I want to take you, the reader, with me.

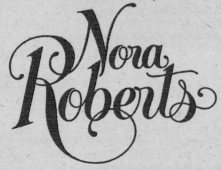
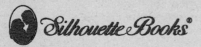

FOUR UNIQUE SERIES
FOR EVERY WOMAN YOU ARE . . .

Silhouette Romance®

Love, at its most tender, provocative, emotional . . . in stories that will make you laugh and cry while bringing you the magic of falling in love.

6 titles per month

Silhouette Special Edition®

Sophisticated, substantial and packed with emotion, these powerful novels of life and love will capture your imagination and steal your heart.

6 titles per month

SILHOUETTE *Desire®*

Open the door to romance and passion. Humorous, emotional, compelling—yet always a believable and sensuous story—Silhouette Desire never fails to deliver on the promise of love.

6 titles per month

SILHOUETTE·INTIMATE·MOMENTS®

Enter a world of excitement, of romance heightened by suspense, adventure and the passions every woman dreams of. Let us sweep you away.

4 titles per month

Bestselling author **NORA ROBERTS** captures all the romance, adventure, passion and excitement of Silhouette in a special miniseries.

THE
CALHOUN WOMEN

Four charming, beautiful and fiercely independent sisters set out on a search for a missing family heirloom—an emerald necklace—and each finds something even more precious . . . passionate romance.

Look for THE CALHOUN WOMEN miniseries starting in June.

COURTING CATHERINE
Silhouette Romance #801

July
A MAN FOR AMANDA
Silhouette Desire #649

August
FOR THE LOVE OF LILAH
Silhouette Special Edition #685

September
SUZANNA'S SURRENDER
Silhouette Intimate Moments #397

Silhouette Books®

SILHOUETTE BOOKS ARE NOW AVAILABLE IN STORES AT THESE CONVENIENT TIMES EACH MONTH*

Silhouette Desire and Silhouette Romance

> May titles: April 10
> June titles: May 8
> July titles: June 5
> August titles: July 10

Silhouette Intimate Moments and Silhouette Special Edition

> May titles: April 24
> June titles: May 22
> July titles: June 19
> August titles: July 24

We hope this new schedule is convenient for you. With only two trips each month to your local bookseller, you will always be sure not to miss any of your favorite authors!

Happy reading!

Please note: There may be slight variations in on-sale dates in your area due to differences in shipping and handling.

*Applicable to U.S. only.

Silhouette Special Edition

proudly hails

WOMEN OF GLORY

from Lindsay McKenna

Soar with Dana Coulter, Molly Rutledge and Maggie Donovan—
Lindsay McKenna's WOMEN OF GLORY. On land, sea or air, these
three Annapolis grads challenge danger head-on, risking life and limb
for the glory of their country—and for the men they love!

May: NO QUARTER GIVEN (SE #667) Dana Coulter is on the brink
of achieving her lifelong dream of flying—and of meeting the man who
would love to take her to new heights!

June: THE GAUNTLET (SE #673) Molly Rutledge is determined
to excel on her own merit, but Captain Cameron Sinclair is equally
determined to take gentle Molly under his wing....

July: UNDER FIRE (SE #679) Indomitable Maggie never thought
her career—or her heart—would come under fire. But all that changes
when she teams up with Lieutenant Wes Bishop!

SEWG-1

SILHOUETTE·INTIMATE·MOMENTS®

IT'S TIME TO MEET
THE MARSHALLS!

In 1986, bestselling author Kristin James wrote A VERY SPECIAL FAVOR for the Silhouette Intimate Moments line. Hero Adam Marshall quickly became a reader favorite, and ever since then, readers have been asking for the stories of his two brothers, Tag and James. At last your prayers have been answered!

In June, look for Tag's story, SALT OF THE EARTH (IM #385). Then skip a month and look for THE LETTER OF THE LAW (IM #393—August), starring James Marshall. And, as our very special favor to you, we'll be reprinting A VERY SPECIAL FAVOR this September. Look for it in special displays wherever you buy books.

MARSH-1